Maggie scanned the crowded dance floor for a long, lean cowboy with a gorgeous redhead pressed close to his chest.

All she wanted was to say good-night and leave.

As for Ross... Ross was certainly free to dance with whomever he wanted. She'd made it clear to him that she wasn't interested in continuing whatever strange kind of relationship they had, so...

So why did she come completely unglued when she saw him dancing with another woman?

Maggie closed her eyes and told herself she didn't know. But she did. It defied all logic, but she did.

He had a record; she was a law-enforcement officer.

He was a hell-raiser; she was a preacher's daughter.

Excellent reasons why she absolutely could *not* be falling in love with Ross Dalton. But she was....

Dear Reader,

Winter's here, so why not curl up by the fire with the new Intimate Moments novels? (Unless you live in a warm climate, in which case you can take your books to the beach!) Start off with our WHOSE CHILD? title, another winner from Paula Detmer Riggs called *A Perfect Hero*. You've heard of the secret baby plot? How about secret *babies?* As in *three* of them! You'll love it, I promise, because Ian MacDougall really *is* just about as perfect as a hero can get.

Kathleen Creighton's *One More Knight* is a warm and wonderful sequel to last year's *One Christmas Knight*, but this fine story stands entirely on its own. Join this award-winning writer for a taste of Southern hospitality—and a whole lot of Southern loving. Lee Magner's *Owen's Touch* is a suspenseful amnesia book and wears our TRY TO REMEMBER flash. This twisty plot will keep you guessing—and the irresistible romance will keep you happy. FAMILIES ARE FOREVER, and *Secondhand Dad*, by Kayla Daniels, is just more evidence of the truth of that statement. Lauren Nichols takes us WAY OUT WEST in *Accidental Hero*, all about the allure of a bad boy. And finally, welcome new author Virginia Kantra, whose debut book, *The Reforming of Matthew Dunn*, is a MEN IN BLUE title. You'll be happy to know that her second novel is already in the works.

So pour yourself a cup of something warm, pull the afghan over yourself and enjoy each and every one of these terrific books. Then come back next month, because the excitement—and the romance—will continue, right here in Silhouette Intimate Moments.

Enjoy!

[signature]

Leslie Wainger
Executive Senior Editor

Please address questions and book requests to:
Silhouette Reader Service
U.S.: 3010 Walden Ave., P.O. Box 1325, Buffalo, NY 14269
Canadian: P.O. Box 609, Fort Erie, Ont. L2A 5X3

ACCIDENTAL HERO

LAUREN NICHOLS

INTIMATE MOMENTS®

Published by Silhouette Books

America's Publisher of Contemporary Romance

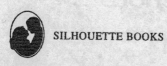 SILHOUETTE BOOKS

ISBN 0-373-07893-5

ACCIDENTAL HERO

Copyright © 1998 by Edie Hanes

This edition published by arrangement with Harlequin Books S.A.

Printed in U.S.A.

Books by Lauren Nichols

Silhouette Intimate Moments

Accidental Heiress #840
Accidental Hero #893

LAUREN NICHOLS

fell in love with Montana thirteen years ago when she and her husband took their three children out west to see "cattle country." Montana has owned a chunk of her heart ever since. While this is Lauren's second published novel, her romance and mystery short stories have appeared in several leading magazines. She counts her family and friends as her greatest treasures. When she's not with them, this Pennsylvania author is writing or traveling with her husband, Mike.

For Karen Rose Smith,
with my gratitude and affection.
What would I do without you?

Chapter 1

Maggie Bristol's heart leaped into her throat as she heard the distant roar of a vehicle approaching the Comfort, Montana, sheriff's office. Nervously, she stuffed the folder she'd been scanning back into the file cabinet, then hurried to her desk to sit. She yanked her policies and procedures manual from a drawer. If the sheriff came back and found her snooping through Ross Dalton's criminal file on her first day on the job, she wouldn't be the dispatcher for long.

The thunder of the engine grew louder, and a dusty black truck fishtailed down Prairie Street, swerved into a parking spot and skidded to a halt five feet from the office's wide plate-glass window. Maggie peered out at the street over the thick volume in her hands.

The alleged lawbreaker was coming in.

Let him be ugly, she wished, hating the way her pulse raced at the thought of seeing him again. Let him be bald and flabby and tattooed. She winced when a little voice inside that completely misunderstood her motives said, *It's been thirteen years, Maggie. Isn't it time your pride healed?* But she didn't let it get to her.

Ross was trouble, and the angry pacing going on inside the sheriff's private office attested to that. Fifteen minutes ago, the too-pretty son of the richest horse breeder in the state had stormed inside demanding Ross's head on a plate.

Now sunlight glinted off the Dodge Ram's chrome bumper as Ross swung out of the truck and slammed the door…

And Maggie saw that her wishes had not come true.

The last time she'd seen him—eleven years ago—she was seventeen. And except for the rugged, angular look that maturity had brought, he hadn't changed much. At thirty-one, Comfort's resident bad boy still had sandy brown hair, still liked tan Stetsons.

Her gaze slid over him, taking in snug jeans, broad shoulders and a beige plaid shirt on a lean, work-toughened frame. Ross Dalton was six feet two inches of cocky attitude and brash good looks—and the night of her fifteenth birthday, she'd been half in love with him. Soon afterwards, she was half in hate, if there was such a thing. His irresponsible behavior in the years that followed had only given her more reason to feel the way she did.

A full thirty seconds behind Ross, the sheriff's white Jeep sped down the street and screeched into the parking space beside Ross's truck. Cy Farrell climbed out, red-faced and agitated. His angry words didn't quite penetrate the front window with its fancy lettering and prestigious seal.

Maggie squared her shoulders and assumed a disinterested expression. Then Farrell waved his suspect on ahead of him, and Ross Dalton blew inside like a wild wind, grinning like a sinner who couldn't get to hell fast enough.

"So what heinous crime am I accused of this time? Somebody stretch plastic wrap over the toilets at the filling station? Tree one of Bessie Holsopple's cats?"

Then Trent Campion burst out of Farrell's office, and Ross's eyes went hard. "Never mind," he muttered. "I know why I'm here."

"I want him jailed," Trent roared. "Assault and making terroristic threats."

Farrell nodded toward the cramped private office that Trent had just vacated. "Inside and sit. Both of you." He turned to Maggie, perspiration beading his upper lip. "Hold my calls, unless it's someone about fixing the air-conditioning." He started to follow Ross through the doorway, then stopped. "And if anyone comes in, give me the high sign so I can shut these two up. I'm leavin' the door open. Good Lord, it must be ninety degrees in here."

It was probably less than eighty, Maggie thought, but Farrell was heavy, and obviously minded the heat more than she did.

"I'll let you know."

At the sound of her voice, Ross turned toward her, his raised eyebrows suggesting that he'd expected someone else to be sitting behind the desk. Maggie felt an unwelcome flush stain her cheeks as his gaze skimmed her black hair, even features, and what he could see of her tan uniform.

"Well, hello," he said softly.

She sent him a cool nod. At least he'd had the courtesy to remember her.

Scowling, Farrell nudged Ross through the doorway and into his office—but not before Maggie heard him say, "New girl's not bad, Cy. Who is she?"

Who is she?

Bristling, Maggie watched Farrell drop into his squeaky swivel chair, while his "prisoner" took a seat opposite Campion. *Ross didn't remember her at all? Not at all?*

Trent's heated allegations from the next room blurred in the wake of Maggie's hurt and irritation. Yanking her manual forward, she tipped back in her seat to read.

But the only thing she saw was that crackling bonfire back at the Daltons' hot spring on the night she'd turned fifteen. All she heard was the bouncy twang of country music, and the raucous laughter of recently graduated seniors splashing in the dammed-up creek. That night, beer had flowed like tap water, crickets had sung backup to Waylon Jennings...and Maggie had melted like warm butter in eighteen-year-old Ross Dalton's arms.

Chills peppered Maggie's limbs as she recalled the heady magic of that night, and her naive pretendings that the party was for her alone—not just a celebration that she and Mary Ellen Parker had nervously crashed. Being with Ross had been a dream come true for an innocent, but well-developed sophomore who'd secretly idolized him for the entire school year.

Maybe that's why she hadn't offered much resistance when he coaxed her down on one of the blankets and slid his tongue deep into her mouth. She was a minister's daughter, and she'd never experienced anything so frighteningly sensual in her life—yet, eventually she'd welcomed him without reservation.

Reservation had come later, when she realized her blouse was open...*and that one of Ross's friends was standing over them.*

Horrified and humiliated, she'd scrambled away, found Mary Ellen, and they'd hurried for home. She'd insisted to Mary Ellen that Ross cared about her, or he wouldn't have touched her that way, but Maggie had never heard from him again. His neglect had crushed and shamed her.

Farrell's anger spiked in the other room, yanking Maggie's attention back to the present. "All right, I've heard Trent's version. What's yours?"

Ross's voice was low and cold, deeper than she remembered. "Not much to tell. He was beating his horse and I took his riding crop away."

"I was *not* beating that horse," Trent shouted. "But

even if I was, he's my property and I'm legally entitled to do it.''

"It's not a question of what's legal," Ross countered. "It's a question of what's right."

The sheriff expelled a scornful laugh. "Quite a statement comin' from a cattle thief."

Maggie's gaze slid to the office again. She knew what Farrell was referring to; it was all in Ross's file. What wasn't in the file had been publicly circulated through the newspapers and rumor mills.

Ross's rugged profile tightened, and Maggie glimpsed the edgy tension lurking beneath his cavalier attitude. She waited for him to defend himself—found herself wanting him to defend himself. But he didn't. He only commented on Trent's accusations.

"I shoved him, he fell, and I told him if I ever saw him beat another animal, I'd cram that crop down his throat so far he'd need a proctologist to get it out."

Trent shot angrily to his feet, and the sheriff held up a hand. "Look, why don't we just let it go at a warning this time. Nobody really got hurt—"

"Except the horse," Ross replied dryly.

"I told you what I want, Cy, now do it!" Campion ordered. "You're up for reelection this year, and my old man won't take kindly to you letting your obligations to this town slide."

"He has a point, Cy," said Ross. "You wouldn't want Ben Campion withdrawing his support in an election year. Better lock me up."

Farrell bolted from his chair and grabbed the keys to the cells. Maggie jerked back to her manual.

"Okay, hotshot," the sheriff muttered. "You just got your wish. Get movin'."

"Don't I get a phone call?"

Farrell herded Ross through the reception area and past

Maggie, heading for the lockup on the other side of the room. "You want a lawyer?"

"Nope, just some food. Take-out from my Aunt Ruby's café will be fine."

Getting redder by the moment, Farrell opened the door and shoved Ross inside, where a row of three cells waited. "Just shut up and get in there."

Maggie heard keys jangle in the lock, then a cell door swing open and bang shut. Breathing hard, Farrell came out and slammed the heavy door, which instantly bounced ajar. He pulled out his handkerchief and mopped his thick neck.

A vague uneasiness moved through Maggie at what she'd just witnessed. Ross was no angel, but she couldn't believe Farrell had caved in to Campion's demands—especially over such a trivial charge. Not that she minded seeing Ross behind bars. For several reasons, she thought, he had some repenting to do.

Farrell spoke to Trent. "Okay, he's locked up. But he'll be out before you know it, and he's not gonna be happy. It's a busy time over at Brokenstraw. They're gettin' ready to brand."

"Then he should have thought about that before he messed with me." With a smug look, Trent turned to leave, then reconsidered and walked casually back to Maggie's desk. His voice took on a warm, persuasive tone. "It's almost noon—time to take a break. Why don't you join me for lunch?"

Maggie had to force a smile. Have lunch with a rich, spoiled, egotistical horse-beater? No, thanks. After her last relationship, she planned to be very selective of the men she dated. Even if she *liked* men who were all surface, no substance, Trent Campion's perfect black hair and movie-star looks didn't appeal to her. In fact, there was nothing about him that she found attractive—not even the wealth he flaunted. Today he wore jeans and a long-sleeved plaid shirt, like those worn by nearly every other man in Comfort. But Campion's were the expensive, tailor-made variety that had never known the sweat of an honest day's work.

Still, she hid her disgust. In this town, antagonizing the Campions was like biting the hand that fed you. Their charitable contributions and investments in local businesses had elevated them to near sainthood in the eyes of the community.

"Thanks, but I brought a lunch with me today. I have a lot of material to go over."

"Maybe another time, then." His green eyes stroked her dark ones. "There's a rodeo at the fairgrounds next weekend. Are you going? I'll be riding."

"Sorry, I don't know if I can. I'm staying with my aunt and uncle, and they'll probably have things for me to do."

"But if they don't...keep the rodeo in mind." Still smiling, he started away. "Take care, now."

"You, too," Maggie made herself say.

To her right and a little in front of her desk, Cy Farrell stood rigidly, watching Campion leave. His eyes were gray ice behind his steel-rimmed glasses. It was clear to Maggie that he'd been pushed into doing something he hadn't wanted to do. And that he resented it.

Cy hiked his uniform pants up over his paunch. "Maggie, I need to see somebody over at the print shop. Think you can handle things around here for a while?"

Well. Yes. She'd been a deputy in Colorado until she'd returned to Comfort last week; Farrell knew she was capable. Besides, he'd already left her alone when he'd gone looking for Ross. "Sure," she said, hiding a twinge of annoyance. "Anything you'd like me to do besides acquaint myself with procedures and answer the phone?"

He handed her the thick ring of keys. "Not on your first day. Joe should be back from Bozeman soon, and Mike's coming in around three." His thoughts turned from his two deputies to the man in the cell, and his disgruntled gaze followed. "And let *him* sit. If he starts hollering in there, check to see that he hasn't hung himself, then shut the door again."

The "hollering" started the instant Farrell fired up his Jeep and pulled out of his parking space.

Determined to be professional, ignoring the long-ago quote about a woman scorned—because it positively did *not* apply to her—Maggie walked to the slightly open door. Tamping down the strange, emotional fluttering behind her navel, she grabbed the knob and stepped inside.

Ross was sprawled lazily on his bunk, back braced against the green cement-block wall, hat tipped forward, worn brown cowboy boots crossed at his ankles. Eyes the color of a Montana sky assessed her from beneath the brim of his Stetson; they looked even bluer than she remembered in his lean, tanned face.

"Is there a problem, Mr. Dalton? Have you changed your mind about a lawyer?"

His smile was utterly charming. "Nope, I have something more effective in mind. But yes, ma'am, there is a problem. I'm just wasting away in here. How about sharing your lunch with me?"

Maggie sent him a chilling look. The door had only been cracked an inch or two, but it had apparently been enough for him to overhear her conversation with Trent.

"By the way, I'm glad you turned down the heir apparent's invitation to dine out. You can do a lot better."

"Who I spend time with is none of your business. As for lunch, I can phone your aunt Ruby's and order something for you."

Ross's gaze narrowed curiously. "You know I have an aunt Ruby? Have we met?"

He'd practically undressed her, but he still didn't have the vaguest idea who she was? How flattering. Maggie fought to keep her poise. "I heard you ask the sheriff if you could order from your aunt's café, Mr. Dalton. Now, what would you like?''

His low chuckle only made her angrier. "Wow, you're tough. It usually takes me a lot longer to tick off a woman this badly. How about a couple of cheeseburgers, a chocolate milk shake and a slice of apple pie?'' Skidding lower on his tailbone, he crossed his arms over his chest and closed his eyes. "I'll pay whoever makes the delivery. Actually,'' he added, "I'd be happy to buy you a hot lunch, too, if you'd quit being so uppity.''

Maggie stared at him for a full moment, wondering how a man who'd been in such deep trouble three years ago could still act like the world spun just to please him. How could anyone go through something like that and not come out changed? "You don't give a damn about anything, do you?''

"Of course I do. I definitely give a damn about going hungry, and I'm beginning to give a warm, fuzzy damn about your long braid and pretty brown eyes.''

"Get up.''

Ross cracked one of his eyes open. "What?''

"Get up and take off your belt.''

A teasing light rose in both eyes as he swept off his hat, tossed a hand through his hair to lessen the crushing effect of the Stetson, and ambled over to the bars where she stood. "You want my belt?''

"Prisoners aren't permitted to have belts, and I suspect you know that.''

"Is that in the manual?''

"The belt.''

"Afraid I'll do myself in, deputy?''

"I'm not a deputy yet. I'm only the dispatcher, and I couldn't begin to guess what you're capable of.''

Ross smiled slowly and undid the flashy rodeo belt buckle, then slid the leather out of his belt loops. "What if my pants fall down, Ms. Dispatcher-who-isn't-a-deputy-yet?''

Maggie reached through the bars, snatched the belt away, and strode back into the reception area. "Then I guess you'll be wearing them around your ankles, won't you? I'll call your order in to the café. The county will pick up the bill." She wasn't sure how Farrell handled the issue, but prisoners the world over were allowed to have lunch—no matter how aggravating they were.

This time when she closed the door, she made sure it stayed shut.

The sheriff was back and ensconced in his office by the time Ruby Cayhill stormed inside carrying a take-out box and a milk shake. A frown deepened the creases in her already lined face. *"Where is he?"* she demanded. She bumped her bony behind against the door, shutting out the early June heat.

At a brisk clip, she gained the reception desk. Aunt Ruby, as she directed everyone to call her, was ninety pounds and four feet eleven inches of righteous indignation, and today it was all directed at her great-nephew.

She passed her spectacled blue gaze over Maggie, then softened her irritation a bit. "Heard you were back in town, Maggie. How's yer uncle Moe? That was a nasty accident."

"He's better now, thanks, but he's really limited in what he can do. I'll be helping my Aunt Lila and cousin Scott for a while." Maggie paused. "I guess you're here to see Ross."

"I guess I am," she answered crisply.

"Then let's go wake him. I'll open the cell so you can hand in his food, but if you want to visit, you'll have to stay in the aisle. I'll bring a chair in for you."

"That young pup's *sleepin'* through this?" Ruby started toward the cells, her red high-top sneakers squeaking on the floor tiles, and her red cardigan flapping like a flag on a pole over her white waitress's uniform. A hair net squished frizzy silver curls to her head.

For the next few minutes, Maggie sat at her desk, thoroughly enjoying the lambasting Ross was getting. Then she quirked her head as the low rumble of his voice carried to her. A moment later, Ruby strode across the reception area to Farrell's office, her strident accusations ricocheting off the walls.

"It ain't bad enough you been harassin' my family since Ross's brother took yer girl away—a girl neither of you needed, I might add. Now you lock up my nephew for defendin' a helpless horse?"

"Aunt Ruby—"

"Don't you 'Aunt Ruby' me when I'm talkin' sense to you. You let that boy out right now, or so help me, I'll get my patrons to vote fer someone else come election day if I have to run for sheriff myself!"

"I'm sorry," Cy offered sincerely, "but my hands are tied. A complaint has been filed—"

"Well, another complaint's gonna be filed soon as I git to my phone, mister, and you're *not* gonna like it." Whirling abruptly, Ruby trooped out of the office, nodded shortly to Maggie, then threw the door open wide and marched out.

The low chuckles emanating from the lockup didn't register in Maggie's mind until Ruby was midway across the street. She hurried to shut the door before the sound carried to Farrell's office.

Ross stood, grinning, his forearms draped loosely through the bars of his cell and resting on the crossbeam, his blue eyes full of amusement. "I warned you."

Maggie paused in the doorway. "About what?"

"I told you I had something more effective in mind than a lawyer, Ms. Dispatcher. Now, may I have my belt back, please? I expect I'll be leaving within the hour."

He was only off by fifteen minutes. Maggie had just hung up on the air-conditioner repairman and had gotten his promise to come by first thing the next morning, when Ben Campion's commanding presence filled the doorway. His brooding son followed him inside.

"Miss," he said, with a gallant tip of his white Stetson. "I wonder if I could have a word with the sheriff?" Campion was sixty-something with gray-white hair and tanned, handsome features. Though he was simply dressed in a short-sleeved shirt and slacks, his gold-nugget string tie and Rolex watch were not-so-subtle reminders that he was a wealthy man.

Cy hurried out of his office, his ingratiating smile making Maggie a little sick. After the good ol' boy backslapping and handshakes had ceased, the elder Campion's forehead lined.

"It seems there's been a misunderstanding." Ben smiled at Trent, but there was no warmth in it. "My boy's decided he was a little rash in insisting Ross Dalton be locked up this morning. He'd like to drop those charges now, wouldn't you, son?"

Trent nodded sullenly, but didn't speak.

Farrell beamed. "Absolutely, Ben. No problem at all. In fact, I think if you ask Trent what I said earlier, you'll find that I thought it'd be a good idea to let bygones be bygones, too."

Campion's shrewd black eyes judged Farrell. "Well, I surely wish you'd been a bit stronger with your objections, Cy. Woulda saved me a trip to town. A sheriff's got to be in control, you know what I'm sayin'? Especially a sheriff who wants to be reelected this fall."

Farrell flushed deeply, but it was an angry flush that said Campion had taken his reprimand a step too far. "Of course, Ben. Sorry for the inconvenience." He turned away. "I'll see if our prisoner's ready to get out of here."

"Appreciate it, Cy."

A few moments later, Ross reentered the reception area, a whisper of a grin still touching his lips. "Hi, Ben, nice to see you. What brings you to town?"

Campion's gaze darkened, and with slow, purposeful strides, he crossed the room to Ross. He lowered his voice, but not low enough. "I put up with your aunt's threats because she's an old woman. But don't you ever interfere with Campion business, or try to embarrass my family again. If you do, you'll be sorry for a long, long time." With a bracing smile for Maggie, Ben walked out, Trent and Farrell following behind him.

Ross strolled over to Maggie's desk. "Guess it's okay if his kid rides roughshod over half the county, as long as he leaves the horses alone. Ben's got a real soft spot when it comes to his prize Appaloosas."

Maggie nodded. When Ross continued to stand there, however, she sent him a questioning look. For some reason, she didn't feel nearly as antagonistic toward him as she had earlier. Maybe because the other men she'd dealt with today were so much worse. "Is there something else?"

"My belt? Unless you'd like to keep it till Saturday night."

Maggie blinked, not understanding. "Saturday night?"

He smiled. "I could pick you up around eight, and we could drive out to Dusty's Roadhouse...have some laughs, dance a bit?"

Not in this lifetime. She'd been down that road before with this man—even if he had no recollection of it. She wouldn't be "picked up" by him again.

Locking her gaze on his, Maggie reached inside a deep desk drawer and withdrew a large manila envelope with his name on it. "Sorry, I don't dance. Here's your belt. Try to stay out of trouble."

Chuckling, Ross withdrew his property, then laid the

envelope on her desk. "Only if you'll do something for me."

"What?"

"Let your hair down a little."

"My hair is down, Mr. Dalton. Now isn't there somewhere else you'd like to be?"

Maggie saw his gaze slip down the front of her uniform to her name tag, and a tingling she hadn't felt in a long time vibrated over her nerve endings.

"Actually, there is. But since the woman I'd like to be there with isn't exactly falling at my feet, I guess I'll just go back to Brokenstraw and round up a few more strays." Smiling, he touched the brim of his hat and headed for the door. "Bye, Miss Maggie. It's been interesting."

Yes, Maggie thought, watching him through the window as he climbed into his truck and drove away. It certainly had been that.

Chapter 2

Maggie pulled her little blue Ford onto the gravel pad beside the house, shut off the engine and got out. She freed the top button of her uniform as she walked up to the wide white porch where her uncle sat, dressed in a work shirt and a pair of roomy pajama bottoms. Moe Jackson was a big man in his early sixties, with a weathered face and hazel eyes, and he was wearing the same "just shoot me, I'm not worth a dang" look he'd been treating his family to since his accident had put him out of commission. His hair was still as black as the day he was born, a Jackson trait Maggie's mother had shared. When she had died four years ago, Amanda Bristol's hair had been that same shade of ebony.

"Hi," Maggie called.

"Hi. Your pa phoned."

"Great. I'll call him back in a few minutes. You're looking good. You're getting some color back." Ascending the steps, she kissed his cheek and plopped down on the porch swing. "The fresh air and sunshine must be agreeing with you."

Moe gestured to his taped ribs and his cast-encased leg, the latter propped up on a wicker ottoman and cushioned by pillows. "Gettin' rid of *this* nonsense would agree with me more. I feel like a useless old woman sitting here on the swing while other folks are out doin' my work."

"I know," Maggie said kindly. "But you can't roll a tractor over on yourself and expect to come out without a scratch. You're lucky it wasn't a lot worse."

"Yeah, yeah," he grumbled. Wincing, he reached for the glass of lemonade on the small wicker table beside him, then took a sip. "How was *your* day?"

"Oh, about as much fun as yours, I imagine. The air conditioner was down, and everyone who came in had an ax to grind. Which makes sense, I suppose. No one visits the sheriff unless he has a problem." Maggie paused for a moment, studying the car keys in her hand. "I did something today I probably shouldn't have done. I kind of overstepped my bounds."

Moe raised a thick black eyebrow, finally interested in something besides his own discomfort. "Oh? What?"

"I pulled Ross Dalton's file and read it."

If he was annoyed before, the mention of Ross's name tripled his vexation. "I expect you would've found better readin' on a bathroom wall. Hell-bent for destruction, that one. Been wild since his momma and old Ross died."

Maggie remembered the small plane crash that had taken the lives of Ross's parents; they'd been members of her father's church. "It had to be hard on him, losing his parents so young."

"His brother Jess turned out fine—and he lost his parents, too." Moe took another swallow of his lemonade. "Why did you want to read Ross's file?"

His rugged face appeared in Maggie's mind and, against her will, a tingle of attraction ran through her. "Oh, just curiosity, I guess. Farrell pulled him in today, and I thought I'd take a peek at what he's been up to lately. There really wasn't much in the file except...that rustling business."

"That rustling business?" Moe echoed. "Those were *my* steers, Maggie, and if the courts hadn't forced those thievin' skunks to make restitution, I'd still be tryin' to recoup my losses."

Maggie inched closer on the swing, feeling a bit odd because she was about to defend Ross. Not because she cared one whit about him—but because he didn't deserve to be lumped into the same category as "thievin' skunks."

"According to the report, he didn't actively participate in the rustling. The file said that when he realized what those men were up to, he refused to have anything to do with it. The court gave him immunity for his testimony— which *did* put the actual criminals behind bars."

"Makes no difference," Moe snorted. "He was weak to get involved with them people in the first place. All that drinkin' and gamblin'—owin' money to the wrong folks. He didn't just put his family's ranch at risk, he damn near got his sister-in-law killed because he couldn't stay away from the cards."

That wasn't exactly what had happened, Maggie knew. In fact, Ross had acted heroically on the night in question. But when she verbalized her thoughts, Moe scowled again.

"Maggie, if Ross Dalton did anything heroic, then he was an *accidental* hero. You keep that in mind." His scowl deepened. "Now—what's he done this time?"

"Nothing terrible. He and Trent Campion mixed it up earlier in the day. Trent and his father came in later to drop the charges."

Suddenly her uncle's tone became a lot more patient. "Now, there's a fella for you, Maggie. Young Campion would be a fine catch."

Trent? She couldn't imagine Trent Campion being a "catch" for anyone, much less her.

"Aside from money, education and him not bein' all that ugly, his daddy's priming him for the state legislature."

"I didn't realize Trent was involved in politics."

"He ain't yet, exactly. But he's up in the capital pretty often lobbyin' for conservation groups and such. When he's ready to run for office, he'll get in. The Campions have some powerful friends." Moe frowned and met her gaze. "Wouldn't hurt you to pay Trent some mind instead of wasting your time readin' about Ross Dalton."

Maggie was about to say that she wouldn't be interested in Trent if his father were priming him for the presidency, when her aunt stepped outside, looking lean and fit in jeans and a light blue T-shirt.

An indulgent smile tipped the corners of Lila Jackson's mouth. "My goodness, but you're ornery today." With her slim build and feathered cap of gray hair, she looked much younger than her fifty-eight years. "And by the way, Your Grumpiness, I'd take ten of Ross over one Trent Campion any day. It wasn't Trent who rode over here the day after your accident to offer his help, now was it?"

"Too little, too late," Moe growled.

"Ross offered to help out, Uncle Moe?"

"Yeah, but I ran him off. I don't need his kind of help."

Lila sighed audibly, then turned a smile on Maggie. "Supper's almost ready, honey. I hope you like shepherd's pie."

"Love it," Maggie said, grinning. "I'll set the table. Is Scott staying?" Moe and Lila's son was married and lived in town, but he still worked the Lazy J with his father.

"Not tonight. He and Marly are having dinner with her folks."

"He's lucky," Moe grumbled. "No self-respectin' cattleman should be eatin' anything called shepherd's pie."

"You're absolutely right, sweetheart," Lila said with a twinkling look at Maggie. "That's why we're popping a toaster waffle in for you."

On Saturday morning, Maggie saddled up her uncle's chestnut gelding and rode out right after breakfast. The day before, Scott and Lila had moved the new calf-and-mother units to the west pasture to make next week's branding more convenient; today Maggie's job was to check for stock that might have been missed.

As she rode, she reflected on her first full week back home. Time had flown by. She'd thrown herself into managing the office, gritted her teeth while she made coffee for the men, and tried to control her envy as Farrell and his two deputies went out on calls. Her evenings were spent tending to the ranch work Scott and Lila didn't get to during the day.

But the nights that she didn't fall asleep the instant her head hit her pillow, Maggie's thoughts somehow found their way to Ross Dalton—which thoroughly annoyed her.

Maybe it was because they were neighbors with the Daltons' Brokenstraw ranch, which bordered the Lazy J to the east. Or maybe it was because she'd spent too many nights thinking about him when she was a teenager, and old habits were hard to break. Either way, there was a physical attraction there that made her nervous. Not that it would ever go further than that, and not that seeing Ross would quash any hopes of Farrell giving her that deputyship. She'd recently ended a two-year involvement with Todd, a man who'd finally admitted that he couldn't take the next steps in their relationship—engagement, marriage, children.

Hitching her wagon to Comfort's commitment-phobic bad boy was just asking for another dose of heartbreak. And she knew from experience that—given the opportunity—Ross Dalton could break her heart quicker than a

Chinook wind could melt a mountainside. He'd done it before.

Pushing her thoughts aside, Maggie crisscrossed the east pasture, centering her efforts on clumps of trees and hillocks as she scanned the area for curly-faced, red-coated Herefords. The sky overhead was a clear, cloudless blue, crows complained noisily, and faint wisps of fog still hung in the deeper depressions of the pasture. The air she inhaled was sweet with the smells of sage and wildflowers.

Suddenly Maggie pulled up as a low mooing drew her attention to a coppice of trees ahead. Then a brief snatch of blue fabric flashed through the leafy cottonwoods. Putting her heels to the chestnut's flanks, Maggie nudged the gelding into a lope. She was sure Scott was still back at the barn. There shouldn't be anyone...

Shock, then anger, ripped through her, and Maggie kicked her horse into a full gallop.

At the sound of pounding hooves, Ross glanced around to see a slender woman with silky black hair thundering across the pasture toward him. He started to smile as he pulled his mount up short, preventing the light-buckskin-colored horse from pushing the last of three steers over the downed barbwire to Brokenstraw property.

Ross's blood began to warm. What was *she* doing out here? Not that he minded. He hadn't been able to get his pretty jailer out of his mind all week.

"What do you think you're doing?" she shouted, yanking back on the reins. The powerful chestnut reared, then danced to a blowing, head-tossing stop as Maggie brought him under control.

Ross's delighted gaze took in her fiery brown eyes, high color, and that sexy tumble of hair falling around her face and shoulders. Then it slipped to her open collar and the pale-yellow cotton shirt and jeans she wore with her boots. "My, my," he breathed softly.

"You shag those cattle right back where they belong, or I'm running you in."

The loathing in her voice withered the smile on his face. A split second later, understanding dawned, and Ross dredged up a bit of loathing himself. "You think I'm stealing these steers?"

"Aren't you?"

"Well, I must be, if a fine, upstanding member of the sheriff's department says I am." He ran his eyes over her body again, lingering rudely on her breasts, hips and long, athletic legs. "Are you tailing me?" Without waiting for a reply, he smirked, and added, "I guess the sheriff decided you'd be better at 'undercover work' than dispatching, Miss Maggie. Might be the first thing Farrell and I have ever agreed on."

"Get those animals back here where they belong."

"I intend to," Ross said, steel lacing his words. "But before you shake out the handcuffs and read me my rights, you might want to check the brand on these steers."

Ross watched Maggie's furious gaze slide to the side and look. When she saw the Brokenstraw brand, new color rose in her cheeks. "I'm...I'm sorry. They're your cattle."

"Yes, they are. And as soon as I'm through here, I'm riding into town and filing a harassment charge. I think I might like being on the other side of a complaint."

"No one's harassing you, Mr. Dalton," Maggie snapped. "I'm out here working, just like you are." She stepped down and ground-tethered her horse, then strode over to examine the rotted post and downed fence line that had allowed Ross's strays onto Lazy J property. "Are you going to fix this fence?"

He sent her a cold look. "Well, now, I'm not sure. I've been trying to decide which would be a better idea—repair it now, or ride two miles out of my way every damn day to shag my strays back home again."

"You're not cute, Mr. Dalton."

"Really? A lot of women think I am."

"So I've heard." Maggie returned to her horse and unbuckled her saddlebag. She withdrew a pair of thick gloves.

"What are you doing?"

"I'm going to help you."

"Why?"

"Obviously, to make sure it's done right. I don't want any more Brokenstraw cattle eating Jackson grass."

Ross swore a blue streak under his breath and climbed down from the buckskin. "And why would you care?"

"Because I'm Moe Jackson's niece."

Ross scowled as he digested that fact and everything it implied. He imagined Moe had filled her head with a lot of unflattering—but unfortunately true—information. Since the rustling, Moe didn't have a very high opinion of him. "I guess that explains why you hate my guts," he said. "*And* the way you ride. I take it you grew up around horses."

Her anger actually intensified. "I grew up around here. *Right* here. I'm *Maggie Bristol*."

"You say your name as though I should recognize it. From where? Did we go to school together?"

Maggie yanked on her gloves. For the first time, Ross noticed that a black cowboy hat dangled against her back. "Possibly. I don't recall. Now are we going to mend that fence, or waste time talking all day?"

Ross gritted his teeth. Bristol. Bristol. He grabbed the bag of tools and the wrapped, lasso-size roll of wire tied to his own saddle, then carried them over to the fence. He was surprised when Maggie took the initiative and dragged the rotted post aside, then suggested coolly that they use a nearby tree for a temporary connecting post.

"Fine." With a bit of grudging respect, Ross joined a length of new wire to old, then motioned for Maggie to hold the barbwire against the trunk while he hammered in staples. He had a stray thought that she was precisely the right height for a woman; if he were to pull her close, her head would slip snugly under his chin. Ross shook off the musing and hammered in another staple.

After a while, he said, "How did you get roped into the dispatching job? Seems like you'd make a fair cowhand."

Her voice still dripped with attitude. "I applied. When my uncle was hurt, I sent out a resume. I was a deputy in Colorado for two years, but this was always home."

"You were a deputy, but you applied for a dispatching job?"

"No, I applied for a deputyship, and Farrell promised me Mike Halston's job when he leaves for law school at the end of summer. Then he mentioned that he was going to be losing his dispatcher, and that if I wanted, I could start sooner at that position."

Ross clipped and stretched the last row of wire, then hammered in more staples. "A female deputy under Cy Farrell? I hate to rain on your parade, but our esteemed sheriff probably forgot that promise two seconds after he made it."

Maggie's tone didn't change. "I don't think so. While memory loss seems to be a veritable plague on some of the men in this town, I believe he'll follow through. Are we finished?"

Ross plucked the wire with a gloved hand, checking its tautness. "I guess. It's not great, but it'll do until I can come out and sink another post."

"Good." Pulling off her gloves, Maggie walked briskly to her mount and stuffed the gloves into her saddlebag. Then she gathered the chestnut's reins and levered herself into the saddle. For a moment, she stared down at him, the muscular gelding skittering impatiently beneath her, while something that he thought looked like...hurt?...churned through her expression. Then, without a word, she gave the horse his head and rode off, leaving the image of fire-dark eyes, cascading hair and a perfect mouth burning in Ross's mind.

He was halfway back to the homestead when it finally hit him that Maggie Bristol was Reverend Tom Bristol's daughter.

Which still didn't explain why she was so hostile toward him—even taking into account his trouble with Moe. The Bristols had moved away quite a few years ago when the reverend was reassigned to another parish. Ross hadn't gone to church regularly since his mother and dad had passed away, so it was unlikely that he would have known Maggie from there. But now that he thought about it…there was something vaguely familiar about—

Like a sudden storm, the memory returned in a rush of splashing water, party music and shrieking laughter. Vince Harper was chuckling to him beside the bonfire. "Nice move, Ross, that was the preacher's daughter you were foolin' with. Man, you're goin' to hell, for sure."

Ross winced as the scene replayed in his mind. Sweet lips…soft voice…warm, responsive body. At least it had been until he'd gotten a little carried away, and she'd scurried for home like a frightened church mouse. No wonder she was in such a snit. No woman—or girl, for that matter—wanted to be so insignificant in a man's mind that she was completely forgettable. And he *had* forgotten her. The minute she and her timid little friend escaped back to their car, he'd connected with an older girl who knew exactly what he wanted—and Maggie Bristol had become a hazy memory.

Ross kept half of his attention on the fence line as he walked his mount through knee-high sweet grass and blue columbine. Eventually, his thoughts took an enjoyable little shift, and he smiled to himself: the preacher's little girl had grown up very nicely.

The woman who'd come galloping across that pasture on horseback bore almost no resemblance to the quiet girl with the prim, pageboy hairstyle and buttoned-to-the-throat white blouse. She was now a raven-haired knockout with a body that was born to the saddle, and a feisty attitude that heated his blood.

Suddenly the excitement of challenge rose in his veins. With a light heel to its ribs, Ross nudged the buckskin along a little faster. That long-ago night at the hot spring, she'd stiffened at first when he'd slid his tongue into her mouth—but if he were still a betting man, he'd lay odds Maggie Bristol knew how to kiss like a woman now. He just had to find a way to make it happen.

Not a very lofty goal, a small inner voice put in.

"Too bad," he muttered, feeling the old bitterness return. This was as lofty as he got these days. After the trial, he'd done everything in his power to make amends for his past indiscretions. But no matter how hard he tried, Comfort, Montana, had labeled him an irresponsible hell-raiser, and any kindness or decency on his part had been held suspect. Now he showed them the face they were comfortable with. No point confusing the natives.

On Monday afternoon, Ross pulled his truck into a parking space in front of the sheriff's office, glanced in the rearview mirror to check his shave, then headed for the door. Not bad, if he did say so himself. Clean shirt, decent jeans and polished boots. Maggie was at her desk, talking on the phone, when he walked in. Her posture stiffened the instant she noticed him.

Scribbling something on a notepad, she rose and said, "I'll see that he gets the message," then hung up.

Ignoring him, Maggie carried the slip of paper into the sheriff's office and put it on his desk. When she came back out, she gave Ross her grudging attention.

"Something I can do for you, Mr. Dalton?"

"Yep. I've come to turn myself in. A gum wrapper blew out of my truck window a few minutes ago, and I figured

I'd save Cy the trouble of hunting me down and bringing me in for questioning." He sent her his most charming grin. "You want to cuff me or anything?"

She wasn't amused *or* charmed. "I'm busy, Mr. Dalton, and unless you have a good reason for being here—"

"As a matter of fact, I do," he interrupted amiably. "I just thought I'd try to lighten the mood a bit before we got down to business."

Maggie shuffled through some papers on her desk, then turned her back on him and went to the file cabinet. "What business could we possibly have that would require lightening the mood?"

"I'm here to press charges against you for harassing me."

Maggie whirled, almost lost the sheaf of papers she was filing, and stared at him, dumbstruck. "You're joking."

"No, ma'am, I'm not. Now, how do I go about this? It's rare for me to be on this side of a legal problem."

Ross watched that blistering anger rise in her eyes and had a hard time holding back another smile. The fact that she obviously hated him made getting her into his bed all the more tempting.

Maggie finished her filing, walked stiffly back to the desk and sat, then sent him a steady look. "I can't take your statement. That's up to the sheriff or one of the deputies, and they're all out on calls right now. But just for the fun of it, perhaps you'd like to tell me what charges you're planning to bring. Harassment isn't going to work because the definition of harassment isn't met under our circumstances."

Ross adjusted his tan Stetson and pursed his lips thoughtfully, thoroughly enjoying himself. "All right... libel, then. You *did* falsely accuse me of stealing my own steers."

"That won't work, either. Libel is damaging a person's reputation in print."

"Slander?"

She sighed impatiently. "Really, Mr. Dalton, for as many times as you've been dragged in here in the past ten years, I would have guessed you'd have some knowledge of the law. Even if I *had* pointedly accused you, there were no witnesses, therefore, your sterling character wasn't defamed, and there was no slander. Now, can't you find someone else to bother today? I'm busy."

Ross glanced at her desk. Aside from a pen, a notepad and an inactive computer, there wasn't a thing on it. "Yes, I can see how busy you are." He made no move to leave—just stood there watching her dig around in a drawer until her irritation erupted again.

"Why are you still here?"

He grinned. "You like me."

Her pretty jaw sagged, and she sent him a bewildered look. "Why on earth would you think that?"

"Because you've obviously been checking up on me to make a statement like you did."

"*What* statement?"

"The one about my fondness for being here. Did you go through my file?" He waved the question aside. "Well, you might have, but to know I've been dragged in here every time Farrell's ego needed a boost, you would've had to talk to someone. Let's see...a deputy, maybe? Mike Halston? He likes to talk."

Maggie felt her cheeks turn to fire. She *had* spoken to Mike about Ross. But she'd only done it out of professional concern for the grudge Cy Farrell held toward the Dalton family. Mike had told her that in the past few years, bullying Ross for sport had replaced Cy's preoccupation with discrediting Ross's brother, Jess. Now Maggie doubted that was the reason at all. Farrell was probably just sick to death of Ross's insolence and was determined to take him down a peg or two.

Maggie picked up her pen, studied it, then rolled it

slowly between her hands. Her gaze returned to Ross. "Speaking of egos that need boosting, why are you really here? Am I supposed to go for this ridiculous hayseed act you seem to conjure up whenever you're looking for some action? Do you think all women are that naive?"

"No, ma'am."

Maggie threw the pen down and stood, coming almost nose to nose with him across the desk. "Stop calling me 'ma'am.' I've had it with your fake drawl and your lopsided grins. In fact, you were a lot more appealing when you were swearing up a storm and swinging a hammer."

Grinning again, Ross bumped his nose to hers. Gasping, Maggie jerked back in shock. "Now we're making progress. You do like me a little. Let's take a ride and talk about it."

"Look," she snapped in frustration, "I'm trying to build a career here, and being seen in public with the sheriff's favorite felon isn't conducive to accomplishing that."

Maggie watched his blue eyes harden, and instantly regretted her words. Until now, none of her comments had seemed to strike home. But that… That was low, considering the fact that he'd paid dearly for his past behavior. Mike Halston had told her that since the rustling, some people still refused to speak to Ross, unable to forget the gambling addiction that had nearly destroyed his life. "Ross, I'm sorry."

But he'd already pushed his reaction behind another cocky grin. "Come on, Maggie," he drawled. "You've been biting at me ever since you came back to town. You still mad because I didn't try harder that night back at the hot spring? Or is it because I never gave you another chance to say yes?"

Maggie's face flamed as she watched him amble out, get into his truck and drive away. He'd finally remembered her.

Now she wished to heaven that he hadn't.

Swallowing, she went to the file cabinet and pulled Ross's folder again, then carried it back to her desk. She reread the information that she'd scanned last week. Because of his gambling, he'd nearly lost his half of Brokenstraw by defaulting on a loan; he'd been dragged into a rustling ring; and he'd been shot trying to save the woman who'd eventually become his sister-in-law from being taken hostage when the rustlers fled town. After that, there had been a court-ordered gambling rehab program and two years of community service.

Maggie closed the file and released a ragged breath, suddenly weary. "You've been a busy man, Mr. Dalton," she said quietly. "But I can't afford to feel any sympathy for you. I just can't."

She also couldn't afford to think about the disturbing things he did to her nervous system when he was around. Oh, yes, she'd thought him appealing when they'd met at that fence line. So appealing that it had been an enormous effort to keep her mind and eyes on the task at hand. His chiseled looks and long, lean body made her warm and jittery; the low timbre of his voice made her pulse race. But nothing could come of it. The next man she let into her life would be stable and dependable. Not an overgrown child with a disarming smile.

When four o'clock finally came, Maggie gratefully left the office in part-time deputy Joe Talbot's hands, and climbed behind the wheel of her car. She opened the collar of her uniform shirt and rolled back the sleeves. The day hadn't been all that busy, but she had needed some time to think, and the constant ringing of the phone had prevented that.

Pressing the gas pedal, Maggie sailed along, passing the town limits, then turning onto the unpaved country road that led to the Lazy J. A plume of light brown dust rose behind her. She was still feeling bothered and embarrassed about her run-in with Ross that afternoon. As her mind played and replayed their meeting, lush green meadows and miles of barbwire zipped by her side window.

Impatience had made her too short with him, and she really did regret it. But she'd needed to make it clear that nothing was going to happen between them, hadn't she? Especially since anything that did happen would be a momentary fling for him. Then he'd turn his attention elsewhere, just as he'd done that night thirteen years ago. She'd heard later from Mary Ellen—who'd heard it from her older sister—that another girl had taken her place the moment they'd driven off. How utterly humiliating. Maggie had finally found her way into his arms and naive lamb that she was—she hadn't been able to go where he'd wanted to take her...

"Then why did he pick me in the first place?" she'd fumed at her friend, trying to cover her embarrassment. "There were plenty of older girls there to choose from."

Mary Ellen, in her sixteen-year-old wisdom, had winced to take some of the sting out of her answer, and guessed, "Fresh meat?"

And that was probably all Maggie was to him now, too—a challenge waiting to become a conquest.

With a satisfied nod, Maggie gave the accelerator another nudge. Okay, now she felt better about calling him a felon.

A tape she'd been listening to on her way to work rattled loosely in the tape deck. She shoved it in the rest of the way, and Celine Dion's powerful voice flowed from the speakers.

What a coincidence, she thought, frowning. Just like Maggie's, Celine's memories were all coming back to her now.

Suddenly the little Ford's "check engine" light flashed on.

Braking quickly, Maggie pulled over to the side of the

road and shut off the car. *Now what?* Reaching down, she popped the hood release, then climbed out just as the dust she'd been raising caught up with her. Squinting and coughing, she fanned a feeble hand to clear the air, then walked to the front of the car.

Fingers of steam curled from beneath her sprung hood.

Chapter 3

"**W**onderful," she muttered. "Just wonderful." It was hot, she was still five miles from her uncle's spread, and this was probably one of the least-traveled roads in the whole state. Why was it that these things always happened when one was twenty miles from the nearest garage?

Maggie raised the hood, and the trickle of steam became a billowing white cloud. It only took a moment to discover the hole in her radiator hose. Sighing, she slammed the hood. Then she grabbed her purse and keys and started walking.

Thirty minutes later, she was breathlessly climbing over a barbwire fence and taking what she hoped was a shortcut across a tree-dotted pasture. She'd spent a little time here when she was a girl, but not really enough to pick out familiar landmarks; staying on the road would have been wiser. But at the rate she was going, it would have been Tuesday—and time to go to work again—when she got home.

She was sweaty, ornery and footsore by the time the

dull drumming of horse's hooves sounded in the pasture behind her. She heard a soft, deep "whoa," then the blowing stomp of the large animal being pulled up short. She knew who the rider was without turning around. It had been that kind of day.

"Out for a walk?"

Maggie turned to glare at him, then faced forward again and kept moving. Right. When she walked she always wore a soggy uniform and a purse slung across her chest like a paperboy's bag.

Ross brought his buckskin mount alongside her as she hiked through the knee-deep grass. He matched the horse's pace to hers. "Guess something happened to your car, huh?"

She tried not to sound out of breath, and failed. "Radiator hose."

"Oh. Sorry to hear that."

She just bet that he was.

"Quite a coincidence, our meeting again today. Buck and I were just heading for home when we saw you."

"Buck" clopped softly along beside her, and Maggie gritted her teeth.

"I replaced that rotted fence post today. Looks like Brokenstraw's cows will be staying on their own side of the fence now."

Buck kept walking, Ross kept riding, and Maggie kept seething. She felt as though she'd spent the last hour in a Navajo sweat lodge, and emerged with none of the curative benefits.

"Well, take care," Ross said, reining his horse around and pointing it in the other direction. "Supper's probably ready by—"

Maggie's angry shout startled half a dozen crows into flight. "*Do I have to beg you for a ride home?*"

Ross held his horse up. "No," he said politely, and she could read the payback in his eyes. "All you have to do is ask." He didn't add a reminder that her reputation was safe—that chances of anyone seeing her out here with "the sheriff's favorite felon" were slim to none. But she'd have bet anything that's what he was thinking.

"All right," she said, swallowing her pride. "I'm asking."

Dismounting, Ross led the horse back to her, then offered her a clean handkerchief from his back pocket. Mumbling her thanks, Maggie blotted her sweaty face. "I'll launder it for you and send it back."

"Just keep it." He paused, assessing her flushed complexion and the long tendrils of black hair that had come loose from her braid. "There's water in my canteen. It's probably warm, though."

"I'd love some, thank you."

He retrieved it for her, and as she drank, Maggie experienced a peculiar feeling knowing that he'd sipped from the same container. She managed a weak smile when she gave it back. "Delicious."

"Old family recipe." After returning the canteen to his saddlebag, he gestured to his horse. "All set?"

Nodding, Maggie mounted up. Her feet didn't reach the stirrups, and he adjusted them. Then Ross swung up behind her, and reached around her for the reins.

"Shouldn't take long," he said, his deep voice burring beside her ear. "Ten minutes, tops."

It was the longest ten minutes of Maggie's life. Even though they were separated by the cantle's hard ridge of leather, suddenly she was fifteen again, and her stomach was quivering as they rode because she was in Ross Dalton's arms...surrounded by his scent...feeling his warm breath fan the side of her neck.

Maggie sat ramrod-straight and gripped the saddle horn for balance, trying to ignore the jostling rub of his forearms against hers. Trying to minimize their contact. But now and then with the change of terrain, she'd bump back against his chest or he'd lean forward to keep his seat. By the time she got to her uncle's place, she was so tense that her shoulder blades ached.

Her aunt Lila opened the screen door and hurried out, as Ross reined his horse to a halt near the path leading to the house.

"Maggie! Thank goodness. We were beginning to worry about you. I called the office and Mike said you'd left quite a while ago." Lila smiled a welcome to Ross from the top step. "Hi, neighbor. Where did you find her?"

Ross slid down off the horse's rump, and Maggie swung her leg over the saddle and dismounted.

"Not too far from here. She had car trouble."

Maggie frowned at him. "I can speak, if you don't mind." She turned back to her aunt. "I had car trouble."

Lila Jackson seemed to hold back a smile as her gaze took in the two of them standing together. "So I've heard. You look like you could use a shower and some supper before we drag out the truck and tow chain. Any idea what's wrong with your car?"

Ross answered again, and Maggie clamped down hard on her molars. "She thinks it's just a radiator hose. If you want, I can take a look."

Moe Jackson appeared behind the screen door, gripping a walker. His voice was gruff. "No need, we can handle it."

"Nice to see you up and around Moe," Ross called cordially. "How's the leg?"

Maggie shifted uncomfortably, hoping her uncle would try to be civil. Regardless of the grudge he held, Moe was a fair man—and Ross *had* helped a member of his family.

"Comin' along," he returned without cracking a smile. "You okay, Maggie?"

"I'm fine. Just a little warm."

"Good. Your aunt was worried about you." Without

another word, he turned awkwardly and moved away from the screen door.

Maggie saw Ross's mouth tighten, then he climbed back into the saddle, ignoring the short stirrups. Though her uncle hadn't been openly hostile, his tone and manner spoke volumes. Moe Jackson would tolerate Ross, but he wouldn't welcome him.

"Well, I'd better get going and let you folks have your supper."

Maggie nodded soberly. If her rescuer had been anyone but Ross, he would've been invited to stay for the evening meal as an expression of her family's appreciation. Maggie knew that Ross was aware of that, too. There was an old saying some Montanans still used: "The latchstring is always out." It just wasn't out for Ross.

Lila sent Ross an apologetic smile as she followed her husband back inside. "Thanks again, Ross. Say hello to Jess and Casey for us."

"I'll do that."

When Lila, too, was gone, Ross dismounted and bent to readjust his stirrups. Maggie felt her heart soften as she watched his strong hands at their task.

"I'm sorry he was so cold. He's still upset about…well, you know."

"You can say it. Plenty of other people still do."

He walked to the other side of the horse, and Maggie followed. "Then that's unfair," she said sincerely, as he adjusted the other stirrup. "You never wanted to be a part of it, and you weren't." She paused. "And I'm sorry I called you a felon this afternoon. That's not true, either."

Ross returned to the left side of his horse and mounted again. He looked down at her. "Only because I turned state's evidence. Otherwise, there would've been an accessory charge, and I would've been serving time now instead of talking to you." The reins chinked lightly against the buckskin's bridle as Ross slowly turned his horse toward home. "Moe has a right to feel the way he does."

Twenty minutes later, Lila Jackson bumped her old Chevy pickup around the bend in the road where Maggie had left her car. And Maggie was startled to see Ross there. He was just slamming her hood and tucking a pocketknife into his jeans.

Maggie found herself battling that strange attraction again. It didn't matter that he was the most aggravating man she'd ever known. He was the perfect American cowboy—long and lean...flat-stomached and gritty in his plaid shirt and dusty jeans. Several yards behind her car, Ross's horse was tied to a fence post and pulling up grass below the barbwire.

Maggie got out of the truck. "Hi."

Ross's reply was cordial and friendly despite his words. "Before you accuse me of trying to steal your car, let me assure you that I'm not interested." He tapped his tan Stetson. "No hat room." His glance slid over her loose hair, clean jeans and pale blue shirt, and Maggie was glad she'd used her time to clean up a bit. "Looks like you skipped supper," he observed.

"I'll eat later. I needed the shower more than the food. So what's the prognosis?"

"It's fixed. Temporarily, anyway. The hole was close enough to the radiator connection for me to cut off a couple inches of hose, then stretch it back on and re-clamp it. But I wouldn't put too many miles on the car before you have the hose replaced." Shifting his eyes, he smiled at her aunt Lila who, for some reason, was hanging back beside the truck. "Got a water can in that bucket of bolts, Lila?"

"You name it, I got it." Grinning, she fetched the can from the bed of the truck. "And you have some respect for this fine piece of machinery," she added. "She's a gutsy old girl. Eight cylinders, and 396 horses. She'll take anything *you* drive.''

''My apologies,'' he said, chuckling.

Ross filled Maggie's radiator, then splashed a little water on his greasy hands and wiped them off in the grass. A few minutes later, Lila was driving off, leaving her niece to follow in her own car.

''So,'' Maggie said when they were alone again. ''I guess I owe you another thank-you.'' Frowning at her sneakers, she considered the offer that she was about to make, then once again met the compelling blue eyes beneath the Stetson. ''I was thinking...that is, if you still wanted to have lunch...that we could drive over to Big Timber on Saturday. My treat, of course. I know this restaurant where the food's great, and—''

His eyes went cold. ''—and there probably wouldn't be a soul around who knew either of us, right?''

Maggie flushed deeply—and lied. ''Ross, that wasn't my reason for suggesting Big Ti—''

''The hell it wasn't. You're scared to death to be seen with me. Fortunately for both of us, I already have a lunch date.'' He moved closer, grit scraping beneath his boots, and something imminent darkening his eyes. ''But you're right. You do owe me another thank-you. I want a kiss.''

Shocked, Maggie tried to backpedal away. But she had nowhere to go. The backs of her knees smacked her front bumper, her legs buckled and her fanny dropped firmly on the hood of the car.

''You give me too much credit,'' Ross said with a shrug. ''But if you need to be sitting for this, fine.''

Before she could say no, one of his broad hands tipped up her face and his warm mouth covered hers. Her response to him was swift and astonishing. A shivery heat flooded Maggie's limbs, and her traitorous lips parted for him. Ross deepened the kiss, vanquishing all her reservations and making her an eager, active participant. The next thing Maggie knew, they were standing, she was in his arms, and their warm bodies were melting together, straining for a closer fit.

When they finally broke from the kiss, Maggie's heart was hammering and her lungs had shut down. Her eyes opened and she gazed into the hazy bewilderment in Ross's. It unnerved her to see that she wasn't the only one who'd been shaken by the kiss. She knew that she should say something, should breathe...but she couldn't do either.

Abruptly, that telling look vanished from his eyes, and was replaced by a perceptive twinkling. Bringing his hands to her shoulders, Ross eased her back down on the hood. "How was that, sweetheart?" he asked. "No tongue to scare you off this time. And no people around to see." Then he walked behind the car to untie his horse, acting as though the kiss hadn't fazed him a bit.

It took a full moment for Maggie's muzzy head to clear. Then rage splintered through her like heat lightning on an August night. He really loved getting under her skin. In fact, for some unknown reason, he seemed to have made infuriating her his life's calling. Well, she would not give him the satisfaction of knowing that he'd gotten to her again. Lifting her chin, Maggie got calmly to her feet, brushed off her seat and got inside her car.

And her feelings suddenly changed.

She shared the blame for the kiss and his cocky taunts. He'd had to do something to snatch back some power after she'd insulted him with her out-of-town lunch invitation. Brash as he was, he still had feelings; a man who kissed like he did had to be capable of a lot of emotion.

Maggie drew a soft breath. Who would've thought that after all these years he could still turn her knees to butter just by taking her in his arms?

Iron horseshoes thudded against the packed dirt road as Ross led his horse up to her open window and peeked inside. A teasing grin still curved his lips. "Waiting for seconds, Maggie?"

Maggie's anger came screaming back. Amazingly, she held it in check. "Actually, I was just sitting here wondering how long it would take *you* to come back for more." She started the engine. "Not that it was all that great, but you obviously enjoyed it."

"Sorry, you're dead wrong."

"I am, huh?" Smiling, she dropped the car into gear. "You don't lie any better than you kiss." Then she buried him *and* his horse in a spin of tires and a thick cloud of dust.

The only thing that made her exit less satisfying was Ross's hearty laughter fading into the distance.

When Maggie reached the sunny fairgrounds on Saturday afternoon, it was bustling with activity—adults and children alike all decked out in wild-West paraphernalia. Chaps abounded, as well as dusty Stetsons and wedge-heeled boots designed to hook securely into stirrups.

Maggie bought a paper cone of French fries and a cola from a vendor, then climbed the metal grandstand. The Charlie Daniels Band blared from the speakers overhead, nearly drowning out the happy cacophony of the crowd. She found an end seat six rows up, just above one of the chutes.

All around her, the fecund smells of dust, hay and animals rode the air, mingling with the aromas of grilling hamburgers and French fries. And in spite of herself, Maggie felt a twinge of excitement. She hadn't planned to come to the rodeo—had never been to one before. But as she'd come out of Hardy's Mercantile earlier, she'd seen the rodeo playbill in Ruby's window, and decided to find out what all the shouting was about.

Maggie pulled her sunglasses out of her purse, then frowned. Yes. Yes, that was the only reason she was here.

"Good afternoon, folks," the announcer's drawl boomed from the booth above her. "Welcome to the preliminaries. We've seen some fine ridin' and ropin' so far, and we'll be gettin' to the bulls pretty quick. So grab your refreshments and take your seats. Trent Campion's up first and he'll be ridin' a nasty bugger called Rampage." An instant later, the music came up again and Charlie Daniels and his fiddle were back to dueling the devil down in Georgia.

An elderly voice shouted over the lively music. "Now, how did you get yerself such a fine seat, Maggie?"

Maggie glanced down to see Ruby Cayhill carrying a bag and spryly angling her way across the bleachers. She still wore a red apron over her waitress's uniform. As she made her way to Maggie, she yelled greetings to friends, and waved a bony arm.

Maggie slid over to make room, a little nervous about Ruby's climb. "I don't know, Aunt Ruby," she said with a smile. "I think it's just a case of 'finders keepers.' No one was here, so I took it."

Ruby pulled a cushion out of her bag, slid it under her bottom and plunked herself down. She peered at Maggie through her spectacles. "Don't recall ever seein' you at one of these things before."

"This is my first time. My dad never really approved of rodeos. He thought that it was prideful for men to risk life and limb for applause."

Ruby shrugged. "Folks are entitled to their own opinions. Me, I fire up my truck and leave the café to my waitresses when it's bull-ridin' time." Her shrewd eyes narrowed on a man walking toward the judges' stand across the arena, and she blew out a disgusted breath. "There's that struttin' peacock Trent Campion. He's a good rider—mostly 'cause he has the whole livelong day to practice if he wants. Hope that bull tosses him on his fancy backside."

Maggie followed Ruby's gaze. "Because of that business with Ross?"

"Nope, just on principle. Him and his daddy both need to find a little humility. Ben was nasty as spit in a windstorm when I phoned him about Trent beatin' that horse. He sure changed his tune when I told him I'd write it up on my menu board if he didn't get Ross sprung by supper time."

Maggie smiled and offered Ruby some of her French fries, which she accepted. She could just see Ruby wiping the daily specials off her chalkboard and replacing them with *Trent Campion's a no account horse beater.* And she could see Ben Campion doing what he had to do to protect his family's reputation. With most of the country's current outrage over political *faux pas,* that kind of publicity wouldn't have been good for Trent's bid for the legislature.

The music stopped, and the announcer's voice blared over the loudspeaker again. "All right, folks. It's time for the bull ridin'. If you were listenin' before, you heard me say Trent Campion was up first on Rampage. Well, Rampage isn't cooperatin' right now, so Trent's gonna wait a bit, and we're gonna move on to the number two rider. Comin' out of the west chute, we have Ross Dalton on Diablo."

Maggie's hand clenched, crushing her cone of French fries.

To the roar of cheering fans, a huge black bull came out of the chute like damnation on Judgment Day, spinning and tossing its massive bulk with Ross hanging on one-handed to a rope tied around the bull's middle. Maggie's nerves went raw as she watched Ross lean back for balance and clamp his legs tight, saw the cardboard number on the back of his vest fly out as the bull churned up dust and convulsed wildly—trying to toss the hazy blue blur that was Ross into the air. Ross's back whipped and jerked but he still kept one arm in the air and stayed on. The bull went into a constant, heaving spin. Then, thank heaven, the eight-second horn sounded and Ross leaped off to the applause of the crowd, while the rodeo clowns hazed the bull back through the gate.

Maggie realized her throat had gone dry, and she gulped her cola. That's why there had been no sign of him when she'd looked around town earlier. And a bull named Diablo had been his lunch date. Good heavens, what an insane sport. What made a reasonably intelligent man trade the thrill of gambling for money for the thrill of gambling with his life? What was this need of his to live life on the edge?

"He'll git a ninety-somethin' fer sure! That was a dandy ride!" Ruby yelled proudly. "A dandy ride!" She waited until the scores were announced, then clapped Maggie firmly on her denim-clad thigh. "Eighty-nine. Not as good as I thought, but good enough to beat whoever rides agin' him." Then she stood and packed her cushion into her bag.

Maggie sent her a curious look. "You're leaving?"

"Got work to do. Now that I know he didn't break his fool neck, I can git back to it."

"You came all the way out here just to see Ross ride?" Maggie smiled. "That was nice."

Ruby's brisk, no-nonsense attitude softened. "He's family, honey, and I love him. After the mess he made of his life a few years back, this is the only place most folks around here accept him. I need to see that." She paused. "And he needs to feel it."

With a nod of agreement, Maggie stood as well. She imagined that Ross did need it, and felt a tug of compassion. "I'll walk you back to your truck." The tiny woman's climb up the bleachers had been accomplished safely, but Ruby Cayhill was close to eighty—if she hadn't already reached that milestone. It wasn't good to tempt fate.

They were only a few feet from the grassy, roped-off parking area when Ruby spied someone that she recog-

nized at the cotton-candy booth. Maggie waited while she
hiked across the packed dirt to chat with a good-looking,
dark-haired man and his family.

Their coloring was different, but the man reminded
Maggie of Ross. Both men were tall, and had that same
loose-limbed look that said they knew who they were and
that they were satisfied with that. Then the hugs and smiles
exchanged all around told Maggie that the man had to be
Ross's brother, Jess. His wife—Casey, her Aunt Lila had
called her—was a pretty blonde, and their toddler was a
carbon copy of her daddy. The little girl looked to be about
two.

Low, muttered voices tugged her attention away. Maggie turned slightly to see Trent Campion and his father
having an animated conversation between two parked
trucks. She almost moved away, afraid Trent would see
her and think she'd come to watch him ride. Then she
heard a familiar name and remained where she was.

"You're ten times the rider he is, now stop whinin' and
do it."

"I wasn't whining, Dad," Trent returned angrily. "I just
said Dalton's score would be hard to beat. And these are
just qualifying rounds for the Founder's Day rodeo in July
anyway."

"If you take that attitude, you're a loser already," Ben
said harshly. "It's high time you realize voters don't get
real excited about also-rans. Or maybe you like being humiliated the way you were at the sheriff's office two weeks
ago. You're a Campion. Now get out there and win."

"That's all you care about, isn't it? Winning and the
Campion name. You certainly don't care about me."

"Don't take that tone with me. If I didn't care about
you, I wouldn't be there to pull your fanny out of the fire
every time you do something stupid. Do I have to remind
you what happened five years ago?" He paused, his voice

hardening. "Ross Dalton took away your manhood. You got to get it back."

The demeaning way Ben Campion spoke to his son made Maggie regret that she'd listened—and made her feel sorry for Trent. Small wonder that he acted the way he did. She saw Ben's gaze narrow bitterly as it settled on someone or something ahead of her, then she heard him say, "Come on. Let's see if that bull's settled down enough to get him into the chute."

Maggie's eyes followed Ben's stare. And a sudden warmth moved through her. Ross had joined his family beside the cotton-candy booth.

He was dusty, and his damp chambray shirt clung to his broad shoulders and lean midsection. He was still the most appealing man she'd ever seen. His thick, feathered hair was sweat-darkened at the temples and his tan Stetson rode low, shading his face.

A surprising tenderness touched Maggie's heart when the little girl in Casey Dalton's arms stretched her wee ones out to her uncle. Maggie saw him shake his head and gesture to his dirty clothing. But the child kept reaching for him. Finally, Ross laughed and took her from her mother, then swung her high above his head and pulled her down fast for a silly bear hug. The little one's giggles and high-pitched shrieks breached the afternoon air.

Abruptly, Ruby motioned toward Maggie, making everyone aware of her presence. She felt that warmth again as Ross turned to her and smiled. Handing the baby back, he waved goodbye to his departing family, then fell into step beside his great-aunt.

"Hi," he said, as they walked up to Maggie.

She returned his greeting warily. "Hi." Out of the blue, an uneasy feeling had come over her—a feeling that had nothing to do with the good-looking man standing beside her. On impulse, she scanned the area.

Cy Farrell was watching her as he mingled with the

crowd near the holding pens. A judgmental frown creased his thick features. For an instant, Maggie caught his eye, and she could imagine what Farrell was thinking—that she'd thrown in with the Daltons, joined the "enemy camp."

Ruby spoke, snagging Maggie's attention again.

"Well, I gotta git movin'." Her pale eyes sparkled with approval as she glanced from Maggie to Ross. She headed toward the roped-off lot. "Thanks for the company, Maggie."

"My pleasure."

"Nephew," she continued over her shoulder, "you know where the keys are if you need my truck later."

"Thanks, Aunt Ruby." After another wave, Ross met Maggie's gaze. "Are you leaving, too?"

Maggie hesitated. Why did she feel as though she would be knuckling under to Farrell's unspoken demands if she did what she'd already planned to do? "Yes, we were both on our way to the lot."

"Then I'd better apologize quick." His smile pushed fine lines into the skin beside his blue eyes. "I shouldn't have baited you the way I did the last time we were together. I'm sorry, but sometimes I just can't help myself."

Sighing, Maggie slipped off her sunglasses and tucked them into her purse. "No, you shouldn't have...and maybe you *should try*." She nodded toward the stands, deliberately looking away from Farrell's cold perusal. "Why are you out here when the bull riding's still going on? Don't you want to see if anyone beats your score?"

"I thought I came out to say goodbye to Casey and Jess. But maybe the fates had another reason for sending me out." He didn't elaborate, and Maggie didn't ask. "And yes, I *would* like to see if anyone beats me. Campion's riding soon." He paused for a moment, seeming to mull something over in his mind. When he spoke again, Maggie detected none of the cockiness that he usually showed her.

His voice softened. "Buy you a hotdog if you watch the rest of the bull riding with me."

Maggie tried to ignore the stirring in her veins. What was wrong with her? She wanted to say yes! But hadn't she vowed to stay away from overgrown children with charming smiles? And how *could* she go—with Farrell watching her like a hawk? Like that proverbial carrot, the deputyship he'd promised spun and dangled before her, a bright red warning tag hanging from it.

Ross's brow lined and his eyes clouded slightly. "Never mind. I won't put you on the spot. Farrell's skulking around here somewhere, and if he sees you with me, it'll probably cost you." He turned away. "Wish me luck."

"Ross, wait."

He stopped, his shadowed expression questioning her beneath the brim of his hat.

Suddenly, Maggie resented Farrell's blatant manipulations. He had no right to pressure her—yet without uttering one word, he was doing just that. When she wasn't in the office, her time was her own. And if Farrell objected, they would have to have a talk about the discrimination laws in this country. It occurred to her that Ross could be doing a bit of subtle manipulating, too, but she didn't think so.

Maggie walked toward Ross, still not one-hundred-percent sure that she was acting in her own best interests. Forcing a smile, she fell into step beside him and said, "I like chili on my hotdogs."

She ended up doing much more than watching the rest of the bull-riding competition with him. When the event was over and Trent had beaten Ross's score by a point, Ross asked Maggie for a ride to his aunt Ruby's, and she couldn't say no.

After tossing his hat in the back seat, Ross folded himself into the small Ford and pushed the seat back as far as it would go. "My truck was loaded with building supplies, so I rode in with Jess and Casey this morning. Then my niece—Lexi—got to be a handful and they took her home for a nap. I'll just borrow Aunt Ruby's truck and return it in the morning.''

"She won't need it?"

"She said she wouldn't. She lives upstairs over the café, so getting to work won't be a problem."

Maggie kept both hands on the steering wheel, unnerved by his presence as she drove from the outskirts toward town.

With his wide shoulders and rangy frame stuffed inside the tiny car, Ross seemed even more formidable than usual. His warm male scent invaded her nostrils, the faint odors of animals and sweat only adding to his rugged appeal. Maggie slid a veiled look his way. He kept surprising her. The only outward expression of disappointment he'd shown when Trent had beaten his score was a wry grin and a shrug.

Turning her attention back to the road, she mentioned it. "I expected you to be more upset about Trent beating you out.''

"If there'd been a nice purse involved, I might have been. But this was only a qualifying round, and the money wasn't all that much." He paused. "We'll both ride in the finals. All I needed today was a decent score."

Maggie nodded. Her mind had already turned to something else. Or rather, *re*turned to something else. They were only a minute away from Ruby's now, and she knew that she was insane for offering, but...

"I was just thinking," she said. "I have to pass Brokenstraw to get to the Lazy J anyway. Why don't I just drop you off? Then you don't have to worry about returning your aunt's truck in the morning."

The look he sent her was startled but pleased. "You don't mind?"

"As I said, I'm going that way anyhow."

"Then sure, that would be great." He motioned ahead of them to where houses and businesses had suddenly sprung up. "There's the café. Want a piece of pie and a cup of coffee before we head back?"

Maggie had to think about that. Sitting in the bleachers with him was one thing. Having pie and coffee was another. She'd already done herself some damage in Farrell's eyes, and if the sheriff happened to see them go into Ruby's, he might attach more importance to their being together than was warranted. On the other hand...her life *was* her own, wasn't it?

"Come on," he teased. "Your reputation's shot by now, anyway. The busybodies who saw you with me today already have you three-months' pregnant, and us on our way to the altar."

Maggie made a squealing U-turn in the middle of the street as something that was half shock, half fear shot through her. Her heartbeat stepped up its pace. Pie and coffee with Ross? What in the world was she thinking? "I have to get back."

His blue eyes narrowed. "Look, it was just a joke—I didn't mean anything by it."

"I know. I—I just need to get home."

Even though she'd thought about how Farrell would perceive their spending time together, she wasn't really worried about rumors. Gossip died down as soon as it ran out of fuel. But his "three months' pregnant" comment had hammered home something she'd managed to ignore all afternoon. She shouldn't be spending time with him at all.

From high school and beyond, Ross had had the reputation of bedding any willing female in the county. Despite her rather puritanical upbringing, she was willing to accept—but not condone—his life-style. As long as he kept his head and no one got hurt, fine.

Conversely, she was twenty-eight years old and ready to settle down—with a man who could commit to a long-term relationship. A solid, steady man who could give her children and wouldn't be eyeing every woman who came down the pike. So why was she watching bulls and eating hot dogs with a commitment-phobic rodeo rider who'd never had a serious thought in his life?

When she looked past his obvious physical appeal, Ross Dalton was the antithesis of everything she wanted—everything she needed.

"Guess that wasn't as funny as I thought it was," Ross said quietly as the silence stretched on between them.

Maggie sent him a small smile. His subdued look said that he would accept her excuse. But he obviously didn't believe it.

Late that night as she tossed in bed, Maggie decided she needed a good, long session on a psychiatrist's couch. Because there Ross was, back in her thoughts again.

Why was she so attracted to a man who—simply by *being*—could ruin her life?

Seeing Ross at the rodeo wasn't happenstance. Just as her noontime shopping trip to Hardy's Mercantile wasn't something she'd done on a whim. Hardy's was right across the street from Ruby's Café—the place that he probably would have taken his supposed lunch date.

When there was no sign of him in town, she should just have driven back to the Lazy J—that would've been the sensible thing to do. Instead, she'd read the rodeo playbill in Ruby's window, remembered the flashy buckle on Ross's belt, and suddenly she was off to the fairgrounds. Worse yet, Farrell had witnessed her momentary madness.

She flipped her pillow to the cool side, then flopped back down again. She had to get a grip on herself.

Maggie climbed out of bed and went to the window of her upstairs room. The drapes billowed gently as the night breeze blew through the screen, bathing her bare legs beneath her white eyelet nightie. What a lovely place this is, she thought. The pale, three-quarters moon was high, illuminating the jagged peaks of the mountains and lighting the dark pine ridges below. Stars seemed to glimmer from every corner of the galaxy.

This was why she'd come back to Comfort…why she'd come back to Montana. Colorado was a miracle of mountain peaks and lush alpine forests. But this was home.

She couldn't let an infantile crush ruin her chances for a solid, productive life here. She had to stay away from Ross Dalton.

Chapter 4

The bell above the door jangled late Sunday morning as Ross walked into the café and scanned the crowded dining room. Like most of the shops and businesses on the restored main street of town, Aunt Ruby's Café had once been something else. In the 1890s when Comfort was a brawling cow town, the café had been one of eight raucous saloons—and the only one with a calliope. Ruby claimed that her breakfast crowds were every bit as noisy. Today, Ross had to believe her. The sounds of silverware clanking and friendly chatter nearly drowned out the twangy country ballad on the radio.

Ruby walked briskly across the floor towards him, carrying two coffeepots. Ross grinned. The skinny little woman liked red. She had to own at least four red sweaters and—come snow or ninety-degree weather—one of them always topped her white uniform. Her truck was red; her sneakers were red; and red, white and black dominated the café's homey decor.

"Mornin', Aunt Ruby. Jess said you wanted to see me about something."

Ruby cocked her cheek for his kiss, then turned a brief, sharp eye on him and kept walking toward a table. "Didn't see you in church this mornin'."

Rolling his eyes, Ross followed along behind her. Her waitresses carried the heavy trays to the tables now, but Ruby still liked to take the coffeepots around herself. "Aunt Ruby, you haven't seen me in church for *years*."

"Wouldn't hurt you to go now and then. Jess, Casey and the baby were there."

"Someone had to water the horses."

"They wouldn't have died of thirst while you were gone."

Sighing, Ross gave up defending himself. He nodded toward the lunch counter. "I'll see you over there when you're finished."

"Don't run off now. This is important."

"Wouldn't dream of it." Ross waved to a few friends who were willing to give a man a second chance, then ambled over to the lunch counter and took a seat. Most of the red vinyl stools were vacant, the Sunday morning "family crowd" having chosen booths and tables. When he took off his hat, he laid it on the stool beside him.

Ruby returned quickly, scooting behind the counter with her empty pots. She glanced at his Stetson. "Savin' that space for some nice, church-goin' young woman?"

So they were back to that again. The "something" that she wanted to talk about became crystal clear. "Nope, I've already got a woman picked out."

"Well, if her name's Maggie Bristol, you coulda seen her earlier if waterin' them horses hadn't been so dang important to you."

Ross's interest piqued. "Maggie was at church?"

"She's the daughter of a preacher and a good, God-fearin' young woman. Where else would she be on Sunday mornin'?"

Ruby grabbed a fresh pot and poured a cup of coffee for him, then slid a spoon and the chrome-and-glass sugar dispenser his way. The twinkle in her eyes said that she thought she had the inside scoop—that he'd finally met his match and was ready to settle down. If Ruby knew a commitment was the last thing on his mind, he thought, she wouldn't be quite so smug.

"So what did Maggie have to say?"

"Oh, some of this, some of that." When he didn't ask for specific "this" and "thats," she cackled and leaned close, peering over her spectacles. "Guess yer wonderin' if she asked about you."

"No, because she probably didn't."

"That's right. She didn't."

Ross felt a jolt of annoyance. So he wasn't on Maggie's mind day and night. So what? He didn't think of her all that often, either. He stirred sugar into his coffee, then clinked the spoon into his saucer.

"You missed the announcement about the church social next Sunday," Ruby persisted.

"Should I care?"

"Well," she said, grabbing a wet cloth and wiping a coffee ring off the counter. "I happened to see Trent Campion in church, and he seemed to care. Has a date already picked out, too, if I read him right."

Ross watched her take the rag over the same stretch of counter several more times, and sighed audibly. "All right, you know you're dying to tell me what's going on, so why don't you just do it?"

Ruby stopped wiping, and her pale eyes lit with mischief. "There's gonna be a box-lunch auction in the churchyard for the single folks. The ladies bring a picnic and the fellas bring a blanket to picnic *on*."

"So?"

"So the fellas bid on the basket they like the best, and the money goes toward the new church roof. The gal whose lunch was bought is obliged to eat with the bachelor." Ruby sent him a meaningful glance. "She ain't allowed to say no. Lots of pretty young things have already signed up fer it."

Ross felt a low stirring in his belly as he finally got Ruby's point. Maggie was participating, and Trent planned to buy her basket.

Well, Ross didn't think so. He remembered how her body had fit so perfectly to his the day he'd kissed her—recalled thinking she'd actually wanted to be with him yesterday at the rodeo. *But afterward, she'd dropped him off at the ranch with all the warmth of an IRS auditor, and he hadn't seen her since.*

Ross took a long swallow of his coffee, then finished it. Maybe it was time to show her that when he wanted something badly enough, he didn't give up until he got it. That's what this town expected of him, right? "So, are there names on these picnic baskets?"

"Nope. It's potluck. Whoever you git, you git."

Ross met Ruby's shrewd blue eyes. "I want to know which one's hers," he said. "Can you find out?"

"It'll cost ya."

It would cost him? Well, this was a first.

Sighing, he stood and pulled his wallet from the back pocket of his jeans. "How much?"

Ruby's long-suffering stare called him a dolt. "I don't want your money, nephew. *I want you to go to church.*" Reaching high, she tugged the light-brown hair at his nape. "And get a haircut before the auction. It's hangin' all over yer collar."

Chuckling, Ross leaned down to kiss her goodbye. "Keeps the sun off my neck, gorgeous." He flashed her another grin as he pulled his hat back on. "How will you find out which one's hers?"

"Did I take care of yer trouble with Trent Campion?"

"Yes."

"Then don't worry about me figurin' this one out, either. You just park yourself in a pew and I'll handle the rest."

After a full, sweaty week of running new wire, sinking fence posts, and branding and vaccinating the new calves, Ross was ready for a sweet, clean distraction.

Maggie didn't disappoint.

He and Ruby were seated midway up the church aisle, with Ruby planted firmly on the end to make sure he didn't "run off." Lexi's low-grade fever had kept Casey and Jess home today, but Ross recognized nearly everyone else. And while there had been a few old biddies who'd whispered behind their hands when he walked in, the roof hadn't caved in and no one had run for cover. Apparently, God was more forgiving than were the locals.

Two pews ahead of him and across the aisle, Maggie held a hymnal and sang softly beside her aunt Lila. She wore a white, gauzy-looking dress that was belted at the waist and fell to just below her knees. Her hair tumbled in silky black waves over her shoulders. Perfect, he thought. Perfect from the feathery bangs brushing her eyebrows to the soles of her heeled straw sandals.

He was still admiring the view when Reverend Fremont wished everyone a good day and invited the congregation downstairs for refreshments, and the auction—single people only participating, of course. Ross couldn't wait for the bidding to begin. Because while he'd been watching Maggie, he'd noticed the overly cologned, spruced-up showboat in front of him eyeing her, too.

As the organist hit a few sharp keys, and the small church reverberated with the swelling strains of the recessional hymn, Trent and his father slowly filed out ahead of him. Ross looked over Ruby's tiny four feet eleven inches, and sent the younger Campion a slow smile. His eyes never left Trent's as he spoke to his aunt. "You're sure about which basket is Maggie's, right, Aunt Ruby?"

"Saw her bring it in with my own two eyes."

Trent expelled a mirthless laugh, and as he shuffled past them, said, "Forget it, cattle thief. My pockets are a lot deeper than yours."

"We'll see. Beaten any horses lately?"

Ben Campion whirled on Ross, then froze, apparently realizing that there was nothing he could do about the remark without creating more of a stir. Then, with a nerve leaping in his jaw, Ben hustled his son past a few curious parishioners who'd caught the exchange.

The very first basket up for bids was a large wicker affair with pale-pink silk roses and a big white bow tied to the side of the handle. The generous contents were covered with a pink-edged, white linen napkin; cut-glass stemware protruded from one side, wrapped in matching napkins and tied with pink ribbons.

Ross started the bidding at twenty dollars.

Trent overbid him at every turn. Anytime anyone went higher, Trent upped the price. Soon it was only the two of them bidding, with Ross sending Trent a curdling look after every increase. Finally, Trent called out a bid, Ross smiled in satisfaction, and cat-lady Bessie Holsopple's pretty basket went for one hundred dollars. The rage in Trent Campion's eyes told Ross he'd made an enemy for life.

Maggie's basket was smaller than Bessie's, with none of the adornments. It was simple and covered with a folded plaid tablecloth—exactly what Ross would've expected from her. She was a no-nonsense woman who lived on a ranch and worked all week long. She didn't have time for silk roses and fluted stemware. Although…Maggie was a class act, and she certainly deserved those things.

"I have twenty-eight dollars," Reverend Fremont boomed in his best gospel voice as he stood over Maggie's basket. A large, beefy man with graying hair and wire-rimmed glasses, Fremont's love of good food was evident in the way his voluminous black robe fit across his belly. "Smells mighty good. Do I hear thirty?"

"Fifty," Ross called.

Surprised chatter erupted all around him, and the reverend stared at him in bewilderment. "But yours was the last bid," Fremont said. "You had it for twenty-eight."

"I know. I'm just sure it's worth fifty, and it's for a good cause." He didn't dare look at Maggie. He'd made such a big deal over buying that basket—and had attracted so much attention—that she'd ream him good when they finally got into the churchyard and he spread his blanket for her.

The reverend's broad face beamed. "Do I hear fifty-five?" When no one raised the bid, he frowned slightly, then happily continued. "Fifty once...twice... It's yours for fifty dollars, son."

Ten minutes later, Ross followed Maggie to a shaded spot under a tree, trying not to smile at her stiff-as-a-fence-post posture. She was annoyed, and she wasn't trying to hide it.

She pointed to the ground, her index finger telling him exactly where he could put his blanket. She hadn't said a word to him since the reverend had sent them on their way. On the other hand, Lila Jackson had seemed fairly amused by their pairing.

Ross spread out the blanket.

Maggie dropped the basket unceremoniously onto a corner of it.

"So what are we having?" he asked innocently.

Snatching the tablecloth from the basket, she revealed fried chicken, potato salad, fruit and chocolate cake. Cans of ginger ale and straws were tucked into a corner, along with a thermos, plates, cups and silverware. Maggie threw the tablecloth in the center of Ross's blanket, then brutalized it until it lay flat.

Eventually she spoke—but she obviously had no intention of being cordial. "Sit. Let's get this over with." Between the tinny ring of silverware and the plopping of food on his plate, she added, "And I'm not going to sleep with you, so get that thought right out of your head."

Ross stared, dumbfounded, then chuckled in surprise. He accepted the plate that she handed him. "You know, you could at least wait until somebody asks you before you refuse. And who says I even want to?"

"Don't insult my intelligence by pretending you haven't thought about it."

He sampled his chicken, made an appreciative sound in his throat, then grinned again. "I won't. Because I have thought about it—often, and in great detail. I just had no idea you were as obsessed with the idea as I am."

Her eyes widened. "I am *not*—"

Ross sighed to the heavens. "Maggie, for Pete's sake, lighten up. What's going on?"

"I'll tell you what's going on," she muttered in an undertone. "You. Your sudden interest in church. Your grandstand play in there, raising your own bid, acting like you were only too happy to contribute to such a worthy cause."

"That's what's bothering you? Maggie, that doesn't even make sense. It *is* a worthy cause. If you said that I embarrassed you because it was your basket I accidentally bought, I could understand—"

"Accidentally, my foot. Ruby saw me set it on the table downstairs and described it to you. And somehow you conned Trent into thinking that Bessie's basket was mine."

"And why would I do that?"

"To make sure he'd already claimed a basket before

mine was auctioned off—which prevented him from bidding on mine.''

Ross took off his Stetson and tossed it on a corner of the blanket, then fluffed a hand through his hair. "Gee. Someone's got a dandy ego.''

Maggie held her tongue.

She'd told him to sit. Instead, he'd sprawled out full-length on his side, his boots hanging off the end of the blanket, his weight supported on an elbow, as he sampled the food she'd prepared. Today, his shirt was a pale blue, rough-weave, button-front with the long sleeves turned back and the collar open at his tanned throat. The chest hair she could see was a little darker than the soft, feathered shag on his head, and she hated the fact that she'd noticed. New jeans hugged his lean hips and waist.

Picking up a few surreptitious—but unmistakably coveting—looks from women on other blankets, Maggie held back a sigh. What made normally sensible women lose their heads over hellions? What made *her* lose her head? So what if they were charming and good-looking? They made lousy husbands—and worse fathers.

Which was really why she was so upset. She'd vowed to stay away from him after the rodeo, and she'd been doing just fine. By Wednesday, even Farrell's grumpy mood had improved, probably because there had been no sign of Ross all week. Then Ross had popped back into her life under seemingly the most respectable of circumstances—a church fund-raiser—and here she was, pulse hopping around like a naive schoolgirl's again, right back on that emotional roller coaster to perdition.

Be honest, Maggie, a little voice inside said. *You're not angry with him. You're angry with yourself because you're dying to take the ride.*

Sitting up, Ross dragged the picnic basket closer, and dug out a plate and silverware. Her long silence had had a sobering effect on him. "Maggie, no one thinks you're with me of your own accord. So whatever you believe is going to happen if you're seen with me...won't.''

He thought that she was worried about gossip? That was the least of her problems—and letting him think that was shallow and hurtful. But how could she admit that the more time they spent together, the more time she *wanted* to spend with him? That kind of knowledge would only make her more vulnerable to him.

Ross took another item from the basket. Adrenaline shot through Maggie when he smoothed a napkin over her lap. He started filling her plate.

"I—I can do that," she stammered.

"That's okay. You did the hard part—you cooked."

Suddenly she was ashamed of herself. What would it hurt to simply be nice once in a while? Despite his Good-time Charlie/Lady-killer reputation, he wasn't a total maverick. She'd seen how hard he worked, and she had watched the honest affection he felt for his little niece and the rest of his family.

A shadow fell over them, and Maggie glanced up to see Reverend Fremont smiling down at them. She'd been so engrossed in Ross, she hadn't even heard the big man approach.

"And how are the two of you getting on?" the reverend asked in his deep baritone. His clerical robes were gone, replaced by a comfortable-looking white-knit shirt and black slacks.

Ross handed Maggie her plate, then respectfully pushed to his feet. "Just fine, Reverend. This was a great idea for a fund-raiser."

The reverend smiled. "Well, money's only part of it. We'll be needing a few able-bodied men to tear off shingles and such. Can we count on you, Ross?"

Ross stared, speechless, and Maggie found herself smiling.

"Just thought I'd ask, since we haven't seen you around

here in a while," Fremont continued. "I'd hate to think you were mad at us."

"Mad?" A flush crept up his neck, pinkening his cowboy tan. "I...no, I'm not mad at anybody."

"Great. Then can I give you a call when we're ready to start? It'll be a Saturday sometime soon."

"Sure."

"Wonderful. With enough willing hands, it'll only take a day." He smiled at Maggie. "And this nice young woman has already agreed to help with the food, so you'll have a friend at the refreshment table." Fremont patted his jutting middle and chuckled. "That's why I'll be helping out." Then he addressed Maggie alone. "Heard from your dad lately?"

"As a matter of fact, we talk on the phone at least twice a week. He's busy. His congregation in Colorado is quite a bit larger than the one he left here."

"But he's doing a fine job, I hear. Good man, your father. I had some deep shoes to fill when I came here."

"Thank you, Reverend. I'll tell him you said that."

Then Fremont was off to blackmail the rest of his flock.

Maggie laughed softly at Ross's ambushed expression, then poked a fork into her potato salad, the food in front of her suddenly more palatable.

"What's so funny?" he grumbled, dropping to his knees, then sprawling out beside her again.

"You are. You've got a wisecrack for every situation and an answer for everyone, but you couldn't say no to the reverend. You know what that means, don't you?"

"I haven't a clue."

"There might actually be some hope for you."

They gathered up their picnic supplies forty minutes later, and walked to their side-by-side vehicles. "Now, that wasn't so bad, was it?" he asked.

Maggie unlocked her trunk, thinking that it had been far

too enjoyable. They'd actually had a normal conversation over coffee and cake, discussing cattle prices and water rights. "It wasn't bad at all," she admitted. "In fact, I had fun."

"But you'll deny it if anyone asks?"

"Absolutely."

After packing her things inside, Ross slammed the trunk. "The food was great. Thanks."

"Worth fifty dollars?"

Ross smiled. "The chocolate cake alone was worth that much." His gaze drifted down to her mouth and lingered there for several long seconds. Then, just as she was getting nervous about the protocol of parting, he touched an index finger to the tip of her nose, climbed into his truck, and left.

Maggie slid into her little blue Ford, frowning at the warm chills prickling her forearms, the airy tug behind her navel. Okay, she'd managed to get through the picnic without throwing herself into his arms and making a complete fool of herself. Now she could go home and put this nerve-wracking afternoon behind her.

Actually, getting reacquainted with Ross had served a useful purpose. During her involvement with Todd, she'd wondered if something was wrong with her. She'd felt an attraction to him, but it was nothing like the mind-scrambling heat that flooded her veins when Ross was around. So did she have a working libido? Yes, she did. And it was working so well that it was very close to getting her into trouble. Thank heaven there was no reason to see him again.

But her relief only lasted until she returned home, opened her trunk and saw his soft Indian blanket folded beside her wicker basket.

On Monday, Ross reined his horse to a stop beside Jess's bay gelding and followed his brother's stare past the herd below to a structure some distance away. Nearing completion, Ross's newly varnished log home gleamed in the mid-afternoon sun, surrounded by pines and aspens. Its wide creek-stone chimney stretched up one side of the house, and a portion of the wraparound porch railing became visible when the wind blew leafy saplings aside.

"It's coming along," Jess said.

"Yeah, it is. I finished putting on the first coat of varnish last night, so tonight I'll start setting the windows. I figure I'll be in by the end of July."

"Great. Then, as Casey says, all you need is a wife."

Ross couldn't hold back a grin. "Tell Casey she's dreaming. I'm one of those Hopalong Cassidy types who only loves his horse."

Chuckling, Jess nudged the bay's ribs and walked him slowly down the hill toward the grazing cattle and the water trough. "If that's why you put in that big loft bedroom, people are going to talk."

"People talking about me? Wow, that'd be big news, wouldn't it?"

"According to Aunt Ruby, you gave them plenty to talk about at the church auction yesterday. Fifty bucks for a lunch?"

"Yeah, well, Bessie Holsopple's went for a hundred. I figured Maggie's should bring at least half."

Jess guided his horse to the trough, stroking the animal's sleek neck as he drank. "So now what? Are you planning to see her again?"

"That's up to her," Ross said offhandedly, letting his horse drink, too. But beneath his disinterested reply, his eager mind was making plans.

He knew that he'd be seeing her again. By now, she'd have opened her trunk and seen his blanket in there. She'd feel obligated to return it. When she did, he'd swear that it was an oversight. She'd fuss and bluster that it was deliberate. He'd apologize and confess that she was right.

Then they'd shrug the matter off and continue tiptoeing through the mounting attraction between them. Manipulative? Yep. But without that blanket as an excuse, she'd never be able to come to him—never maintain the skimpy thread of a relationship they had going.

Ross knew that she wanted to. He also knew that she was wary of the attraction she was feeling—something Ross had never encountered before. Most of the women he'd dated were in it for the thrills and chills—no rings, no promises. Not that he expected to make a convert of Maggie overnight, but he was willing to spend the time trying. Because when she finally did come around...they'd be great together.

"Wake up."

Ross jerked his attention back to the amused eyes beneath Jess's black Stetson. "What?"

"I asked if you wanted some help tonight after supper."

"With what?"

"Putting in your windows."

Ross laughed. "Anxious to get me out of the homestead so you and Casey can run around in your birthday suits?"

"No, anxious to see you settled and raising a playmate for Lexi. Maybe Maggie's the one."

Laughing again, Ross reined his horse away from the trough. "Don't let her hear you say that. When she gets her blood up— Well, she's nothing like any minister's daughter I've ever known."

"How many ministers' daughters have you known?"

"One. But if I didn't know she belonged to Tom Bristol, I'd swear her dad was a drill sergeant. I've never met a woman who was so ready to go to war—at least with me."

Jess grinned as they walked their horses into the herd to cut out the steers they'd chosen for auction. "Sounds like she's exactly what you need."

Casey Dalton was playing in the grass with her daughter when Maggie drove in on Tuesday evening and parked her car in the driveway. Rising and dusting off the seat of her jeans, Casey walked down to meet her—Lexi tagging behind and trying valiantly to blow the stubborn fuzz off the dandelion that she held.

"You're Maggie," Casey said with a smile as Maggie got out.

"And you're Casey. Hi."

"Hi."

Maggie's glance dipped to the tiny, silky-haired brunette in the pink-and-white Minnie Mouse shorts set. "And I'll bet you're Lexi," she said.

Lexi hid behind her mother's leg, and laughing, Casey scooped up her daughter for a kiss and a squeeze. "I'm such a wuss. I can't pick her up without kissing her."

"Nothing wrong with that," Maggie said, liking the picture the two of them made. They were as different as night and day, with Casey's almost-Scandinavian coloring a stark contrast to Lexi's dark, glossy hair and big brown eyes. "She's darling."

"Thanks, we think so."

After a pause, Maggie drew a breath, then said as matter-of-factly as she could, "Is Ross at home?"

"Well…yes, and no." Casey laughed, intercepting the dandelion stem that was on its way to her daughter's mouth. She tossed it back in the grass. "He's not here, but he is at his own house."

This was a surprise. When he'd found her cutting through the pasture two weeks ago, he'd implied that he still resided at the homestead.

"Ross's home won't be finished for a few weeks yet," Casey continued, "so technically, he still lives here. Actually, we were just going out to the house to pick up Daddy—" she smiled at Lexi "—weren't we, sweetie?"

Lexi grinned shyly, then ground her face into her mother's shoulder.

she wanted desperately to stay. She didn't want to be
drawn any further into Ross's life than she already was—
yet she couldn't say no to Casey's intriguing invitation.
Why, she wondered, hadn't she just followed her first impulse and mailed the blanket back to him?

"All right," Maggie agreed. "Just let me get the blanket
from my back seat, and—"

"Actually, you'd be better off leaving the blanket
here." Casey motioned for Maggie to follow as she
bounced her giggling daughter on her hip and walked toward the house. "All of Ross's things are still here, and
he'd just have to cart it back again. You can give it to him
later."

Okay, that made sense. Swallowing, Maggie followed
Casey through the screen door and into the cheery kitchen.

What *didn't* make sense, she thought, was agreeing to
tour the home of a man whose sexy smiles and rangy good
looks kept testing her conservative upbringing.

Chapter 5

The house was a two-story architectural dream with a broad porch, high peaked roofs, and gleaming log walls—all tucked into a sheltering grove of pines, cottonwoods and aspens.

Casey carried Lexi up the porch steps and through an open, unfinished wooden door to the spacious living room. Maggie followed with the pump canister of lemonade and paper cups. The smells of new wood and varnish tinged the air, but the multipaned wood windows were open, letting in the constant Montana breeze as well as the pinkening hues of sundown. Soft male voices burred from a room down the hallway.

A massive, polished creek-stone fireplace stretched up an outside wall, and halfway across the smooth plank floor a gleaming staircase with a narrow log handrail led to a loft.

Maggie glanced upstairs at the smooth, varnished twig fencing that ran the width of the loft. *Yes, Maggie,* murmured that patronizing little voice that she'd come to loathe, that's probably where his bedroom will be.

"Okay," Casey said in a conspiratorial whisper as she put Lexi down. "Now, scoot into the kitchen and tell Daddy and Uncle Ross that the juice ladies are here. Can you do that for Mommy?"

Lexi nodded enthusiastically, then streaked into the hallway, her high-pitched baby voice squeaking, "The juicy ladies are here!"

Deep, hollow laughter rang through the house, raising gooseflesh on Maggie's arms. Casey rolled her eyes. "Well, she tried."

A moment later, Jess, then Ross walked into the great room, Lexi clinging to her daddy's hand and bouncing up and down at his side.

Jess Dalton was lean, tanned, good-looking and shirtless—and it didn't faze Maggie a bit.

Ross was, too. And Maggie felt the warm attraction right down to the soles of her feet.

Late at night when her restless mind refused to find something safe to focus on, Maggie had imagined him as he was now: tanned, broad-shouldered and rawly male— not a spare ounce of fat anywhere. Sweat glistened in the curly brown hair covering his chest, the gradually tapering *V* pattern trailing downward and disappearing into the waistband of his jeans. The faint scar Casey had mentioned on the drive here showed on his left side, just below his rib cage.

Ross smiled, and devastating blue eyes and perfect white teeth made her nerves vibrate and her stomach go weak.

"Hi. This is a surprise."

"Hi," Maggie said, glad that she had the thermos to hang on to. "I just stopped by the ranch to drop off your blanket, and Casey persuaded me to come with her and Lexi to see your house."

"And it wasn't easy to convince her," Casey scolded, "so behave yourself." Her words were for Ross, but her smiling eyes feasted on Jess. It didn't take a mind reader to know her thoughts had taken the same route as had Maggie's. But Casey had the luxury of openly drinking in her husband; Maggie was asking for a peck of trouble if she looked at Ross that way.

"Juice, Daddy?"

Chuckling, breaking eye contact with his wife, Jess scooped up his daughter and kissed her nose. "Not right now, baby. Daddy needs to talk to Mommy. Can you and Uncle Ross play a game for a minute?"

Lexi bobbed her head "yes." "Bunny hop game?"

"Maybe. You'll have to ask Uncle Ross." Jess sent Maggie a grin. "Hi. I guess you're Maggie. Nice to see you."

"Same here."

"Back in a minute," Casey called, laughing. Then Jess tugged his grinning wife across the floor and deep into the hallway. Without rugs, furniture or drapes to absorb them, the sounds of low chuckles and kissing filtered out to the great room.

"Bunny hop game, Uncle Woss?"

"Okeydoke, sweetie pie."

Giggling, Lexi latched on to Ross's thick index fingers, and he stretched her arms high. Then he lifted her off the floor and bounced her, again and again, in a silly zigzagging route to Maggie. Lowering his voice, he cast an amused glance into the hall. "I'm always amazed that I don't have at least one more niece or nephew."

Maggie thought the closeness Jess and Casey shared was special, and she said so.

"Yes, it is," Ross agreed. "What they have is great. For them."

"But not for you?"

"What do you think?"

She thought a deeply committed relationship was the last thing on earth he wanted, but she didn't say so. For some reason she didn't want to say so. "How long have they been married?"

"Three years in August, and I don't think they've regretted a day of it." He nodded at the thermos and cups that she held. "If you carry those over to my fancy dining-room table, I'll buy you girls a drink."

His "dining-room table" was two wide boards stretched across a pair of sawbucks. A heavy circular saw sat atop the makeshift tabletop; after ordering Lexi to stand her ground, Ross unplugged the saw and moved it to the floor. He brushed some sawdust off the planks, and Maggie put down the canister.

"Okay, Lex," Ross said, opening his arms. And Lexi ran to be lifted high again. After hugging her close, he tipped her back. "Tell Maggie, honey. Do you ever touch Uncle Ross's tools?"

"No," the child murmured seriously, her little brow furrowing behind wispy black bangs.

"Why not?"

"Get hurt."

"That's right. Good girl." The skin beside his deep blue eyes crinkled as he brought the two-year-old close to his face. "Now can I have a kiss for doing the bunny hop game?"

Lexi giggled and pulled on his cheeks, stretching them like rubber. "Yes."

"How many can I have today?"

"Five!"

And Maggie's heart flooded with warmth as, between the two of them chanting out numbers, Lexi smacked five noisy kisses on Ross's lips.

Ross put her down and spoke to Maggie. "Better fill all five cups. I have a feeling when Jess and Casey come up for air, they'll want to drink fast and run."

Maggie slid the first cup under the canister's spout and pushed the pump, hiding her disappointment. She wasn't ready to go just yet. "Then I'd better drink fast, too. My car's at the ranch."

He ambled a little closer to her, and Maggie picked up the musky scents of warm man and hard work—not at all unpleasant.

"You haven't had the tour yet."

"Yes, I know."

"If you want, I can drive you back."

Not looking at him, Maggie bent to give Lexi the first cup of lemonade, her pulse racing. "Sure," she said with feigned indifference. "As long as I'm here, I might as well look around. What I've seen is beautiful. Although—"

Lexi reached for the cup with both hands, and Ross said, "Tell Maggie 'thank you.'"

"Thank you."

"You're welcome, sweetheart," Maggie said.

"Although, what?" Ross prompted, pulling their conversation back a few sentences.

"Although...they could stay."

"Oh, they'll leave," Ross said quietly, and a rush of anticipation warmed Maggie's limbs.

Ross was right.

A moment after he'd made the statement, Casey and Jess came out of the hallway, drank their "juice," and announced that it was getting late, that Lexi hadn't had her bedtime bath yet.

Now, keeping her distance from the bare-chested man showing her around, Maggie was glad Jess and Casey had gone. She knew that she was flirting with disaster, but the feelings she'd been battling since she'd seen Ross again were too exciting to keep tamping down. She'd only had one serious relationship in her life, and none of the emotional chaos she felt with Ross had ever been present with

Todd. Her father had always said that life was a gift to be cherished and celebrated. And tonight, that's what Maggie intended to do—celebrate. At least a little.

They went from room to room, and Maggie was aware of his pride as he showed her the things he'd done with his own hands—and pointed out the things others had done for him. The polished fireplace with its smooth gray, rose, and beige creek stones had been well beyond his talents, and Ross had found someone to build it for him. But every shiny, dovetailed hemlock log in the structure had been placed by Ross and Jess.

"It's taken me nearly two-and-a-half years and most of my spare time," he said. "But in a few weeks I'll have a roof over my head." He paused and said with emphasis, "My *own* roof."

When they went upstairs to the loft and looked out the window, Maggie couldn't imagine a lovelier setting. The same high, snow-capped mountain peaks she saw from her bedroom at her uncle's home were shown against the sky, dark pines creeping up the lower ridges to timberline. Nearer, there was a mixed stand of trees, and blue columbine and pink timothy dotted the wispy grasses below the window. Maggie thought she saw a ribbon of water winking in the fading light of the sun. "It's breathtaking, Ross. All of it."

"Thanks," he said with a pleased smile. He came up behind her, and Maggie's senses sharpened. Though there were several inches between them, she could feel his heat against her back, feel his breath fanning the hair at her temple. "The sun's going down. If I'm going to wash up before I take you back, I'd better do it now." Taking her hand in his larger callused one, he led her downstairs. Maggie didn't pull her hand away.

She had seen raw plumbing, but so far there were no sinks, showers or tubs in the house. Where was he planning to wash?

Ross grabbed a small duffel bag from behind the front door, then guided her outside to a well-traveled, wooded path behind the house.

Suddenly, Maggie knew where they were going, and a prickly uneasiness swept through her. She hadn't made the connection when she'd seen the water shining from the window in the loft. But now she knew. She was all for celebrating life—she really was. But with his reputation, and feeling the way she did tonight, the celebration could easily get out of hand where they were headed. "You don't really need to wash up."

"Yes, I do." He flashed her a grin. "If I don't, neither of us will survive the ride back."

Maggie nodded her wary assent and continued to walk through the tall grass beside him. She heard the soft rush of water before she saw it, before she smelled its freshness.

Tall cottonwoods and pines shaded the bubbling creek and the clearing she'd visited thirteen years ago, preventing all but a few stalwart patches of grass from growing in the packed dirt grotto.

Still holding her hand, Ross guided her to a fallen, peeled log beside the stone fire ring. Without being told, she sat. Several yards away, beckoned the pretty, dammed-up creek bed with its underground hot springs. Full darkness was a good hour off, but a few crickets were already practicing their night songs.

"Now if you face *this* way—"

Startled, Maggie instinctively grabbed his shoulders as Ross half lifted, half spun her on the log to face the other direction.

"—you won't get embarrassed."

He was going to undress? She leaped up quickly. "Look, maybe I should meet you back at—"

"—the house?" Ross's deep laughter mocked her modesty. "Can't trust yourself not to peek, huh, Maggie?"

Belligerently, she sat right back down. "Get over yourself. I wouldn't care if you danced naked through the streets. I was just trying to be a little considerate of your feelings."

"Sure you were." Taking a seat beside her, he pulled off his boots. The socks came off, too, and he rolled them in a ball, then stuffed them into his boots. "Watch these for me?"

"All right," she said stiffly, "but I can't imagine why anyone would want them."

Then he dug soap and a towel out of his bag, and with a wink moved toward the creek.

Maggie's posture grew even more rigid as she tried to ignore what was happening behind her. But the chirping of the crickets and the rushing sound of the creek couldn't cover the unnatural metallic noise of his zipper sliding down, or the clink and jangle of his pockets' contents as he kicked out of his jeans and underwear. At least, she hoped he'd been wearing underwear.

"Sure you don't want to join me?" he called. "It's nice and deep where it's dredged out—chest high when you sit down."

"No, thanks." Maggie heard the splash of his bare feet as he entered the water, heard his deliberate sigh of pleasure as he settled into the eddy where hot jets turned the gold-and-green creek bed into a natural hot tub.

Maggie focused on the break in the woods where the dusky, mauve-streaked sky shone through. The surrounding quiet seemed to call for a soft tone from her when she finally spoke. "You have a scar on your side."

"My appendectomy?" he called. "You did peek."

"I did not!" Maggie replied impatiently. "I'm talking about the one beside your waist. I didn't know you had an appendectomy scar."

His laughter mingled with a few soft splashes. "I don't."

Irked, Maggie whirled around to respond, saw a brief

flash of soap and a raised arm, then jerked her head back. She counted to ten—another of her father's precepts. "Casey told me what happened with the rustlers."

"Yeah? Well, you didn't have to hear it from her. I'm sure the whole juicy story's right behind your desk in one of Farrell's filing cabinets."

"It is," Maggie admitted, feeling obligated to be honest with him. "You were right before. I did pull your file."

The low sound he made wasn't damning—but just an acknowledgment of her statement.

"I always thought—when my family lived here before, that is—that Belle Crawford was a nice woman. I even have a gold cross my dad bought me from her jewelry store."

Ross expelled a humorless laugh. "Then the souvenir you got from her is a lot prettier than mine. She was a busy woman. By day, pillar of the community. By night, queen of the cattle rustlers and madam to the girls down at Babylon."

Casey had told her about Babylon, too. The private gaming club and brothel in the deep woods outside town had been shut down for quite a while now. But three years ago, Belle's cronies—the men Ross had owed—had held Casey captive in one of the old pleasure cabins to make sure that Jess wouldn't turn them in to the sheriff. Luckily, Casey was a fighter, and had escaped before anything could happen to her.

"Casey said you were shot trying to keep those men from taking her hostage."

"Didn't do much good. I failed."

Maggie turned around, no longer uneasy about watching him bathe. "But you tried. You put your own life at risk to save hers."

"Yeah, I'm a real saint." Ross splashed some water on his face and combed his wet hair back with his fingers. Then he grinned and changed the subject. "As long as you're not doing anything important, want to wash my back?''

Maggie smiled, beginning to like him—as opposed to just being attracted to him. ''No.''

''My front?''

Her smile grew and she shook her head. He was cheeky and insolent, and annoyingly happy. But she was starting to see his cocky smiles and teasing repartee as a shield, hiding the man inside that—for some reason—he was afraid to reveal. She'd occasionally glimpsed that man when his guard was down, or when he hadn't realized she was watching. The vulnerability that he tried so hard to hide was there in the devotion he showed his little niece, in his regret at not being able to save Casey, in the sweetness he showed his aunt Ruby. And whether or not he knew it, his sturdy log home was a monument to his need for something solid in his life. He might be a hormone-happy womanizer, but he did have a depth to him that Maggie wouldn't have suspected had she not ridden out here with Casey tonight.

''Coming out.'' Ross tossed the soap onto the grassy bank and started to rise. Quickly, Maggie averted her eyes again.

Just when she'd decided he had *some* class, he had to do something outrageous again. Although…he had risen out of the water a lot more slowly than he might have.

By the time he'd toweled off behind a tree, pulled his jeans back on, and walked, barefoot, to the log where Maggie sat, the sun was gone from the sky, and night's deepening shadows had fallen around them. He grabbed clean socks and a shirt from his bag, rolled his soap, underwear and old socks into the towel, then stuffed the roll into his duffel. When he pulled on his shirt, he left it unbuttoned.

Ross sat down beside her to pull on his socks. Maggie couldn't look away from the soft mat of dark brown spanning his well-formed pectoral muscles…the ribbon of hair arrowing down to his navel. The towel-dried hair on his head was still damp, falling in thick strands over his forehead and collar. Maggie's head felt a little light as she breathed in the masculine smell of his soap, mingling nicely with their woodsy surroundings.

When he finished yanking on his boots, Ross rolled the sleeves back on his cotton shirt. Most cowboys, even in summer, wore long sleeves to keep from sunburning.

Finally, he looked at her, and Maggie looked back.

Suddenly, they were both aware of the heady silence between them, aware that they were alone out here with only the crickets to witness what went on.

Ross's gaze ran slowly over her long, loose hair, returned to her eyes, then settled with obvious interest on her mouth. For a moment, he seemed to measure the wisdom of proceeding.

Maggie swallowed.

Then he inched toward her—slowly enough to give her a chance to back away. She didn't. Maggie's heart pounded so hard, she half expected it to burst through her chest. She felt her arms go weak, felt her breasts grow heavy. She could smell the lemonade on his breath now, see the day-old stubble shading his firm jaw.

He kissed her. Softly, sweetly, without touching her anywhere else, only their lips blending. His tongue slid languidly along her closed lips, which she kept sealed. He presented his tongue again.

Maggie's stomach was a hard knot behind the zipper of her jeans. Her breath grew shallow. And she wanted...oh, yes, she wanted...

Ross broke the soft kiss, but didn't back away. A rustle of night air cooled her lips where his tongue had traced them. "Why are you here with me, Maggie?" he murmured. "You could've gone back with Jess and Casey."

Maggie didn't recognize her own trembling voice. "Curiosity. I wanted to see your home."

Ross shook his head, then slid his warm, broad hands down her sides to the waistband of her jeans. He spanned her hips, stroked the side seams of her Levis with his fingertips. "I don't think so," he whispered, once again parting his lips over hers.

Ross gathered her close, trapping her arms at her sides. Automatically, Maggie's hands fumbled up between them to grip his shirt. But it wasn't shirt that she touched. A tingle swept through her as her fingertips encountered smooth, taut skin and soft chest hair. Maggie drove her fingers into its warmth.

Ross's tongue darted and thrust at the seam of her lips, determined to penetrate them, daring her to take it. "Taste me, Maggie," he rasped, breaking away for a moment. "Let me in."

Maggie's inhibitions sailed away like a hawk on thermals. Mind spinning dizzily, she opened for him, welcomed him inside, and let his slick tongue and hot mouth take her senses back thirteen years.

Ross slid one of his hands into her hair, pulling her closer to make the mating of their mouths more intimate. The other hand, Maggie began to realize, was sliding along the curve of her hip, the tips of his strong fingers grazing her left buttock. Prickly gooseflesh danced down her leg, and she didn't stop him…until his hand slipped under her T-shirt and his thumb started stroking the side of her breast.

Maggie broke from the kiss and stilled his motion, struggling to bring her rapid breathing under control. She eased his hand from under her shirt, then placed it on his thigh and covered it with her own hand.

In a heartbeat, he reversed their hands and hers was on the bottom, pressing into his warm thigh.

"I can't do this," she whispered shakily. She tried to pull her hand away, but he held it fast.

"You're doing fine."

"No, I'm not," she answered. This time she succeeded in tugging her hand away. "It'll be dark shortly. If we don't leave soon, we won't be able to see where we're going."

"We could feel our way."

Maggie stood, her knees threatening to buckle beneath her, the cooling night doing little to allay the heat still suffusing her.

Ross coaxed her back into his arms.

"Just one more kiss," he murmured, his breath warm on her skin as he nuzzled her ear. "Then I'll take you back to the ranch." He tipped her chin up, and their eyes met. Even in the fading light, she could see that his were cloudy, uncertain, a question in them Maggie didn't understand. "Come on," he whispered, tracing a finger along her lower lip, and setting new fires along her nerve endings. "Just one more, then we'll go. I promise."

Maggie's heart pounded. She could kiss him one more time—just once more. Kissing on the log had been exciting. But much of the excitement had come from their inability to slide closer to each other, from the shivery straining of their bodies in the twilight secrecy of the woods. And, heaven help her, she wanted that intimacy, had longed for it since that first kiss beside her car. Maggie's eyelids closed and her lips parted.

Ross covered her mouth with his, the warnings of the crickets and night calls of a nearby owl going unheeded. Then their hands were moving, examining sloping muscles and gentle curves. When one of Ross's hands slid to her bottom and pressed her into the hard saddle of his hips, Maggie didn't pull away. She dragged in thin air as the kiss went on and on, and the primitive pressure of his hips became a sweet ache in hers.

Gasping, he broke away. "Let's go back to the house. I keep a sleeping bag in the loft for times when I stay overnight. We'll be more comfortable there."

"I can't."

"Maggie, I want you."

"No."

"Why?"

Somehow, she found the strength to push out of his arms and back away from him. "Because you want everybody. How many other women have shared your sleeping bag?"

Ross stared at her for a long moment—a moment in which clear thought made a shaky comeback for both of them, and their labored breathing settled down to a manageable level. Finally, he nodded, and without answering her question or denying the accusation he said, "We'd better go. Jess and Casey are probably wondering what happened to us."

No, they weren't, Maggie thought a few minutes later as she sat glued to the passenger's door on the silent ride back. Right now, they were probably wrapped in each others' arms, praying between soft sighs and kisses that their baby would sleep soundly and that Ross wouldn't return too soon. After three years of marriage, they still had that snap and sizzle between them—the kind of chemistry she hoped to have someday with her own husband.

Maggie glanced at Ross. His brow was furrowed beneath his Stetson, his chiseled profile faintly lit by the glowing panel on the truck's dashboard...his thoughts hidden. A flutter of arousal curled through her belly, and Maggie drew a soft breath and turned away—back toward the dark sky and shadowy mountains and rows of barbwire illuminated in the peripheral glow of the headlights.

Please, she begged the first new stars. Please let the man I'm destined to marry show up before I make the biggest mistake of my life.

Ross drew a deep breath, breaking into her thoughts. "There was no one but me," he said.

"I'm sorry?" she asked, not understanding.

"In the sleeping bag. There was no one but me."

Chapter 6

Maggie drove home while fighting the deep, gnawing urge to turn around and go straight back to Brokenstraw. Her nerves still vibrated. Her lips still felt the commanding pressure of Ross's mouth. Her cheeks and chin still tingled from the scrape of his beard.

What would her father say about such wantonness with a man who was not her husband? Maggie released a burdened breath. The reverend—as her mother used to call him—had sent Maggie a few not-so-subtle looks during the two years she'd dated Todd—but not because Todd wasn't a supporter of organized religion. Reverend Tom Bristol was a good, gentle man who wasn't opposed to people cleaving to their own personal beliefs as long as they led decent lives. But he was adamantly opposed to couples having premarital sex—even in relationships where the near certainty of marriage existed.

Her behavior would have mortified him had he seen her tonight.

She could almost hear her father's troubled, but loving

"Don't mind Lex," Casey said, rocking her close. "It takes her a while to warm up to people—but then, look out." She paused. "Why don't you ride out to the house with us? It's not that far—only about a quarter of a mile from the hot spring, if you know where that is."

Oh, yes, she knew. "I don't think—"

"I just made a huge thermos of lemonade," Casey added. "All I have to do is grab it and get a sweater for Lex."

"Thanks, but I just stopped by to return Ross's blanket. It ended up in my trunk by mistake." Maggie flushed at the implication of her words and hurriedly explained. "There was a box social at the church this past Sunday and—"

"Yes, I know. Ross bought your picnic lunch. Did you have fun?"

Maggie hesitated, feeling a bit awkward. She didn't know what Ross had said about her, and she didn't want to give anyone a false impression. "Yes. I had a good time."

"Great. I think Ross did, too." Casey sent her an engaging smile. "Come on, change your mind about riding out to see his house. He'd love a chance to show off for someone besides family."

"He built it himself?"

"From top to bottom—with a little help from Jess and an electrician. He even did his own plumbing." She laughed. "Boggles the mind, doesn't it?" Casey's smile faded a little. "Too many people have a dated opinion of Ross. They can't imagine that he's anything more than what he shows them on the surface. But they're wrong." She paused thoughtfully, then said, "If you ride along with us, I'll tell you a story. You might find it interesting."

Even though the heat of the day still held, chills chased up Maggie's arms. Lord help her, she wanted to run to her car, gun the engine and drive away—and at the same time, voice. "Honey, think about this. You're a minister's daughter, and you're involved with the town hell-raiser— a man who, by his thoughtless actions and frequent liaisons, says he doesn't believe in rules, and he doesn't revere women. You are also—unsettling as it is to me—an officer of the law. What sense does it make for you to be with this man? Maggie, if you aren't careful, this could hurt you spiritually, physically and vocationally."

"I know," she sighed as she parked near a utility shed beside her aunt's truck, well short of the ranch house with its lighted windows. "I really know, Dad."

Clicking on the Ford's interior light, she glanced into the rearview mirror to check her appearance. What she saw made her groan. How on earth could she walk inside looking like this? A quick brushing would fix her hair. But her puffy lips and the distinctive red scrapes on her chin and cheeks left little to the imagination. Whisker burn didn't look like anything else.

Taking a brush from her purse, she pulled it several times through her hair. Then she snapped off the dome light and got out of the car. Her heart sank when she heard the low murmur of voices coming from the porch.

Twenty yards ahead, she spotted an expensive-looking vehicle parked close to the house. To Maggie's chagrin, Trent Campion's deep voice carried to her over the greetings of her uncle and aunt. "Hi, Maggie."

Maggie managed a small smile as she took the path, then climbed the steps, thankful that Lila's dislike of dive-bombing moths kept the porch light off. Although, now that she looked, she could see a few valiants fluttering near the citronella candles. She stopped short of the candlelight near the porch's thick support post.

"Hello, Trent. This is a surprise."

"A nice one, I hope." He seemed unusually pleased as he took in her hair and courteous smile.

Moe chuckled heartily—one of the few displays of

delight Maggie had seen from her uncle since her return from Colorado. "Now that you're home, Lila and I are gonna stop borin' this young fella with our stories and go inside." With Lila's help and a grunt of exertion, Moe hoisted himself out of a wicker chair, then latched on to his walker. Trent hurried to open the screen door.

"Why, thank you, Trent," Lila said, then let Trent help Moe inside while she took a few steps closer to Maggie. Her curious gaze swept Maggie's face. "There's still some lemonade over there on the table, honey, and a clean glass on the tray." She lowered her voice. "Why are you standing way over here? Are you all right?" Lila stared at Maggie a little longer, a little harder. Maggie's uneasiness with her perusal seemed to prompt Lila to reach for a candle and bring it closer. "Oh, my," she said softly.

Any skin on Maggie's face that wasn't already scraped and red, turned scarlet. "It's not what you think."

"Just a little sun poisoning?"

"Something like that. Poison, anyway."

"Ross?"

Trent came back outside, sidelining their conversation.

"You know," Lila chirped as she blew out the candle, earning Maggie's gratitude, "I'm beginning to believe these nasty old moths think citronella is an invitation to a party." She walked to the remaining candles across the way and blew them out, too. "I'm canceling their invitation right this minute. You two don't need candles out here anyway with the hall light shining through the screen door."

"You won't get any objections from me," Trent answered.

Maggie winced. If Trent had misinterpreted her aunt's motives, and thought Lila was encouraging something romantic, Maggie would have to straighten his thinking out in a hurry.

"Good night, then."

"Good night, Mrs. Jackson. Thanks for the lemonade."

"'Night, Aunt Lila." When the door had closed behind her aunt, Maggie slipped her leather bag from her shoulder and walked over to the wooden porch swing. She dropped her purse there—then nearly sank down beside it before she thought the better of their seating arrangements. Instead, she chose the chair her uncle had just vacated.

Trent took the chair next to Maggie's. "I guess you saw my car," he said, that incredibly pleased smile still lighting his face.

Maggie still didn't understand his delight. "Yes, I saw your car," she answered, wondering why that was significant. He'd needed some sort of transportation to get here, hadn't he?

"That's what I thought. You know, I wasn't sure I was reading you right at the sheriff's office a couple of weeks ago. But you are interested in me a little, aren't you?"

Maggie's throat worked, but no sound came out. *Why would he think that?*

"When I saw you stop to fix your hair for me, I... Well, that was nice, Maggie."

She still couldn't say a word. Trent certainly wouldn't like hearing the reason that she'd had to pull herself together. And Maggie wasn't all that sure she wanted to tell anyone—with the exception of Lila, who'd guessed on her own. Easy guess. Lately, there'd been enough heat and friction between her and Ross to start a small range fire.

Thinking of him sent a trickle of awareness through her again, and Maggie got up and walked to the wicker parson's table. Before she could reach for the lemonade pitcher, Trent was there, pouring. His aftershave was strong—almost overpoweringly so—making Maggie remember how good plain soap smelled on a man's skin.

She accepted the glass he offered, then took a long sip. "How long have you been waiting?"

"Not too long. Your uncle and aunt kept me amused."

Had that sounded arrogant? Maggie frowned and shook off her misgivings, determined to be more understanding. After hearing the discussion between Trent and his father at the rodeo, she pitied Trent. From their first encounter, she'd suspected Ben's toothy smiles and country friendliness were put on. But she never would have guessed at his cruelty—especially toward his own son.

Maggie carried her glass back to her chair, remembering the taste of lemonade on Ross's lips...on his tongue. She cleared her throat. "So, did you have a special reason for driving over here tonight?"

"Actually, I did. I wanted to apologize."

"Apologize? For what?"

"First of all for not coming to see you sooner. I had to be in the capital for a few days. And second," he said, scowling, "I wanted to apologize for that disastrous box social." He met her eyes earnestly. "I thought the basket I bought was yours. I would *never* have paid a hundred dollars for Bessie Holsopple's picnic lunch." He made a disgusted face. "There was so much cat hair on the tablecloth, I was afraid to eat the food."

Maggie had to hold back a smile.

"The long and short of it is, I'm sorry you had to put up with a jerk like Ross Dalton. Whenever I looked over at the two of you, I could see that you were trying to be gracious, but you shouldn't have had to do that. Unfortunately, after I'd bought Bessie's basket, I couldn't buy another one."

Maggie studied his shadowed face in the darkness, waiting for the words that should have followed. He didn't say them, so she did. "And of course, that would have hurt Bessie's feelings."

After a blank look, Trent seemed to catch himself. "Oh, absolutely. And I wouldn't have wanted that to happen." He chuckled. "She was all giddy and flustered that a Campion had bought her basket."

Maggie was sure he was right. Bessie was a thin, plain woman with a houseful of cats and little to do but keep the books in the library dusted and catalogued. But it was heartless of Trent to hint that she'd gushed over his attention. Somehow she knew that if Ross's plan hadn't worked out, and he'd been forced to buy Bessie's basket, Ross would've been sweet and decent about it.

"Trent, if you don't mind, I'm really tired and I need to get some sleep. It's been an incredibly long day."

"Sure," he answered, obviously disappointed. "But let's not wait so long before we get together again." He took her glass and placed it back on the table, then drew her to her feet. "Why don't I come by tomorrow morning and pick you up for breakfast? The café opens at six. You could still be at the office by seven."

"Trent—" Maggie eased her hands out of his and made an excuse "—I'm really not ready for another relationship right now. Just before I came back to Comfort, I broke up with a man I'd dated for two years, and I really think I need some time."

He looked disappointed again, but he managed to shrug it off. "Okay, I can accept that. But there's no reason we can't be friends, is there? At least until you're ready for something else."

"No reason I can think of," she said, unable to turn him down cold. She doubted that Trent had many friends, and extending a little kindness never hurt anyone. But when she was ready for "something else," it wouldn't be with Trent Campion. "It was nice of you to stop by."

"I'm glad you think so. I plan on being nice pretty often from now on."

Maggie was relieved when he said good-night and drove off. She was also relieved that Lila wasn't waiting for her when she went inside. She'd be able to escape to the shower and crawl into bed. Even though her aunt wouldn't have expected an explanation, Maggie would have felt obligated to offer one, and part of her was embarrassed at having to justify her actions with Ross tonight.

The rest of her wanted some time alone to hold the breathless memory of his kisses and touches close, and to relive them, over and over again.

"Sure you don't need any more help?" Jess asked late Wednesday afternoon.

Ross glanced up at his brother. He and Jess had just finished wrestling the bathtub into the ceramic-tiled alcove and finished the plumbing. "Thanks, but that's it. I can take care of the caulking." He peeled a manufacturer's sticker from the side of the white tub, then stood, folding the glossy paper between his fingers.

"So, what's on the agenda for tomorrow night?"

"Set the vanity and connect the pipes, then plumb the kitchen sink." Ross tossed the sticker into an old plastic wastebasket. "And sometime soon, I need to put another coat of sealer on the exterior logs." He met Jess's eyes thoughtfully. "I've been thinking about spreading the finishing work around a little."

"Oh?"

"Yeah. I'd already decided to let a professional do the carpeting and floor tile anyway—Ed Hanley's coming tomorrow morning to do the bathroom. But Aunt Ruby mentioned one of her customers was having a hard time financially, so I thought, what the heck. The guy's always worked construction, and I borrowed more than enough from the bank to put up the house. I figure, as long as I'm making payments, I might as well be living here."

Jess's easy reply had an underlying concern in it, but it was so faint that Ross might not have noticed if he hadn't known his brother so well. "So why the sudden urge to move in? For the past two-and-a-half years, you've been saying you're in no hurry."

"Well, now I am."

"Planning a private little housewarming?"

Ross stared hard at Jess, suddenly irritated by the knowledge that he saw in his brother's eyes. He'd never kept his exploits a secret from Jess. In fact, like a braying jackass, he'd even bragged about a few of them—something he wasn't proud of these days. But now the thought of being with Maggie was too personal, and Ross felt the need to protect her.

"No, I'm not planning a housewarming. Were you planning to give me one?"

"You know what I'm talking about."

"Yes, I do, and it's none of your business."

Jess regarded Ross soberly for a moment, then nodded. "You're right, little brother, it isn't. Just don't do anything without thinking it through first. She's not Brenda."

No, she wasn't. Maggie was as classy as they came. Brenda, on the other hand, was sex personified, and she and Ross had safely enjoyed each other's attentions dozens of times over the past ten years. But only because sex to Brenda was nothing more than an aerobic workout. She enjoyed Ross's company, but the attention of another cowboy would have interested her just as much, and vice versa. Ross hadn't been with her since... He frowned. Since the gambling and rustling and shooting had made him more cautious about the things he did. In fact, he hadn't been with *anyone* in a long time. Maybe that's why he was so obsessed with getting Maggie into bed—good old-fashioned lust.

"You're ticked at me for butting in," Jess said.

Ross shook his head. "It's okay. You were only looking out for her. I can't be mad about something like that." He nodded toward the opening in the bathroom wall that still awaited a door. "Let's grab a beer. I have a couple in the cooler."

A few minutes later, they were standing on Ross's three-sided porch, leaning against the thick twig rails that fenced in the perimeter.

"Wonder why they call these 'twigs'?" Ross asked, running a callused thumb over the rough knots in the varnished wood. "They're a good four inches in diameter."

Jess drank a moment, then shrugged. "Gotta call them something, I guess." He looked up at the cloudless blue sky. "We need some rain."

Ross nodded. The creeks were down, and irrigating the hay fields would soon become a problem. "Northern California and Washington are hoarding it all."

Jess grinned wryly. "Not by choice." He finished his beer and tossed the can into the recycling barrel. "Well, I'd better get back. I promised Casey we'd go to Aunt Ruby's for wings tonight."

"That's right, it *is* Wednesday." Ruby's legendary hot wings were still six cents a piece on Wednesday nights, and she served them to a packed house. "Need a sitter for Lex?"

Jess headed down the steps. "Thanks, but we're taking her along. Aunt Ruby'd have a fit if we showed up without her." Once inside his truck, he poked his dark head out the window and grinned. "If you're so nuts about kids, why don't you have one of your own?"

Ross rolled his eyes. "Correct me if I'm wrong, but didn't you just tell me that was a lousy idea?"

"Not if you do it the right way."

Ross's chest tightened as he grinned and watched his older brother wave and drive off. Jess had it made—a beautiful wife, a sweet little daughter, and the kind of life songwriters put to music. He tossed his own beer can in the recycling bin and strolled back inside to load his caulking gun.

The right way? The "right way" meant marriage, and there was no chance of that happening. Some people—like

Jess and Casey—were cut out for that sort of thing.

Some people weren't.

On Thursday afternoon, the phone at the office rang and Maggie picked it up. "Good afternoon, sheriff's office. This is Maggie."

"Hi, honey. My, but you sound professional."

Maggie winced her way past the word "professional" and smiled warmly. "Well, hello. I didn't expect to hear from you today."

"Why not?" Reverend Bristol replied, an answering smile in his tone. "It should be an ordinary occurrence for a daughter to pick up the phone and hear her dad's voice."

"Well, maybe not at the sheriff's office. Besides, I just spoke to you two days ago."

"I guess you have a point," he said, chuckling. "I won't keep you long, at any rate. I just phoned the ranch and Moe said you were working. Optimist that I am, I keep hoping your interests have shifted to something besides law enforcement."

Oh, her interests had shifted all right, she thought guiltily. But not in any direction her father would approve of. Though it was obvious that her dad still wanted her to marry, have babies, and leave certain occupations to the men of the world, Maggie suspected that, if forced to choose, he'd pick her police work over an involvement with Ross. Ross Dalton was a love 'em and leave 'em, Stetson-wearing Romeo who would never give Tom Bristol grandchildren, much less marry his daughter.

"Anyway," her father continued in a sober voice, "on to the reason I called. I hope you won't be too disappointed, but I can't get away for the Fourth. The parish council wants to have the summer festival on Independence Day, and I really should be there—" he sighed "—This will be the first Fourth of July we've missed spending together since you were born."

"I know," Maggie said, disappointed, too. Reverend

Tom Bristol didn't put emphasis only on religious holidays. He was a family man, too, and from the time Maggie was a child, the two of them had always delighted in fireworks displays.

"I'll miss you, honey. Find something fun to do."

"I will. There's supposed to be some sort of street dance, so I'll probably go. But I'll miss you, too."

"Two weeks. Then we'll have a belated celebration."

"With sparklers?"

"Absolutely."

The other line buzzed and, frowning at the interruption, Maggie said, "I'm sorry, Dad, there's another call coming in. I have to take it."

"No problem, I'll talk to you soon. Love you."

"Love you, too," she said, then hung up and punched the button for the other line. "Sheriff's office."

It was the print shop down the street saying that more of the sheriff's reelection paraphernalia was ready to be picked up. Maggie transferred the call to Cy's office. It wasn't long before Cy left the mountain of paperwork on his desk and walked eagerly into the reception area. "I'll be back in a few minutes. Did Mike call in to say how serious that accident was?"

"No, but he didn't request an ambulance or fire department assistance, so it was probably just a fender bender."

"Outta-staters?"

"That's what he said. Fishermen in an RV."

"Okay. I'll be over at the print shop if you need me." He clipped his radio to his belt and headed out the door. "Be back soon."

Maggie mouthed his last sentence even before he said it. Cy was out of the office more than he was in it these days, what with ingratiating himself with area businessmen, and taking trips to the printer for cards. It was only the first of July, and Farrell's campaign was already in full swing.

Maggie returned to her computer screen. What made a man who was running unopposed do something like that? Was he more interested in *being* the sheriff than in doing the sheriff's job? Or was he just plain bored? Comfort, Montana, was hardly a hotbed of intrigue—and the monthly list of arrests and call-outs she was typing for the newspaper attested to that. Maggie punched in the "print" command, then remembered that she needed to change the ribbon in her printer, and canceled the job.

The ribbons in her drawer were the wrong size. Someone had inadvertently put the ribbons that fit Cy's printer in her desk. Which seemed to suggest that she would find her own ribbons in Cy's office. Grabbing the cellophane-wrapped stack, Maggie strode into Cy's office and started opening drawers.

She grinned when she looked inside. The first and second in the drab gray metal desk were filled with stationery supplies, packaged cupcakes and an assortment of hard candy. When she opened the third drawer, she found the ribbons she'd been looking for. Plucking them out, she traded her ribbons for his, and was about to close the drawer when her knuckles rapped against the metal bottom, and she heard a hollow sound. Frowning curiously, she rapped it again, deliberately this time. Peering inside, she estimated the drawer's depth to be ten inches, then closed it and compared that depth to the outside, which measured between twelve and fourteen inches.

Cy Farrell's bottom drawer had a false bottom.

"Which is really none of your business, Maggie," she murmured, then grabbed her ribbons and hurried back to her desk.

She had just snapped a new cartridge into the printer when Ross walked in. Maggie felt her face heat as memories of the last time they were together swirled vividly through her mind. His mouth on hers…his warm hand beneath her shirt. *Her vow to put a stop to this insanity once and for all.*

Clearing her throat, she tried to be the professional that her father had just said she was. "Good afternoon. What can I do for you today?"

Ross ambled up to her desk, a teasing response forming behind his eyes as he shed his Stetson.

There should be a law against men looking that good in a simple cotton shirt and jeans, Maggie thought. The deeper his tan, the bluer his eyes, and the jumpier her nerve endings.

"For starters, you can say 'yes' to the question I'm about to ask you."

"Ross, don't start."

"Here?" He glanced around in amusement. "This is a little public, even for me."

Maggie felt herself being dragged into his familiar craziness and knew that she had to finally take a stand—for her own emotional well-being. She couldn't keep flirting with the devil and not expect to face the consequences. Besides, today she really did have work to do, and Ross's mere presence was enough to blow every thought from her mind except the ones she shouldn't be thinking.

"Ross," she said, more coolly than she intended, "if you have something important to say, I'd really appreciate it if you'd just say it so I can get back to work."

His smile faded, and his eyebrows raised in rebuffed surprise. "Sorry. I just stopped by to tell you that when I was over at the feed store picking up supplies, I ran into Reverend Fremont."

"And?" she prompted.

His eyes narrowed on her, his rugged face losing its genial lines and his mouth thinning. Suddenly a solemn Ross, dusty from loading bags of feed, was more sensual and unnerving than the grinning man who'd teased her.

"And," he replied, "Fremont's decided to replace the

church roof this Saturday if we can get enough people to do it.''

Maggie's heart sank, along with the hope that she could finally put some distance between them. The reverend's recruiting speech to Ross on the day of the auction had—fairly or unfairly—included Maggie's participation as part of the deal. She and Ross would be there together, further cementing the disturbing bond between them.

"Why so soon?"

"Why not? If the man has enough money to pay for it, why put it off?"

"Because some people just might have plans, that's why. Ranchers and farmers have full days this time of year." A nerve leaped in Ross's jaw at her irritable tone, but she'd decided to make the break and she had to continue. "An activity like this should be scheduled so people aren't caught unaware. My *father* would never have sprung this on anyone."

Ross's eyes went cold and flat. "Every man, woman and child in the county isn't coming, Maggie. Only those who can, and only a handful at that. Most people are able to adjust their schedules when something important comes up. If you can't, I'm sure another woman could step in and handle things in your place."

That shouldn't have hurt, but it did. Swallowing, Maggie murmured, "I'm sure another woman could—very easily." And she was no longer talking about preparing food and filling iced tea glasses for thirsty men. "Do you have someone in mind?"

Ross ignored the question. "If you change your mind, we're starting at nine o'clock. Since most people around here are up at the crack of dawn, that should give the ranchers and farmers time to see to their livestock and take care of their kids."

He walked to the door, his spine straight and his shoulders rigid. Just before he left, he turned around, his eyes hard on hers. "You know, I don't have a clue as to what just happened here. Or why you wanted it to happen."

Then he was replacing his Stetson and striding outside, presumably heading back to the feed store.

Maggie brought the heels of her hands to her forehead and pressed at the pain growing there. Right on cue, up popped that aggravating little voice—the one that loved to point out her faults. *Congratulations. You really handled that well. The man's probably wondering if you have a personality disorder or just a raging case of P.M.S.*

She brought her hands back down and clasped them on her desk. Well, how was she supposed to handle it? Just tell him outright that it wasn't a good idea for them to see each other anymore? He'd probably laugh his head off and point out that they had never even had a real date—so how could they "stop" seeing each other? She could hardly tell him the truth—that she couldn't look at him without wanting him, and that she couldn't have him because he was the kind of man who wouldn't be "had" for long. She'd already wasted two years on someone who'd bolted like a young colt when she'd asked him about their future. She didn't intend to repeat that mistake.

Cy Farrell stormed inside, red-faced and blustering. "What the hell did *he* want?"

Holding back a sigh, Maggie asked "Who?" though she knew full well who Cy meant.

"Dalton. What's he sniffing around here for? You'd think he'd get tired of lookin' at these green walls."

Maggie loaded a stack of paper into the printer. "He just stopped by with some church news from Reverend Fremont."

Cy released a sarcastic laugh. "Church news? You and the town renegade thinkin' of gettin' hitched, Maggie?"

Maggie gritted her teeth. Cy didn't believe that for an instant, and she knew it. He just had to remind her that he knew there was something between her and Ross—and that he didn't like it.

"He came by to tell me that the reverend wants to start the new church roof this Saturday. He knew I'd offered to prepare some of the food."

"And Ross Dalton's gonna help with this roof?"

"As a matter of fact, he is."

"That oughta be some roof. Accordin' to the women in this town, his specialty's never been carpentry."

Maggie felt like lashing out and tearing up at the same time. Cy was doing everything in his power to make sure Ross kept his distance from the hired help, and enjoying every moment of it. He needn't have worried. Maggie had taken care of that herself. She just wished that she felt happier about it.

"I hope you don't mind," she said, changing the subject, "but someone put my printer ribbons in your desk by mistake. I swapped them with the ones they left in my drawer."

The color drained from Farrell's face, then returned two shades redder than normal. To Maggie's surprise, he turned, walked into his office and closed the door—something he rarely did.

When he came back out, he was more composed, but gruff. "My mistake," he grumbled. "I put the new ribbons away when I picked them up the other day. That one workin' out okay?"

"It's fine," Maggie said, indicating the sheets coming out of the printer. She eyed him curiously. Why was he so churned up? Was making a mistake and being found out by an underling that disturbing?

Or was Cy afraid that she might have discovered the secret of his bottom drawer? Her pulse leapt. Was he hiding something in there? Something he didn't want anyone to know about? Something incriminating?

Maggie frowned wryly at the clandestine path her

thoughts were taking, as she took the sheets from the printer. Her suspicions were just plain silly. If there was anything in the drawer at all, it was probably a girlie magazine. She obviously missed detective work more than she realized.

It was nearly quitting time when Farrell shuffled out of his office, pursing his lips around a toothpick that he plucked out of his mouth. "By the way, Maggie—you still plannin' to take that deputy position when Mike leaves for law school in the fall? I know we talked about it some."

The question stunned her. Farrell *knew* she was still interested. And they hadn't "talked about it some." He'd promised her the job.

"'Cause if you're content bein' the dispatcher, one of Harvey Becker's boys is interested in gettin' into police work. Just got outta school with a degree in criminal justice. Did real good, too. Third in his class."

The blood in Maggie's veins turned to ice. It was an enormous effort for her to keep her tone pleasant. Farrell was trying to manipulate her again, and he wasn't being very subtle about it.

"Yes, I'm still planning to take Mike's place. In fact, I'm really looking forward to it."

"Great. Because with your two years of experience, you'd naturally be my first choice. Unless…"

"Unless?" she repeated.

"Unless you decided that it wasn't what you wanted after all. Sometimes the hours get long, and the work gets risky—especially for a woman who might want a family someday. You start wonderin' if you really want to put yourself in the line of fire when you've got little ones."

With a folksy smile, he ambled over to her desk, scanned the arrest report she'd printed for the paper, then put it back down. "Not that it's dangerous all the time. I just wouldn't want you to take a job like that unadvised." The green eyes behind his glasses cooled. "Still want it?"

"Yes. I still want it."

Farrell was either strengthening his warning to stay away from Ross, or he was trying to force her out. Maggie just didn't know which.

Chapter 7

Unable to sleep, and too restless to wait for her shift to begin, Maggie parked in front of the sheriff's office nearly an hour early the next morning, then walked to the door. At 4:00 a.m., she'd been awakened by a disturbing dream, but by the time she was fully awake, she could only recall parts of it. The only clear thing in her memory was Cy Farrell's accusing face.

Opening the door, she stepped inside to hear angry shouts coming from Cy's private office. Maggie froze in the doorway, instantly recognizing the voices.

"If you think I'm shelling out this kind of money for a rally, you're out of your blasted mind!" Ben Campion bellowed. "It's bad enough that it's only July, *you're running unopposed,* and you've already had cards, buttons, pencils and God-knows-what-else printed up!" He'd run out of breath at the last, and now he sucked in another deep one. "Well, I'll foot the bill for that crap, but that's it. I'm telling you for the last time, this rally isn't going to happen!"

Farrell lowered his voice, steel running through his words. "Then your son isn't going to the legislature."

Unnerved, Maggie slammed the door to alert the two men that someone was in the office. Had she heard Farrell right? Had he really threatened Ben Campion? Quick boot heels sounded on the floor tiles, and Cy strode into the reception area.

"Maggie," he said, obviously trying to hide his irritation, "you're early."

Smiling as though there weren't a thing wrong, Maggie walked over to her desk and slung her purse on top of it. "I know. I couldn't sleep, so I thought I'd get a head start on finishing those monthly reports. That is, if it's okay with you."

Farrell stared at her for a brief moment, then nodded. "Of course. But I'm in the middle of a meeting, so I'd appreciate not being disturbed for a while, okay?" He glanced into his office, and Maggie followed his gaze. Campion stood beside Farrell's desk, looking relaxed in a white shirt, khaki chinos and his ever-present white Stetson and string tie. He nodded cordially at Maggie, and she smiled back.

"No problem," she answered cheerfully. "I'll just put a pot of coffee on, charge up the computer, and stay out of your hair."

Cy nodded, then went back inside, closing the door behind him. Maggie's heartbeat began to slow down. What was going on? She *couldn't* have heard Cy correctly. No one in their right mind messed with the Campions. Besides being the benefactors of half a dozen local charities and businesses, they had loyal, powerful friends. That could be the kiss of death for a man who wanted to be reelected.

Maggie dug under a cupboard for coffee and filters, keeping her attention on the closed office door. The sound of arguing still rumbled behind the walls, but it was too low for Maggie to understand what they were saying. She

heard a hard thump—something that might have been a
fist banging a desktop—and a moment later, Ben threw
open the door and walked out. He held several sheets of
paper, crushed like an hourglass, in one of his meaty
hands. Farrell followed him out.

"So are we all set for the rally?" Farrell persisted, giving Ben a companionable slap on the back.

Ben stared at Cy as though he were a bug to be squashed
beneath his boot. "Send me another copy of the figures.
I'll look them over again." His mood quickly reversed
itself when he realized he had an audience. Smoothing the
papers, he tucked them into his pocket, then turned another
smile on Maggie. "You're looking exceptionally pretty today, Maggie."

"Thank you," she said, returning his smile. But she
didn't want compliments from this man. Lately, she'd begun to think that he was dangerous. Or was the dangerous
man the stocky, uniformed sheriff smiling benignly at his
side?

Maggie's thoughts tumbled slowly, as Campion took his
leave, and Cy returned to his office. Maybe she'd misunderstood the whole thing. Walking in on an argument, then
drawing conclusions based only on the part she'd overheard, meant making hasty judgments. She could easily
have misinterpreted the conversation. She just didn't think
so.

Because the image of that strange drawer with the false
bottom kept creeping into her mind.

She didn't see Cy again until nearly lunchtime. When
he came out of his office, he was whistling cheerfully.
Taking the tan cowboy hat that matched his uniform from
a hook on the wall, he smoothed his thinning brown hair,
then pulled his hat low. "I'll be out for a while, Maggie—
got some business with the folks at the Gold and Silver
Exchange—" he winked "—Then I'm gonna walk over

to the Donut Shop and see how Mike's comin' with crowd control.''

Cops-at-the-donut-shop humor? From Farrell? Scoring a victory over one of the most influential men in the state had certainly improved his disposition. ''Sounds like a great idea. In fact, when Mike comes back, I might see you over there.''

Chuckling, Farrell headed for the door. Suddenly, he stopped, smacked his forehead in an absentminded gesture, and turned around. ''I swear, I'd forget my head if it wasn't attached,'' he said through another chuckle. He went back into his office. A moment later, he called her.

''Maggie, could you come in here for a minute, please?''

''Be right there.'' Maggie saved the data on her computer, then walked around her desk and into Farrell's office. She was surprised to see him bent over that bottom drawer. ''Yes?''

Cy glanced up briefly as he dug around for something. ''I want to show you this. Reckon it's time you saw it if you're gonna be my new deputy in the fall.''

Was she? After yesterday, she wasn't so sure. ''What is it?'' she asked, feeling uncomfortable with the question because she already knew the answer.

Cy beckoned her around to the back of the desk where he'd unloaded the computer ribbons, preprinted forms and other contents of the drawer, laying bare the false bottom she'd discovered yesterday. With the forms out of the way, Maggie could see that it was a two-piece metal affair with a hinged center. Cy took a key that was duct-taped to the bottom of the drawer above it and inserted it into a keyhole. Then he lifted the front of the metal plate to reveal a four-inch-deep space and a small coin collector's album full of silver dollars.

''If you ever need to bring anything of value into the

office, this is the place you'll want to put it for safekeeping."

Warily, Maggie stared at the Morgan Dollars behind the plastic sleeves. Was it just coincidence that the day after she'd discovered it on her own, he'd invited her to take a look at this drawer? Had he really "forgotten" his coins? Or was Farrell simply showing her something so that she could cast aside any possible suspicions? She recalled Farrell's extreme reaction to her removing the printer ribbons yesterday—and she couldn't help wondering if there'd been something other than silver dollars in the drawer then.

After retrieving his booty, Farrell locked the flap and replaced the drawer's contents. "Now you saw where I keep the key, right?"

"Yes. I did."

"Good. Now, like I said, if you need to keep something safe for a couple of hours, this is the place you'll want to store it."

"Thank you, I'll keep that in mind."

Farrell slipped the key under the duct tape again, pressed it tightly to the drawer bottom, closed both drawers, then accompanied Maggie back to the reception area. "I won't be long," he said. "Forty-five minutes at the most."

Maggie walked to her desk and sat down numbly. The man's inconsistency was setting off all kinds of alarms in her mind.

The phone buzzed. Reaching for the receiver, she thanked heaven that the next day was Saturday, and that she'd be able to relax a little. Then she remembered the church roofing, and realized her nervewracking week wasn't over. She had to see Ross again.

"That it for the shingles, Ross?" Scott Jackson called.

"Yep."

"Guess we need another bundle, then."

"You stay put. I'll get them."

"Thanks. I keep wondering why he picked black. Cheaper?"

"You got me," Ross chuckled. "I'm just thankful my aunt Ruby didn't pick them out. They'd be red."

On the ground, Maggie overheard their conversation and smiled. Wending through the chattering women busing platters of food to the tables, she lugged the huge iced tea dispenser over to the shaded beverage station. She cast a veiled glance at Ross as he climbed down from the scaffolding and grabbed another square of shingles—then jerked her head forward again when he caught her looking.

Fighting a flush of embarrassment, she set the dispenser in her arms down beside a stack of plastic tumblers and a large lemonade dispenser. To her right, a gray metal washtub held a mountain of crushed ice and assorted soft drinks.

Maggie ventured another look at Ross. He was on the pitched roof again, opening the bundle as the noonday sun baked his powerful shoulders and smooth, tanned back. Unbidden, a rush of arousal seized her and suddenly she was back at the hot spring, hearing his soft laughter…watching him bathe…feeling his hard mouth on hers…

To her mortification, Maggie felt her nipples harden, and she turned away to add more soft drinks to the gray washtub, shoving the cans deep into the ice. She had to stop thinking these ridiculous thoughts before she made a spectacle of herself.

Though it had disturbed her to do it, all morning long she'd continued to be polite but distant to Ross. It was the only way that she could break free of the emotional quagmire she felt herself slipping into. She was glad that her cousin Scott was treating him well, though. Her Uncle Moe was into holding grudges; his son Scott was the kind of man who looked at a situation, reasoned it out, and moved on. Maggie knew that in Scott's mind, Ross had paid for his sins.

"So where do you want this tray of sandwiches, gorgeous?"

Maggie held back a groan as Trent approached her for the fifth time since he made an appearance half an hour ago. She appreciated his help, but the things he chose to do could have been handled by any of the women in attendance. On the other hand, the men working on the roof could have used a hand lugging shingles, and dragging away the old tar paper and nails lying around the church. Not that Trent was dressed for that kind of work.

Maggie wiped her wet hands on her jeans and raised her voice over the noisy hammering. "It'll be fine right over there," she said, pointing to an empty space in the chain of picnic tables. Several yards away, an assortment of salads and desserts, as well as sliced ham, cheese and bakery rolls, stretched deliciously from the first table to the fifth.

She and Bessie Holsopple had covered the tabletops with the roll of heavy white paper they'd found downstairs in the church's meeting room, then taped the ends down tightly to keep the wind from tearing them up. They needn't have bothered. In a land where gusting winds were the norm, today there wasn't even a hint of a breeze. Ross—and the other men, too, of course—could have used one. The temperature was approaching eighty, and the humidity had been high for days. Where was the rain the weatherperson kept promising?

"All right, gentlemen," the reverend announced in his booming voice. "It's noon—time to eat, drink and thank the Lord for the delicious bounty these kind ladies have provided."

There was some light opposition to quitting in the middle of a task, but the reverend overruled the objections. "Come on, you've been at it for three hours. Neither God nor I want anyone keeling over from sunstroke."

Ross wiped an arm over his damp face and crawled

down from the scaffolding again. "At least not until the roof's finished, right, Reverend?"

Fremont chuckled and shook a finger as Ross took his shirt from a bar on the scaffolding and pulled it on. "Now don't put words in my mouth, son."

When everyone was quiet and assembled, Fremont gave the blessing, then ordered one and all to sit down and fill up—which everyone did. Except Ross. In the middle of the friendly chaos of noisy chatter and platters being passed around, Ross grabbed a ham salad sandwich and walked over to Maggie. He took a plastic tumbler from the stack, then grimly slid it under the dispenser.

"Is this the iced tea?"

"Yes."

His tone was as cool as hers had been all morning, and Maggie didn't really blame him. Averting her eyes, she tried to keep her pulse from running away with itself, and pumped tea into his glass. She wished he'd buttoned his shirt. Seeing him standing there with the brim of his hat shading his eyes, and sweat collecting in his chest hair made her think too much...remember too much. Why did he have to look so *good?* And why did he have to look that good all the *time?*

Before she'd finished filling Ross's glass, Trent grabbed one of his own and shoved it close, nearly knocking over Ross's drink. "Gee, excuse me," he said coldly.

Maggie watched Ross's amused gaze scan Trent's irate expression and inappropriate clothing—from his expensive-looking pale-green shirt, string tie and tan slacks, to the mirror polish on his hand-tooled Western boots. The two males were a study in contrast. Trent's black hair was smooth and stylishly cut, while rivulets of sweat trickled from the thick brown hair at Ross's temples.

"Expecting the press, Trent?"

Trent's face reddened—as it should have, Maggie thought. Even the women had dressed casually today.

With a sardonic smile, Ross wandered a few feet away to grab another sandwich from the platter. Trent took the opportunity to move a little closer to Maggie, speaking in a smooth, familiar voice that she realized was meant to be overheard.

"I really enjoyed our visit on Tuesday night, Maggie. Particularly after your uncle and aunt went inside and we had the porch to ourselves." He chuckled softly. "I still haven't figured out why your aunt blew out all the candles and left us in the dark like that."

Maggie stared at him, stunned. Trent had heard Lila's "bothersome moths" excuse, just as she had. He was trying—for Ross's benefit—to make it sound like more. Maggie flicked an anxious look at Ross to see if he'd heard, but there was no reaction from him. He was eating another sandwich, drinking his iced tea, and—it seemed to Maggie—studying the church roof as though he'd like to get back to it.

After she'd handed out cans of soft drinks and filled glasses for several more people, Trent spoke again. "I don't know if I mentioned it the other night, but your aunt Lila's lemonade is the best I've ever tasted. I don't know anyone who makes it with fresh lemons anymore."

Move on to another topic, Maggie wanted to shout. He wasn't saying anything that wasn't true, but that low voice of his made the evening sound too cozy. Especially since she'd spent the first part of Tuesday evening at the Daltons' hot spring. "I'll be sure to tell her how much you liked it," she replied evenly.

"Do that. You know, I had a nice talk with her while we were waiting for you to come home. I think we really hit it off. And that uncle of yours is a great storyteller."

Why was her stomach in knots? Why did she even care if Ross heard? She'd been trying for weeks to discourage any more contact with him, hadn't she? *Well, this should do it,* her conscience remarked.

Ambling over to the booth again, Ross extended his glass for a refill, a flat, unreadable expression in his eyes. "I had a pretty fair Tuesday night, too."

"No one cares," Trent replied dryly.

"Oh, I don't know about that. Maggie might."

Maggie flicked Ross a pleading look as she refilled his glass. But he either didn't understand, or didn't care that he was making her uneasy.

"I worked on my house for a while," he said offhandedly. "Then it was so nice out, I walked back to the hot spring and went skinny-dipping for a whi—"

Trent's features contorted in anger. "*As I said before, no one cares.* Go tell your smarmy Tuesday-night story to Brenda." He expelled a disgusted breath. "Never mind, she was probably with you."

Maggie's nerves vibrated like tuning forks. *Brenda? Who was Brenda?*

"Actually there *was* someone with me," Ross said, smiling. "Someone beautiful, and bright—"

"Here's your drink," Maggie cut in, pushing the glass toward him. "There's chocolate cake over on the table if you'd like to have a piece."

"Did you make it?"

Red-faced, Trent spoke again. "If you don't mind, we were having a conversation."

Ross shrugged amiably. "Sorry. Don't let me keep you from it." Downing his drink, he tossed the plastic tumbler in a trash bin, then walked back to the church to pick up the tar paper and discarded green shingles from the ground. Eventually, other men began trickling back to work, too. It wasn't long before the staccato hammering and the yells of the men rang through the wooded churchyard again.

The sun had slipped behind the jagged peaks of the mountains, and the church roof was finished before Maggie had another opportunity to speak to Ross. At that, she'd almost missed him when she'd gone inside to grab her aunt Lila's cake carrier.

He was halfway across the parking lot, strolling toward his truck and pulling on his shirt, when Maggie caught up to him.

"It wasn't what you thought," she said falling into step beside him.

He kept walking. "What wasn't what I thought?"

"Trent and me," Maggie said. "I didn't want you to get the wrong idea."

"I didn't."

"Yes, you did. He was waiting on the porch for me when I got back from your place that night. I know he hinted that we'd been…well, close…after Uncle Moe and Aunt Lila went inside. But absolutely nothing happened between us."

Ross stopped beside his truck and looked down at her. There was a detached expression in his blue eyes as he buttoned his chambray shirt. The honest odors of hard work and potent male carried to her in the gathering dusk. "Why are you telling me this?" he asked.

Maggie's lips parted but nothing came out. Why *was* she telling him this? "Ross—"

"I know nothing happened. If anything was going to happen that night, it would have happened with me."

She didn't know whether to slap his egotistical face or thank him for not thinking she was easy. Although the tone of his voice hadn't really sounded arrogant. Maggie held back a sigh of frustration. She'd never known anyone who could throw her off balance so often, and with so little effort.

With a weary shake of her head, she turned away from him, walked the remaining distance to her car, and left.

The smoke, music and noise level inside Dusty's Roadhouse that night was staggering, even for a Saturday. Ross sat at the bar nursing his second beer and tried to block out the raucous voices and braying yee-haws from the dance floor. He was trying to remember the title of the old Billy Ray Cyrus song that the band was playing. Oh, yeah…"Achy Breaky Heart."

Ticked-off Heart was more like it. He just didn't know who he was more ticked off *at*—himself or Maggie. Probably her. She'd started this whole cold-war thing with her ice-maiden routine.

When she'd come after him with that explanation about her and Campion, he supposed he could've been a little warmer. But why get all revved up over her again when it wasn't going to get him anywhere? Apparently, she felt safer drinking lemonade with Trent Campion than tempting fate with the town hellion.

Frowning, Ross glanced around the bar. Until he and Brokenstraw hand Ray Pruitt had walked in thirty minutes ago, Ross hadn't been here in months. But Dusty's Remington and C. M. Russell prints still hung on the rough wood walls, and the burn marks from a dozen local branding irons still mottled the roadhouse's rough support posts. Vintage nail kegs and other wild West memorabilia still gathered dust on the high shelf running the perimeter of the room.

Ross helped himself to some pretzels from the bowl on the mahogany bar, then slid the bowl closer to Ray's empty stool. When the band played, slick, dressed-in-black Pruitt had to be out on the dance floor, dazzling the ladies.

Yep. Everything was the same around here.

Except him.

A husky female voice murmured near his ear. "Time to shake a leg, cowboy."

Ross thanked heaven for the constants in life, and spun his bar stool around. Wearing snug jeans and a fringed, green-satin Western shirt, Brenda Larson slid onto his lap and looped her arms around his neck. Thick red hair tumbled in wild ringlets around her exquisite face and shoulders, framing her green eyes and glossy red lips to perfection.

This was why he'd come tonight. It had been a long time since he'd been with a woman, and beautiful Brenda always looked like she'd just crawled out of bed—and couldn't wait to get back in.

"Been a while," she drawled, pushing her soft, full breasts against the front of his shirt. "Miss me?"

"Like crazy," he growled, trying to find the "old" Ross as he tugged her even closer. He burrowed into her hair...rubbed his nose along her perfumed neck...waited for her soft sighs and throaty chuckles to make him ready. Dammit, he was through playing games with a prim, standoffish woman who was scared to death to take what she wanted. He slid his hands over the silky back of Brenda's blouse, remembering the spattering of freckles that dotted her pale shoulders. How ironic that three hours ago he'd been shingling a church roof, and now he was—

Trying like hell to crank up his libido—and failing.

Ross's hands stilled against Brenda's back. Why hadn't her heavily sprayed ringlets ever before reminded him of barbwire? And why hadn't the musky smell of her perfume ever turned him off the way it did tonight?

"Your hands stopped movin', sweetheart," she cooed into his ear. "Maybe we should take this out on the dance floor and get you warmed up a bit."

Suddenly, he realized that he could never get that warm. Not for what she'd want afterwards, anyway. "Hey, Bren?"

"Hmmm?"

He eased her away from him. "I gotta take off."

Brenda's eyebrows rose, and she blinked as though he'd lost his mind. "What?"

"How about a rain check for that dance?"

"A rain check?"

"Sorry."

With a pouty look, she slid off his lap and kissed him lightly, then used her thumb to rub away the traces of her lipstick. "What happened to you, Ross Dalton? You used to be fun."

"I used to be a lot of things," he said, sighing. But he sure as hell wasn't anymore. Ross pushed his beer away and started for the door. "'Night, Brenda. Tell Ray I'll see him back at the ranch."

There wasn't a sign of a cloud as he walked out onto Dusty's moon-drenched deck, then took the short set of steps to the rutted parking lot. The night air was still warm and heavy, but after the smoke inside the bar, it was almost refreshing.

Tugging his keys from the front pocket of his jeans, he made his way tiredly to his truck. So much for his stud status around here. Why had he ever thought that hazy memories and hangovers were fun? Now he'd wasted the whole damn night when he could have been working on his house, or—something foreign and surprising tightened his heart—

Or gone looking for Maggie.

Two days later, on July third, Maggie returned home from work to find a narrow package from her father sitting on the kitchen table. Beside it, the afternoon newspaper lay opened to the second page. A photo of Trent appeared above the church-roofing article.

Maggie skimmed swiftly past Trent's broad smile to the blurred form of a lean, shirtless man working some distance behind him. Her pulse leaped, and her heart started to pound. Then abruptly, she closed the paper, forced Ross from her mind, and turned to the package from her father.

All in all, it hadn't been a bad day. Farrell was still treating her well and hadn't enumerated again the dangerous elements of a deputy's job. But hearing from her dad made a good day better.

"See the paper?" Lila asked, coming into the kitchen from outside.

"Yep." Maggie peeled the packing tape from her package.

"Bet Trent's disappointed he only made page two."

Maggie glanced up in surprise. "I thought you liked Trent."

"He's okay. I just like other people more. By the way, he phoned today—wanted to take you to the street dance tomorrow."

"I know. He called the office, too. I told him no." But she *had* promised him a dance, just to get him off the telephone.

Maggie peeled the brown paper away and laughed. "My goodness. Is he allowed to send stuff like this through the mail?"

"What is it?"

"Sparklers. Two boxes—red for me, gold for him." She faked a look of regret as she glanced over at Lila. "Sorry—none for you and Uncle Moe, but I'm willing to share."

Lila chuckled. "Don't bother. Was there a note?"

"Nope. Guess he felt the sparklers said it all." Smiling at the memory that surfaced, Maggie laid the sparklers back on the table. "Mom never liked these things. She was always afraid they'd start a fire, or I'd drop one, pick up the wrong end and burn myself. Not Dad, though. He's still a big kid about fireworks."

"Good thing, too, because he's *way* too serious about everything else." Lila pulled a platter of steaks from the refrigerator and handed them to Maggie. "How about putting these on the grill, honey? We'll fix your uncle Moe a real cattleman's supper tonight."

"Oh?"

"Yep. I'm baking potatoes in the oven in the basement to keep it a little cooler up here, and the salad's almost ready. I just have to add a few tomatoes."

"No more shepherd's pie?"

Lila chuckled. "After the big stink he made last time? Not for a while."

Maggie went out back and fired up the grill, then arranged the thick steaks on the rack. Lila was right; Maggie loved her dad dearly—but he *was* too serious about everything else.

Her smile broadened as she recalled the time he'd caught her wearing Mary Ellen Parker's lipstick. She was thirteen then, and all the girls in her class were experimenting with makeup—except Maggie, of course. Her father had hit the roof. She had thought she'd have to make a pilgrimage to the Holy Land to settle him down.

Her smile slowly faded. Then there was the night she'd crashed Ross's party...

It had been late when Mary Ellen dropped her off at the parsonage, and Maggie had been torn between going inside, and standing in the dark forever. She was still fighting the mortification of being seen with her blouse undone. When she did go in, all she'd wanted to do was get past her parents and run to her room. Unfortunately, when she'd kissed her dad good-night, he'd smelled beer on her breath.

"Honey?" he'd said. "Do I smell alcohol?"

She'd ended up admitting that she'd tried some beer, just to fit in. Her mom had understood. But Maggie had never seen her father so disappointed, and it nearly broke her heart.

Later, he'd clicked on her small bedside lamp, and pulled a chair up to her bed. "Disobedience, sweetheart? Sneaking around? That's not like you. What made you want to attend such an inappropriate party?"

She'd shrugged miserably because she couldn't tell him

that she was hopelessly in love with that wild Dalton boy. That would have upset him even more.

"And the beer? Maggie, you're only fifteen—there are laws. What if the party had been raided? What then?"

That was when she'd realized that her parents—especially her father—would have been shamed. And she'd broken down.

"Don't cry," he'd murmured, kissing her forehead and holding her close. "It's all right. Just listen to one small piece of advice from your dad?"

She'd nodded, unable to speak.

"In the next few years, you're going to encounter many temptations, and some of them will be incredibly difficult to overcome. But do you know what will get you through them?"

Again, a head shake was all she could manage.

"Your respect for yourself. You have a good heart, Maggie. All I ask is that when temptations arise, you ask yourself two questions: Will my actions hurt anyone else? And, can I live with my decision without guilt if I go ahead with this?"

"That's all?" she'd whispered through her tears.

"That's all. Now give your old dad a big hug, and try to get some sleep."

But after all her tears and all his words, when her father left her room that night, Maggie still thought about Ross…and the frightening but bone-melting feeling of being in his arms.

The spitting sizzle of the steaks on the grill snapped Maggie out of her thoughts, and she quickly grabbed the long-handled fork and flipped them over. But before she'd laid the fork aside again, an empty feeling that was residue from her daydream came stealing back. Turning to the east,

Maggie looked out at the fertile grasslands that rolled from the Lazy J all the way to Brokenstraw.

Why did it seem that, in some way, shape or form, everything in her life was tied to Ross Dalton?

Chapter 8

Lila Jackson sighed and pulled two denim jackets from their hangers in the hall closet. "Moe, I still think we should have rented a wheelchair. You'd be a lot more comfortable."

"Lila Marie, there is no damn way I'm gonna show up for this shindig in a wheelchair. Maggie!" he bellowed. "You ready?"

Suppressing a smile, Maggie came downstairs carrying a lap quilt and her purse. Like Moe and Lila, she was dressed in jeans. But instead of the plaid shirts they wore, Maggie had chosen a white, lightweight cotton sweater with a scooped neckline. The cross and gold chain that her father had bought her years ago at Belle Crawford's jewelry store circled her neck. Her black hair fell in long, loose waves over her shoulders.

"You look lovely, honey," Lila said.

"Thanks. You two look nice, too."

"Did you put them three foldin' chairs in the back of the truck?"

"No, Uncle Worrywart, I put two of them in there. I don't need one." Maggie glanced teasingly at Lila before she added, "You probably won't need one, either. I saw the volunteer firefighters setting up a huge tent earlier today, and it's full of picnic tables and benches. You might like sitting in there better."

With a scowl, Moe moved toward the front porch, thumping his walker over the runner on the dark hardwood and hobbling along behind. "Oh, the two of you'd like that, wouldn't you? Plunkin' me down in the middle of all them bingo-playin' biddies." He snorted. "Well, it ain't gonna happen." Then Maggie's heart warmed as he turned, grinned, and winked at her. "The only biddie I want to spend time with tonight is your pretty aunt, here."

Maggie was still smiling as she followed Moe and Lila toward town. There hadn't been room for all three of them in the cab of the truck, with Moe's leg still in a cast, but that was fine with Maggie. After seeing her aunt's beaming smile at Moe's proclamation, she was glad to give them some time alone. Moe Jackson was a tight-lipped western man through and through, and he didn't often say endearing things. But he loved Lila, and Lila loved him. A man and woman couldn't get much luckier than that.

It was nearly seven-thirty when they arrived at the crowded parking lot at the base of Frontier Street, and every available space was taken. Deputy Mike Halston was there, though, directing latecomers to a grassy overflow lot. After joking that Maggie should be handling his job—and Maggie telling him that this was one time she was glad *he* was still the deputy—Mike flagged them into the lot. They parked near a grove of trees bordering the skinny creek at the edge of town.

Maggie got out of her car, and retrieved Moe's walker and the two folding chairs from the back of the truck. Then, together the three of them made the slow trek up restored Frontier Street, where motorized vehicles were forbidden and flags waved from the vintage 1890 store-fronts.

In a town of fewer than six hundred, everyone knew everyone. For a while, they chatted with friends, sampled funnel cakes and sarsaparilla, and visited booths and crafts displays. Then, when dusk settled in and Moe tired, they found a spot midway up the street where they could park their chairs, listen to the music the first band was playing, and wait for the fireworks display.

Now, as Maggie sat on the raised wooden boardwalk beside her uncle's chair, a bright slice of moon crowned the midnight blue sky, and faux kerosene lanterns began to glow. Up and down the street, they lit weathered clap-board buildings and quaint specialty stores, reminding Comfort of its not-so-distant history. Maggie's attention was caught by the billowing canvas tent at the end of the bricked street. One hundred years ago, it might have housed a revivalist preacher set on bringing the Lord's word to a town fraught with sin and corruption.

A new band took over, and they were primed to party. The tempo picked up, the music got louder and, suddenly, laughing couples were breaking away from friends and joining others on the cordoned-off "dance floor." The band was on its third number when Maggie noticed Moe tapping his good foot.

"Having fun?"

"Sure am," he answered. "He's no Willie Nelson, but that young fella singin' knows this stuff. How 'bout it, Lila?"

"Yes, he does."

A familiar voice intruded. "Dance, Maggie? You did promise me one."

Glancing up, Maggie met Trent Campion's eager gaze and toothpaste-ad smile. Tonight, he wore a red, white and blue plaid shirt and white neckerchief with his jeans and

NO RISK, NO OBLIGATION TO BUY...NOW OR EVER!

GUARANTEED

PLAY "ROLL A DOUBLE" AND YOU GET FREE GIFTS! HERE'S HOW TO PLAY:

1. Peel off label from front cover. Place it in space provided at right. With a coin, carefully scratch off the silver dice. Then check the claim chart to see what we have for you – TWO FREE BOOKS and a mystery gift – ALL YOURS! ALL FREE!

2. Send back this card and you'll receive brand-new Silhouette Intimate Moments® novels. These books have a cover price of $4.25 each, but they are yours to keep absolutely free.

3. There's no catch. You're under no obligation to buy anything. We charge nothing – ZERO – for your first shipment. And you don't have to make any minimum number of purchases – not even one!

4. The fact is, thousands of readers enjoy receiving books by mail from the Silhouette Reader Service™. They like the convenience of home delivery...they like getting the best new novels BEFORE they're available in stores...and they love our discount prices!

5. We hope that after receiving your free books you'll want to remain a subscriber. But the choice is yours – to continue or cancel any time at all! So why not take us up on our invitation, with no risk of any kind. You'll be glad you did!

The Silhouette Reader Service™ — Here's how it works:

Accepting free books places you under no obligation to buy anything. You may keep the books and gift and return the shipping statement marked "cancel." If you do not cancel, about a month later we'll send you 6 additional novels and bill you just $3.57 each, plus 25¢ delivery per book and applicable sales tax, if any.* That's the complete price — and compared to cover prices of $4.25 each — quite a bargain! You may cancel at any time, but if you choose to continue, every month we'll send you 6 more books, which you may either purchase at the discount price...or return to us and cancel your subscription.

*Terms and prices subject to change without notice. Sales tax applicable in N.Y.

If offer card is missing write to: Silhouette Reader Service, 3010 Walden Ave., P.O. Box 1867, Buffalo NY 14240-1867

BUSINESS REPLY MAIL
FIRST-CLASS MAIL   PERMIT NO. 717   BUFFALO, NY

POSTAGE WILL BE PAID BY ADDRESSEE

SILHOUETTE READER SERVICE
3010 WALDEN AVE
PO BOX 1867
BUFFALO NY 14240-9952

NO POSTAGE
NECESSARY
IF MAILED
IN THE
UNITED STATES

boots. But as Maggie detected Ben Campion's calculating looks at his son, she wondered if Trent had chosen his clothes, or if they'd been handpicked by his father. Was Trent's wardrobe a reflection of honest patriotism? Or a fledgling politician's eagerness to project the right image?

From everything Maggie had heard—and overheard— since she'd been back, Ben Campion was packaging an all-American product to sell to the people of Montana in the next election. His son was a good-looking, church-going, hard-riding rodeo star, and a charismatic lobbyist and supporter of the environment. That was a hard-to-beat combination for any man running against him, let alone an aging incumbent.

Smiling at Trent, and lifting her voice over her uncle's invitation to join them, Maggie stood and made her apologies. "I'd love to dance, but we just sat down a few minutes ago. Maybe a little later?"

Her refusal didn't seem to faze him. In fact, it was almost as though he were going through his paces, marking things off an invisible checklist—and dancing with her had been one of his assignments. "Later's fine." He dug into his breast pocket. "I still have some lapel pins to hand out, anyway." Trent gave one to Moe, and Moe smiled broadly.

"Well, thank you," he said through an enthusiastic chuckle. "I'll put it right on."

"You're very welcome, sir. I did have some red, white and blue carnations for the ladies—" he shrugged and sent Lila a grin that begged her forgiveness "—but I'm afraid they went pretty fast. Sorry."

Lila assured him that that was perfectly all right, and Trent turned again to Maggie. "I'll be back in a little while, okay?"

"Sure." Again, Maggie felt a twinge of sympathy for Trent. Because the real Trent—whoever he was—couldn't

be himself for a moment while there were potential con-
stituents around.

Moe cleared his gravelly voice as he pinned the tiny
American flag to his shirt. "You know, Maggie—"

"I know, Uncle Moe," she sighed. "He'd be a great
catch."

Maggie remained standing, enjoying the performance of
the line dancers as they went through their practiced
"vines" and "stomps." When the song was over, the
bandleader grabbed the microphone.

"Okay, ladies," he called. "Here's your chance. Everybody knows that Sadie Hawkins Day falls in November.
But you'd have to be loco to come to a street dance then,
right?"

There were noisy shouts of agreement.

"Right. That's why we're havin' our own Sadie Hawkins dance right now—for one song, anyway. So you
ladies grab the cowboy you've been moonin' over all night
before some other filly nabs him. You've got about—" he
turned to the drummer "—how long is this song, Boone?"

"Four minutes."

"You heard him. You got four minutes to convince him
you're the gal he should watch the fireworks with, 'cause
they're startin' soon as we finish this pretty tune." Then
he counted down the song, and the band eased into John
Michael Montgomery's pretty country ballad "I Swear."

As the pattern of the crowd shifted and changed, Maggie
watched through a space of onlookers as brave smiling
women—and a few shy ones—coaxed their chosen men
onto the brick dance floor.

Suddenly the recurring loneliness of the last few days
was upon her again. The music was lovely, night was falling, and her heart longed to swell with the same dreamy
emotion she saw on the faces of those women.

Against her will and all good sense, Maggie thought of
Ross, and knew that even on the bricks, even in cowboy

boots, he would move languidly against his partner as they danced. There was a lithe, male grace about him. It was in his walk, in the way he'd brought her close that night at the hot spring and melted into her.

Suddenly Maggie stopped breathing, and chills ran the length of her body.

He was here.

Ten yards away, Ross and his partner danced into Maggie's field of vision. For an instant, she almost thought she'd conjured him up.

The woman flattened against him was as long-legged and slim-hipped as a Barbie doll, with enormous breasts that she was currently trying to shove through Ross's chest to his backbone. Her arms were looped high around his neck, and a wild tangle of red hair framed her face and spilled in gypsy ringlets over her shoulders.

Maggie watched his hands grip her waist, saw the tight press of their hips.

And something that was half hurt, half anger—and all jealousy—splintered through her and left her without a sane thought. Maggie tore her eyes away at the exact moment Trent reappeared, passing out more lapel pins. Impulsively, she left her aunt and uncle, and strode to his side.

"I'm ready for that dance now, if you are," she said brightly.

If his smile was any indication, he was delighted. Trent pocketed his pins and took her hand. "I've been ready for weeks," he said. In a moment, they were turning slowly to the music with the other couples on the dance floor, and Maggie was surreptitiously scanning the crowd for a long, lean cowboy with a redheaded succubus attached.

"What brought this on?" Trent asked, smiling down into her eyes. "Not that I mind."

Maggie's head began to clear. This was wrong. He didn't deserve to be used like this. No man did. "Actu-

ally,'' she said after a moment, ''I should have said 'yes'
before. My uncle's getting tired, and we'll probably leave
after the fireworks. If they're starting right after this song,
I wouldn't have had a chance to make good on my promise.'' The reason she gave was true—if recently thought
out.

''Then you didn't suddenly fall head-over-heels in love
with me?''

Maggie opened her mouth to speak, but he grinned and
let her off the hook. ''Never mind. I don't want to hear
your answer.''

Now thoroughly ashamed of herself because he was being so decent, Maggie just wanted the song to be over so
that she could say good-night and leave. As for
Ross...Ross was certainly free to dance with whomever
he wanted. She'd made it clear to him that she wasn't
interested in continuing whatever strange kind of relationship they had, so—

*So why did you come completely unglued when you saw
him dancing with that woman?*

Maggie closed her eyes and told herself that she didn't
know. But she did. It defied all logic, but she surely did.

He had a criminal record; she was a law enforcement
officer.

He was a hell-raiser; she was a preacher's daughter.

He'd associated with the dangerous men who'd shot at
her uncle and stolen his cattle; she loved and respected
Moe Jackson as much as she did her own father.

Three excellent reasons why she absolutely could not be
falling in love with Ross Dalton.

But she feared that she was.

When she opened her eyes, Ross was staring straight at
her—and he wasn't happy.

Maggie made herself nod politely. Grimly, he nodded
back.

It was then that she realized Ross wasn't a willing participant in the snuggle-and-press business that was going on. He was doing everything in his power to keep the woman's thigh from insinuating itself between his legs, moving her hips away while she laughed up into his eyes and sent messages not even a blind man could misinterpret.

When the song finally ended, and Trent walked Maggie back to her aunt and uncle, she was relieved that he didn't stay to watch the fireworks with them. She was too shaken from seeing Ross to be much of a companion.

Thirty minutes later, when the fireworks ended, Maggie supposed they'd been impressive. She really couldn't say for sure because her attention had been elsewhere. Whenever a spray of color lit the night sky, she'd searched the crowd for Ross, her stomach clenching as she wondered if his dance partner had eventually convinced him to take what she was offering. She'd spotted Casey, Jess, Ruby and the baby. But Ross was nowhere in sight.

Now as she, Moe and Lila walked to the overflow lot, leaving most of Comfort still partying, Ross's absence bothered her like nothing else had these past few days—Farrell's strange behavior included. Where was Ross? And who was he there with?

Maggie loaded the chairs and her uncle's walker into the truck's bed, then closed the door when Moe had settled in the passenger's seat. "Comfy?" she asked.

"Close enough," Moe answered.

"Good. You two lead the way." Lila started the truck and pulled on the headlights. Maggie stepped back. "I'll be right behind you."

She watched for a moment while the truck rolled slowly out of the lot and onto the road. Then frowning, she pulled her keys from her jeans pocket and strolled closer to the tree-sheltered creek where her car waited. The unnatural swishing of the long grass nearby made her jerk around.

Maggie drew a startled breath as a man's shadowy form stepped out from the trees and walked unerringly toward her. "Don't say anything," he murmured, tossing his Stetson on the hood of her car. "And please don't pull away. I just need this." In one smooth motion, Ross drew her into his arms and kissed her, and Maggie filled her hungry arms with him.

His mouth was warm and coaxing, his tongue tender and seeking. Maggie inhaled deeply, pulling the tangy smell of his aftershave straight into her belly. She stroked his back, slid her fingers into the soft, shaggy hair at his nape, buried all her reservations in his scent, his taste, his strength...until she heard the low, guttural sound of his passion in his throat.

Maggie trembled as one of his hands slid down the slope of her bottom and brought her close, making her as aware of his growing arousal as she was of her own. He was denim, she was silk, and the seductive friction along her nerve endings was too powerful a force to refuse. She'd wanted this for hours...days...weeks. She began to move against him.

Ross broke the seal of their lips and pressed his forehead to hers, his breathing hard and labored as he struggled for control. He relaxed his hold on her bottom, slid his hand up to a more respectful position at the base of her spine.

The breezy rustle of the cottonwoods managed to register, despite the roaring in Maggie's ears and the bouncy tune the band was playing a short block away. Such an inappropriate song for this time...this place...this moment, she thought.

"I wanted it to be you tonight," he whispered. "Not her."

Maggie's mind spun. This was madness: they hadn't even spoken since the church roofing. She searched his eyes, and her voice came out a tattered whisper. "Ross, what are we doing?"

"Damned if I know," he breathed. He hesitated for a moment, his eyes still on hers. Then he released a reluctant sigh. "You'd better go. Your folks'll get nervous if they don't see your headlights behind them soon." He kissed her again, softly this time. "Be careful driving home." Then he slid a hand over her hair, picked up his hat, and walked back toward the lighted street and the still-celebrating crowd.

Maggie shivered in the warm night air. Her nerves were buzzing and her blood was racing through her veins like a flash flood through a dry wash. Ross was right: she had to leave soon or Lila would worry. But how could she when she was trembling so hard that keeping her car on the road would be a major feat? Drawing a shaky breath, she got in and closed the door.

She sat there for a full minute before she fumbled the key into the ignition and started away.

Two days later, as Ross flopped his saddle over a low partition in the stuffy tack room, he was still browbeating himself for that kiss in the trees. He wiped a sleeve over the perspiration dotting his upper lip. She must have thought that he was insane, sneaking up on her like the reincarnation of Errol Flynn.

What was wrong with him? Why couldn't he get her out of his system? She was only a woman, and he'd kissed plenty of them in his time. But not one of them had ever gotten to him the way Maggie did. It had to be the heat. Or his hormones. Or the barometric pressure. Hell, it had to be something, didn't it?

They were finally going to get the rain that the weather forecasters had been promising for days. Good thing, too. The humidity was so high that everything he owned was sticking to him. When he'd come in to straighten up and spread fresh hay around a while ago, the late-afternoon sky had already darkened, and the wind had begun to pick up.

The sound of hooves outside broke Ross's thoughts. Jess led his bay horse and Ross's buckskin past the tack room and into the barn. "We've got a bad one coming," he called through the doorway, "and it's coming quick."

"How bad?"

"Flash-flood warnings in low-lying areas, damaging winds, maybe some hail."

Ross creased his forehead and looked outside. Ray Pruitt was leading his horse and Hank Lewis's to the barn. He watched grizzled old Hank, Brokenstraw's other cowhand, lock the gate on the corral, then fight a gust of wind for his hat. Three more horses danced skittishly in the packed dirt as they waited to be brought up, their ears pricking and nostrils scenting the air. The sky wasn't just dark now. Some distance off, it was roiling and bruised, thunderheads stacking on the horizon like fat, dirty cotton balls. It had all happened within the space of ten minutes.

Ross saw to the other horses and helped Jess batten down doors and windows in the outbuildings. Then he ran into the house and directly to the phone in the den. When they were working on the church roof, Scott Jackson had mentioned being away this week for a wedding in New Mexico—which meant his parents were alone at the Lazy J. With Maggie working and Moe laid up, preparing for the storm would fall to Lila alone.

He punched in the number, got a busy signal. He tried again a moment later: still busy.

Jess came inside, shedding his hat. "Who are you calling?"

"Moe and Lila. They might need some help. Scott's away this week." Ross looked around. "Where are Casey and the baby?"

"In the kitchen making lunch."

Ross dialed again. This time he got through.

"Maggie?" Lila's anxious voice came to him before Ross had a chance to say hello.

"No, Lila, it's Ross. I just called to see if you and Moe need any help over there with the storm coming."

"We're fine. I'm just worried about Maggie. I called the sheriff's office to tell her to stay in town tonight because of the storm warnings, and Farrell said she wasn't there. He sent her up to Clearcut a few hours ago to serve a summons, and she's not back yet."

Ross got nervous. Clearcut wasn't even a village; it was a three-home settlement. And it was only twenty miles from town, which meant she *should* be back. Worse, with flash-flooding a near certainty, low-lying Clearcut was the wrong place to be. Situated between two ridges, the road acted like a trough that caught every drop of water that rolled down the granite slopes—and the tiny creeks nearby were notorious for overflowing their banks and washing away anything in their paths. "Didn't Farrell radio her when she didn't come back?"

"He couldn't. She took her own car. Cy thinks she's just holed up somewhere waiting for the storm to pass."

She could be, but then again… "Do you know where she went to serve the summons?"

"The Addams place. Do you know it? They don't have a phone."

"Yeah, I know it. I'll find her, Lila." Ross hung up to the sound of her thanks, then strode to the mudroom off the kitchen for his rain slicker. He grabbed a second one, just in case.

"Where are you going in this weather?" Casey asked, concerned.

"Maggie's stuck somewhere between here and Clearcut, and Lila's worried. I said I'd find her."

Casey moved quickly. "You might have to ride out the

storm there. The weather service said we're in for a real siege." She grabbed several cans of soda from the refrigerator and loaded the stack of sandwiches she'd just made into the empty bread bag. She seemed to realize that he wouldn't wait for her to wrap them individually.

"Thanks, Casey." Then to Jess, he said, "Don't give me that look. I'll be fine. If it gets too bad, there's some high country nearby." He bent to kiss Lexi's little upturned face. "See ya later, alligator."

She giggled and answered the way he'd taught her. "Affer while, cocca-dile."

"Be careful," Jess called, as Ross waved and headed out the back door.

"I will."

His truck would keep him drier—no doubt about it, Ross thought a few minutes later as he threw the saddle blanket over his horse. But trucks couldn't climb mountainsides or take short cuts across pastures, and horses could. Besides, in the event of flash flooding, a vehicle could wash away in a heartbeat. Which made him worry again about Maggie's little Ford.

"Sorry, Buck," he murmured as he cinched his saddle, then climbed aboard. "Maybe with some luck, we'll find her before the storm hits, and we can all come back home."

He estimated that he only had about fifteen minutes before the rains pounded down in earnest. Though it was twenty miles from town, Clearcut was only six or seven miles from Brokenstraw. He would cut through the woods until he reached the Clearcut road, then travel the route Maggie would've taken. Pulling the hood of his roomy yellow rain slicker over his hat, Ross put his heels to the buckskin's ribs and let him run, flat out.

Twenty-five minutes later, through a pounding curtain of rain, Ross rode down from the hills to the blue Ford he'd seen through his binoculars. Why was she just sitting there? The ditches were already filled, and water was running over the uncrowned dirt road. A fierce bolt of lightning splintered the sky.

Inside, the windows were steamed, and he watched as Maggie wiped a spot and peered out. Tucking away the information that she seemed relieved to see him, Ross dismounted, hurried to the passenger side, and jerked open the door.

"Come on!" he shouted over the rain drilling down on the car's metal roof. "We have to get out of here."

"No, we'll be safer inside!" she yelled back. "It's starting to lightning."

"It's also starting to flood, and your car isn't going to be here for very long. Now come on!" Ross shoved the extra rain poncho at her, then took the blanket she'd been wrapped in and stuffed it under his slicker. She was already soaked to the skin.

"I tried to fix it the way you did!" she shouted as she looped the long strap of her purse over her head and pulled on the poncho. "But there wasn't enough hose left. Then I started walking back to Clearcut, and the rain just pounded down." Maggie stepped out of the car and into ankle-deep water. She slammed the door.

The radiator hose had blown again? She hadn't gotten it fixed?

"And don't you dare tell me how stupid I am for not getting it fixed!" she shouted. "I've already told myself that a hundred times since it happened."

The rain was deafening against the plastic hood. "We'll talk about it later. Just get on the horse!"

Climbing on behind her, he pointed the buckskin back the way Maggie had come.

"Wrong way," she yelled.

"*Dry* way," he shouted back. "I know a place."

Heart pounding, Ross urged the buckskin up onto the high bank alongside the road, and headed him toward the dim gray hill in the distance.

Chapter 9

The rain blew at them in driving sheets, pounding the slippery mountainside with a vengeance. Loose rocks washed away in the running mud, and the horse's hooves scrambled for solid footing. They'd been traveling for nearly five minutes now, and Ross continued to coax the buckskin into the sparsely timbered foothills, staying as far away from the trees as possible. He swore as hail joined the flashing lightning and thunder.

Pulling Maggie closer, he tried to shield her as best he could. He could feel her trembling beneath the yellow plastic rain poncho, but didn't know how much of that was fear of the storm and how much was the cooler air that the rain had brought. Though she was partially protected by the hood that hung large and baggy over the top part of her face, she'd been wet when he'd found her, and she was chilled. He wanted to reassure her that they'd be okay, tell her that it was less than half a mile to cover now. But with the lightning, the thunder crashing around them, and leaves and thin branches being torn from trees, his words wouldn't have been worth much.

A bolt of lightning rent the roiling sky and crashed with resonating fury to earth. Buck reared and wheeled, tried to bolt, and Ross yanked hard on the reins. Thirty yards away, a thick Douglas fir snapped like a matchstick.

Maggie whirled around, her face white in the strobing flashes. The smell of ozone laced the air.

Ross pointed forty yards up the mountainside. "You can't see it from here," he shouted to her. "But there's a cave up there. We'll be okay!"

She nodded, her expression fearful.

"It's getting too steep for the horse," he yelled again. "We'll go the rest of the way on foot!"

Ross slid off the horse's rump, the wind snatching and pulling at his slicker, the rain determined to wash them down to the road-turned-river below. As if it wasn't bad enough that the rain was falling at a deadly rate and the streams below them were flooding, the Clearcut road was collecting every ounce of water that ran down from the peaks.

Keeping the reins, Ross snared Maggie's hand with his free one, and they hurried toward the fold in the mountain, where he knew there was shelter. He'd never in his life seen this much water come down so fast.

"I see the opening!" Maggie cried.

"Go!" He watched her scramble up ahead of him, then hurry under a broad rock shelf that broke the unrelenting rain. A few more feet, and she was inside the mouth of the cave. Ross followed, tugging hard on the reins when Buck would have shied away. The horse slipped on the loose stones, whinnied and fought for purchase, then finally obeyed.

After the pelting sound of the rain on his hood, it was eerily quiet inside. It was also a good fifteen degrees cooler.

Ross met Maggie's relieved eyes as they stood in the dim afternoon light just inside the cave.

"That wasn't f-fun," she said, quaking.

"No, it wasn't." Ross imagined that, to Maggie, the cave had looked relatively small from the outside—the craggy opening only twelve feet wide, the height, fifteen feet at the most. But inside, it opened to a spacious, cornucopia-shaped room. Not as large as he remembered, Ross thought, but plenty big enough for a full-size horse and two wet adults. There was a smaller exit in the back where the cave narrowed and tapered downward, and it provided the cross-ventilation that kept the cavern from smelling dank and musty.

Ross looked to his right and was relieved to see the bench seat he and friends had built fifteen years ago—a notched-out log stretched across two boulders. He was more relieved to see the stone fire ring with the remains of a recent campfire. The cave was still being used, which meant there could be a wood stash inside.

"How do you know this p-place?" Maggie asked, shivering and hugging herself.

Ross shed his hood and hat, then unsnapped the raincoat and pulled out the blanket he'd brought from the car. It was *his* blanket, he suddenly realized—the same one Maggie had planned to return on the night she'd come to the hot spring. He laid his raincoat on the ground, wet side down, tossed his Stetson on top of it, and held on to the thick Indian blanket. It was a little damp on one side where she'd wrapped it around herself in the car, but it was a lot better than her drenched clothes.

"When I was a kid, a bunch of us hung out in this area. We used to fish those streams below, then later come up here to party." He nodded at the half-charred log in the ring. "Looks like someone else has claimed it in the meantime."

"I th-thought you partied at the hot spring."

Ross frowned, thinking that back then they'd partied anywhere it was convenient. "Not always... You're freezing. Take off your wet things."

"That would be everything," she said, trying to grin. "Skin included."

With a sympathetic smile, he shook out the blanket. "I think you can leave the skin on." Maggie eyed him warily as he held out the Indian blanket dressing-screen fashion. Ross softened his voice. "Come on. I won't look, and I won't take advantage of the situation. You can get hypothermia at any time of the year. Once you lose your body heat, you can't get it back if you're wet. When you're ready, grab the corners of the blanket and wrap it around yourself."

"I can't go home in a blanket."

"I know that. We'll work something out."

Chills wracked her as Maggie fumbled with the wet, knotted tie on the poncho, managed to free it, and then article by article peeled off her soaked uniform and tossed it on his raincoat. She hesitated uncertainly when she was standing there in nothing but a lacy white bra and thin bikini panties. Then she told herself that she had to trust him, and took off her underwear, too.

Finally wrapped in his blanket, she watched as Ross unloaded his saddlebags, unsaddled his horse, and wiped Buck down with the coarse saddle blanket. Then he grabbed a flashlight from his small stack of supplies, shone the broad beam back into the darkness, and led his horse several yards into the rear of the cave. Maggie had heard the echoing splash of water inside, but she was still surprised when she heard the horse drinking.

A few minutes later Ross returned, clicked off the flashlight, and tethered his horse to a boulder some distance away. "We've got a small pond in the back where the rain's dripping in, but it tapers downward so we'll stay dry." He lugged his saddle over to the cave's entrance.

Then he plopped it close to the wall and dragged his rain-coat in front of it. "Go ahead and sit. I'll start a fire. I saw some dry wood in the back." He was already retracing his steps, the flashlight illuminating his path again.

Maggie went to his saddle and sat, then tucked the thick flannel around her freezing feet, pulled her wet braid out of the blanket, and snuggled deeper into it.

When he came back the second time, he was carrying several sturdy branches that had apparently been stored for such an emergency—or for the next party, Maggie thought more realistically. Soon, kindling was teepeed around the charred log, and they had a small fire at the mouth of the cave. In another ten minutes, the log had caught, and Ross was looping his lariat over a jagged outcropping about five feet off the floor and tying it to his saddle horn. He was all grace and efficient movement.

When he bent to pick up her clothes—or more precisely, the bra and bikini that were on top of the pile—Maggie pushed quickly to her feet.

"Thank you, but I can take care of those."

Ross straightened, amused by her modesty. "Okay," he said, grinning. "You hang up your things—spread them out nice and neat so they dry quickly—and I'll hold the folds of your blanket shut."

Maggie sat back down and let him hang her underwear.

Outside the freak storm raged and howled; inside, the fire was beginning to warm and light their little refuge. Even though Ross had worn a raincoat the entire time, it had fanned out behind him as he rode, covering the saddle and saddle blanket. His shirt was dry, but his jeans were wet from crotch to ankle. Now he stood near the fire, dry-ing them as best he could without taking them off.

"As soon as the storm lets up a little, I'll go out and find some more wood," he said, then nodded at the fire. "That should take care of drying your things, but we'll need the light when night falls."

When night falls? "We aren't going back until tomorrow?"

"Can't," Ross said soberly. "Even if the rain stops, it'll be impossible to get out in the darkness."

Maggie nodded. Logically, she'd known that all along. It was the prospect of their spending the night together that had made her ask the question—and hope for a different answer. Not surprisingly, a heady chemistry had crept into the cave as it warmed—as *she* warmed—and those male-female undercurrents were making them both entirely too conscious of her nudity beneath the blanket. Too aware of the intimacy of their circumstances.

Almost as though he could read her thoughts, Ross moved restlessly in front of the fire, then checked his wristwatch. "Casey sent sandwiches and cans of soda—ginger ale and cola, I think. Are you hungry? It's nearly seven o'clock."

"Sandwiches sound wonderful," she answered, not really hungry but realizing that eating would give them something to focus on besides each other. She was fast discovering that, once recognized, awareness was a very difficult thing to ignore.

The sandwiches were ham and cheese, and they were delicious. The conversation was strained because they had to work so hard to maintain it.

Ross talked about his teenage outings in the area, rambling about fishing for cutthroat trout and, on one occasion, tipping over a friend's canoe. Maggie acknowledged that for someone who'd grown up in Montana, she'd done very few of the things most Montanans took for granted. She'd never been in a canoe, never seen a rodeo before two weeks ago, never held a fishing pole in her hands.

When their food and drinks were gone and they'd run out of childhood adventures to relate, that smothering feeling of being alone descended again, and Ross got up to reposition her clothes for the twentieth time.

Domestic touches from the town hellion? Maggie wondered. Or merely a man keeping his hands busy with incidentals to avoid doing other things?

"I would never have imagined you doing anything like this," she said quietly.

"What's that?"

"Fussing with laundry."

"Oh, I'm just full of surprises." Though his smile tried to conceal it, Ross's expression reflected his growing uneasiness as he took her dry underwear from the line and added the horse's blanket. "I used to do laundry all the time. Until Casey moved in, Jess and I did all the housekeeping chores. Of course, I was a pain in the butt back then, and Saint Jess ended up doing the lion's share of the work."

"I thought you got along with your brother."

"I do." Ross frowned. "Actually, I don't know why I called him that just now. I used to all the time."

"Because he did most of the housework?"

"Because he always did the right thing—nine times out of ten, anyway."

Maggie had changed seats during "supper"—moved from the saddle to the peeled log-and-stone bench that Ross had placed before a similar campfire years ago. Ross took a seat beside her, then held out her underwear. His disturbing gaze clung to hers.

Self-consciously, Maggie reached through the fold in her blanket to take them. "Thank you."

"You're welcome."

Her heart began to pound. In the strange way a tiny thing could spark giant emotions, she realized that they were both suddenly too conscious of the snippets of fabric in her hand. When she'd disrobed before, there had been no dancing nerve endings, no pulses throbbing in all the wrong places. She'd been chilled to the bone, he'd been concerned about hypothermia, and all she'd wanted to do

was get warm. Now she was comfortable, the cave was a
cozy hideaway where they would be together all
night…and those dangerous feelings of arousal were thick-
ening the air, wrapping them both in a snug little web of
"maybes" and "what-ifs."

Something moved across Ross's eyes—a flash of desire
that took Maggie's breath. Then, abruptly, he stood again
and walked the ten or twelve feet to the cave's entrance
to look out at the weather. He cleared his throat. "You
might feel more comfortable if you put those back on. Just
let me know when it's safe for me to turn around."

They'd both feel more comfortable if she put them back
on, Maggie thought. But safe? When night fell and they
were forced to recline and get some rest, possibly huddle
together for warmth if he couldn't find more wood…
clothes or no clothes, she knew what could happen.
Quickly, Maggie pulled on her underwear and wrapped
herself in the blanket again. "Okay," she said. "You can
turn around now."

But when Ross turned and met her eyes, Maggie saw
that nothing had changed. His gaze was troubled. Striding
to the wall where his saddle lay, he scooped up his raincoat, laid his Stetson on the saddle, and shrugged into his
rain gear. "I'd better see about that wood."

"Now? Shouldn't you wait until the rain lets up a little?"

"It could go on like this for hours," he answered
gruffly, and pulled up his slicker hood. "If I wait too long,
any wood I find will be soaked clear through." He started
into the unrelenting downpour, then glanced back at Maggie. "We passed some brush on the way up. I won't be
long."

He was in such a hurry to get out that Maggie wasn't
even sure whether he heard her murmur "okay."

Fifteen minutes later, keeping his head down against the
pelting rain, Ross grabbed the pile of branches he'd gath-

ered and headed back to the cave. He should take his hood off, he thought. Hell, he should strip to his birthday suit and take the cold shower he needed to get through this night. Except that if he got hit by lightning and they found his fried body out here, it would just give people more to talk about. Not that he hadn't given them plenty to gossip about already. Small towns had long memories.

Hurrying his steps in the encroaching darkness, his thoughts returned to the fire in the cave—then to the blaze in his belly. He had to be losing his mind. He had *never* made a promise to a woman like the one he'd earlier made to Maggie. Not taking advantage of a beautiful, naked female was as foreign to him as…as hobnobbing with the clergy and going to church picnics. He scowled as he approached the cave's entrance, and a staggering thought occurred to him. Good God, he was turning into his straight-arrow brother.

Ross walked to the fire and dropped the bundle of wood, then shed his dripping raincoat and tossed it aside.

And the instant he looked at her, that airy sensation he'd been fighting for the past two hours rolled through his gut again.

In his absence, she'd freed her hair from the braid she'd worn to work; now she was combing her fingers through silky black strands, drying them by the fire. His blanket was wrapped around her like a bath towel and tucked in at the front, and her bare feet rested on the trailing material. White bra straps shone against her lightly tanned skin and smooth shoulders.

Swallowing, Ross hunkered down across the fire from her, opened his pocketknife, and concentrated on stripping the bark from the thick branches he'd found…while the crotch of his damp jeans got snugger and snugger.

"I was thinking we should make some plans," Maggie said quietly.

Ross kept stripping and peeling, relieved to find dry wood beneath the bark. "What kind of plans?"

"We need to think about our sleeping arrangements."

"Well," he said, instantly picturing a more satisfying scenario than the one he was about to suggest. "Buck's blanket should be dry soon. It won't cushion you much, but it's better than lying on the cold floor. And your clothes are probably dry enough to put on now. You can use the saddle for a pillow, and you've already got a blanket—" he looked up from his task and, with an effort, forced a smile "—All the comforts of home."

"What about you?"

"What *about* me?"

"You...you didn't mention where you'd be spending the night."

"I'll stretch out beside the fire."

"On the ground? Without a blanket?"

"It wouldn't be the first time. Though, now that I think about it, I don't remember much about those other nights."

"Too...inebriated?" she asked.

"Unfortunately, yes."

Maggie walked around the stone ring to his side of the fire, holding the blanket to her breasts. Her hair fell soft and touchable over her shoulders, her cheeks faintly flushed from the fire. Ross couldn't breathe.

He watched her test the saddle blanket's dryness, then take it from their makeshift clothesline and spread the coarse rectangle of fabric out in front of his saddle. Then she returned, gathered her socks and uniform, and stepped a few feet behind him.

She never announced her intention—never told him not to look.

Ross's blood pumped hard as he pictured her in her pretty lingerie, heard the soft rustle of cotton as she slipped on her shirt and slacks. He didn't move a muscle—at least none of the muscles he could control.

Okay, this is good, he told himself. She'd be dressed, he'd be dressed, they'd spend the night together, and there wouldn't be any heavy breathing or morning-after guilt. Tomorrow, he'd take her back to the Lazy J, untouched, and apply for the Medal of Honor.

Maggie stepped out from behind him, fully dressed now, speaking in a sensible tone as she folded the blanket. "I think if we can keep the fire going, we won't need to cover up with this. We can put it on top of the saddle blanket to help cushion our backs."

"*Our* backs?"

"Yes."

"Not a good idea."

"It's better than yours."

Laying his knife down, Ross tossed aside the sturdy branch he'd been stripping. "We're alone up here."

"I'm aware of that. But you're an honorable man, and—"

He expelled a dry laugh. "You think I'm honorable?" She wasn't much of a mind reader, that was for sure. "Believe me, if you did one of those man-on-the-street interviews the newspapers are so nuts about, you wouldn't find many people who shared your opinion."

"I'm not interested in what anyone else thinks."

"Not Farrell? Not your uncle and aunt?"

"No. My aunt likes you, and my uncle *would* if he could get past what happened three years ago. As for Farrell—" she paused "—you were right about him. When the time comes, Cy will find some excuse not to give me that deputyship, no matter what I think or do."

Ross pushed to his feet and walked to her, his boots soft on the floor of the cave. Maggie held her breath as he took a lock of her hair and rolled it between his fingers. His somber gaze held hers. "Don't trust me too much, Maggie," he warned softly. "I'll only disappoint you."

Chills raced up her arms as she looked into his rugged

face. His eyes were so dark, his deep-blue irises nearly swallowed up as his pupils drank her in. Firelight flickered over his lean features, accenting his high cheekbones, his firm, strong jaw...his perfect mouth.

Moistening her lips, she took a step back, and Ross released her hair. "Maybe we should try to get some sleep so we can get an early start in the morning," she said nervously. "Moe and Lila must be worried sick."

"When she told me where you'd gone this afternoon, I promised her that I'd find you."

"She'll still worry. I'd really like to leave at first light."

"Sure. If the storm quits and we can travel safely."

Maggie nodded. With the sensual storm inside, she'd forgotten about the very real downpour beyond their stone walls. Lightning still flashed and pulsed in the night sky. Thunder still rumbled in the distance.

Ross moved toward his saddle. "Let's move your bedroll a little closer to the fire. The rocks will stay warm for a while after the fire burns down."

"We don't have enough wood?"

His voice softened in apology. "Not for the whole night. But I'll keep the flashlight handy in case we need it. Use the blanket to cover yourself."

"But if it's going to get that cold in here, we should share the blanket."

"We'll share the saddle," he said firmly. "I'll use one side for a pillow and you can use the other."

Maggie finally agreed. At least he'd have some comfort tonight. And with his feet pointed in one direction and hers in another, they could keep safely away from each other.

Several hours later, when the fire dwindled to hot coals, Maggie awakened to the chill temperature and her stiff muscles. She was astounded that she'd slept at all after lying there for what seemed forever, listening to the sound of the fire cracking and spitting…listening to the erratic beat of her own heart.

Cautiously, she sat up, then slowly leaned close to look at Ross. She jerked back in surprise when he said, "Are you all right?"

"No," she said after a moment. "I'm cold. Aren't you?"

"I'm okay."

Another moment ticked by. "Ross?"

"What?"

"Can I come over there with you?"

He didn't speak for a while. Then she heard his ragged sigh, and he said, "Stay there. I'll come to you."

Maggie scooted to the right of the saddle blanket to make room for him. Then, as if their movements had been previously choreographed, Ross stretched out on his back, pillowed his head on his saddle…and opened his arms. Maggie filled them. She positioned herself stiffly on her left side, shivering as he put his right arm around her and pulled the Indian blanket over the two of them. His jeans were still cold and damp.

"Okay now?"

Hearing the underlying strain in his voice, she wanted to say yes. But that wouldn't have been true. "No."

"What's wrong?"

"I…I don't know what to do with my right arm."

Ross grazed her thigh as he felt for her hand beneath the blanket, then placed it on his warm chest and held it there. Maggie drew a careful breath. She was now curved against him, her breasts pressing into his side. She swallowed, trying to blot out his male smell, his disturbing nearness. "I don't hear the rain anymore."

"I know. It stopped about an hour ago. The sky's clear."

"It is?" she asked breathlessly.

"Yeah. We've even got a moon out there now. I took Buck outside."

Moment by moment, senses were rekindling, needs re-awakening. Maggie was suddenly too conscious of his rigid form, too aware of his warm breath fanning her bangs and his heartbeat pounding beneath his chambray shirt. Ross's cautious respirations were now as shallow and deliberate as were hers.

"Ross?" Maggie whispered.

"Yeah?" he whispered back.

She couldn't remember what she wanted to ask. The simple act of turning her face up to speak to him had brought their mouths too close. Breaths mingled for just a heartbeat, then suddenly there didn't seem to be anything either of them could do to stop their parted lips from finding one another.

Ross's fevered mouth covered hers, hot and wet and possessive, and like a flash fire, Maggie answered his fervor with an urgency of her own. She held him fast as they turned and shifted beneath the blanket—tried to make the melding of their bodies as complete as was the melding of their mouths.

Maggie's heart swelled to near bursting. This was what she'd wanted, what she'd longed for, almost from the moment her young arms had held him thirteen years ago. To touch him, to taste him, to feel what it was to be a woman in Ross Dalton's arms. Back then, she'd been too naive and inexperienced to answer his needs. Now her needs were as great as his, but with an overpowering and undeniable feeling of love joining the desire in her blood.

Because, heaven help her, she did love him—whether loving him was wise or not.

They strained closer, their blanket billowing as hands moved in ever-widening circles to explore each other's bodies. Soon they were both drifting on a sea of sensation that pleaded for fulfillment.

Maggie broke from the kiss, her whispered voice so thready that she barely recognized it as her own. "Ross, take off your jeans—they're still wet."

Groaning, he buried his face in her hair. "I can't, Maggie. This sainthood thing is just too new to me."

"Then don't *be* a saint."

He stilled. He fought for breath. "Are you sure?" he rasped. "I'm nobody's Prince Charming. I can't make you any promises."

"I'm not asking for any."

A second later, they were kissing mindlessly again, saying goodbye to the last shreds of control as shaky fingers fumbled with buttons and zippers, cast aside denim and lace…until there were no more barriers to their lovemaking. Ross yanked his wallet out of his jeans and fumbled inside for their protection.

Maggie lay back for a moment, then reached for him. But with a whispered, "No, the floor's too hard, I'll hurt you," Ross pulled her astride him. Closing her eyes, Maggie drew a shaky breath as they joined in the darkness. Then she slid her arms around his neck and pressed her body close—while they kissed and tongued, while they immersed themselves in the pleasures of touching and being touched.

She was gentle slopes and swells; he was hard muscle and sinews. Maggie gloried in the feel of his callused hands on her breasts, sucked in a trembling breath when he pushed them high and kissed the swells he'd created. She let her fingers examine his tense shoulders and strong back—urged his face up to rain frantic kisses over his throat. She'd waited so long for this. Waited so long… She began to move against him.

Ross tried to hold off—tried to concentrate on the last bright embers snapping in the fire ring and on their dim shadows on the ceiling of the cave. But her body was too sweet, her sighs too needy. The fire in him became a full-blown blaze. Taking her face in both of his hands, covering her eager mouth with his own, Ross finally gave up trying...and let Maggie carry them both to Eden.

When she was lying against him again and their breathing had finally slowed to a tolerable level, Maggie released a contented sigh. Her bones still felt liquid, her muscles, nonexistent. Her heart, full.

"Well," she laughed softly, "I'm finally warm."

Ross's head was pillowed against the saddle again, with Maggie's hair spilling over his right shoulder. His deep, low voice was as mellow as was hers. "That's good, because if you were still cold, the best I could do right now would be to pull the blanket higher around us."

After several more minutes of touching and kissing, Maggie eased away, a little of her joy fading. Something she'd thought about only fleetingly before had again occurred to her.

"You were prepared for our being together tonight. Did you... Did you have that in the back of your mind when you came for me?"

Ross's hand stilled on her hip. "Maggie, I didn't plan for this to happen. In fact, I honestly tried to stay away from you. The reason I had protection with me was—" He hesitated.

"Never mind," Maggie murmured, feeling her heart sink as her mind filled in the rest of his statement. "It's not important."

Ross rolled onto his side, straining to see her in the near darkness. "Yes, it is important. Maggie, the night of the church roofing, I was so churned up, I didn't know what to do with myself. I—" He stopped, drew a breath, then continued. "I just needed to get you out of my system any way I could. I went to Dusty's."

Tears stung her eyes. "You know, I really don't need to hear this right now."

"Yes, you do. I found a woman. She was more than willing, but I couldn't go through with it. Because I still wanted you." Smoothing her hair, Ross eased down to kiss her softly and repeated in a whisper, "Maggie, I only wanted you."

Chapter 10

Chapter 10

Later, as they sat snuggled in the saddle that they'd moved just outside the cave's broad entry, Maggie's heart was still rejoicing. He'd had the opportunity to sleep with someone else, and he'd said no because he'd wanted her. That had to mean *something,* didn't it?

"Tired?" Ross murmured as she curled on his lap. With his back resting against the exterior stone wall and their blanket tucked high around them, they gazed out at the clear night sky.

"Just a little," she admitted. "But let's not go back inside just yet. It's really pretty out here." Slipping her hand inside his unbuttoned shirt, she stroked the soft hair on his chest. They'd dressed a few minutes ago, but she wasn't willing to give up their easy intimacy yet. It had been too long in coming.

Overhead, a myriad of stars gleamed like diamonds in the vast, black sky, and a silver half-moon crowned the jagged mountain peaks opposite them. Below, in the rain-drenched valley, Maggie hoped no one had been hurt and that the loss of property hadn't been too high. No one should be troubled on a night like this. Not when the air was clean and fresh with pine and sage, and her heart was brimming with love. "Do you know what time it is?"

Ross reached for the flashlight beside him, clicked it on to check his watch, then turned it off again and replaced it. "Almost three o'clock. Does it matter?"

"No, just curious." But it did matter. Things would change when dawn arrived and they had to leave this special place to go back home. How much, she wasn't sure. But there would be changes.

The winking green lights of a jet appeared above, and its reminder of civilization made Maggie draw closer in Ross's arms. He hadn't said that he loved her, hadn't said anything to make her think this had been more than a night of mutual sharing. But he did care for her; she knew it as well as she knew her own name. "Hey," she said quietly, "do you believe in UFOs?"

"UFOs?" Ross chuckled softly. "Where did that come from?"

Maggie laughed, too, and their mirth echoed off their rocky surroundings. "That plane up there. I saw the lights, and my mind just kind of moved on. So do you believe in them or not?"

"Let's see now," he mused teasingly. "Do I believe that aliens in flying saucers swoop down on unsuspecting humans, beam them up, and have profound telepathic conversations with them?"

"No, smarty-pants, do you believe there are other lifeforms out there somewhere?"

"Oh. Probably not. But a lot of people in Rachel do."

"Rachel?"

"Rachel, Nevada. It's a small town in the desert near a high-security air force base. Supposedly there have been mysterious sightings in the area. It's a real Mecca for alien enthusiasts. The local motel's called the Little A'le'inn."

"My, my. For a nonbeliever, you certainly do have the scoop. How do you know about this?"

Ross's uneasy pause before he replied told Maggie that this wasn't something he wanted to discuss. By the time he answered, his posture had stiffened faintly, and regret had altered the low timbre of his voice.

"A few years ago, when I was still Comfort's reigning jackass, Ray Pruitt and I were in Las Vegas. We heard the UFO rumors and decided to drive up there. Rachel's only about a hundred and forty miles north of Vegas. Anyway, we went...both of us all tanked up after losing at the tables." Disgust laced his voice as he added, "I did a lot of stupid things that trip."

Yes, she imagined he had, Maggie thought, noting the time frame. But that was the past. And the fact that he obviously regretted those things spoke volumes about the man he'd become. "I think it's safe to say that everyone on the planet's done something they wish they hadn't at some point in their lives."

"Not like I did," Ross answered quietly. "I gambled away my half of the ranch."

He didn't speak for a few moments, almost as though he were waiting for her to say something judgmental. When she remained silent, he went on. "After we drove back to Vegas, I was absolutely convinced that I could recoup my losses. So along the way to my big win, I signed forty-seven thousand dollars worth of markers to the wrong people."

She wasn't shocked by the amount, because she had already read the transcript of his court testimony. Nonetheless, she had to comment. "You must have been very upset."

"I was. I was sick to the soles of my feet. Then my luck changed. I met a rich doctor in a Vegas bar that afternoon, and ended up spilling my guts—told this fancy Chicago cardiologist my whole life story. He offered to lend me the money to cover my markers if I put up my half of Brokenstraw as collateral. Before I knew it, I was in a lawyer's office making it all legal.

"Then—jerk that I was—I asked for sixty grand. I figured the extra thirteen thousand would be enough for me to win everything back, and pay the doc before his convention ended and he left town."

"I guess it didn't work out that way."

"Nope. I lost the thirteen grand, too. The doctor—Casey's first husband—was killed going home from that convention. Turns out, he was a piece of work, too. When he died, Casey was left with nothing but that loan agreement and a mountain of bills."

"So Casey came out here to collect on the debt?"

"Mmm, hmm. That's how she met Jess."

"Quite a saga," Maggie murmured after a moment. "Is there a happy ending to this story?"

"Yep. For the next couple of years, all I did was work and sleep—took every extra job I could find. I'll finish paying Casey back in August. And I don't gamble anymore."

"Not at all?"

"Not at all. I can't trust myself to stop once I start. Maggie, I can't even buy a lottery ticket because I'm afraid that the next time I'll buy fifty. I don't gamble. Period."

"Good," she said, relieved. She wanted him strong. Strong enough to earn back the respect of his friends and neighbors. Because whether he knew it or not, he needed their respect. His aunt Ruby had even alluded to that weeks ago at the rodeo. "So now, instead of gambling, you build beautiful log homes and shingle church roofs. Better watch out. The town council will want you to run for mayor."

Ross released a short, flat laugh and readjusted the blanket around them. "Fat chance of that happening. Folks around here have long memories. I'm still the guy who

did the unthinkable—a rancher who got involved with cattle rustlers.''

"They have to know you regret that."

"What they know is that leopards don't change their
spots.''

"Not everyone believes those old clichés."

"Yeah, well…enough people do."

Maggie lifted her chin and faced him. "I don't."

Ross held back a sigh, wondering if she'd say that with
such conviction if she realized that even after three years,
staying away from the tables was still a battle for him.
Like an alcoholic with a yen for booze, his hands still
itched to hold a deck of cards. Because the playing, the
betting, was fun. At least, it had been when he was winning. But admitting that to Maggie meant revealing just
how pathetic and weak he really was, and pride wouldn't
let him do that.

The bright half-moon threw her features into bold relief,
and Ross drank in the dark beauty of Maggie's eyes, the
lips she parted in subtle invitation. She wanted him
again…and he wanted her. Even with the distraction of
every cricket in the valley chirping, and a universe full of
stars overhead, the warmth of her against him was first in
Ross's thoughts. But repeating their lovemaking would be
a mistake. She was a respectable woman who deserved
better than a man who would make getting her into bed
his own personal challenge—which was what he'd done.
She was a minister's daughter; he'd been trouble in boots
for most of his life.

He should never have touched her.

Ross brought his forehead to hers and closed his eyes.
"Oh, damn, Maggie," he sighed. "I told you not to trust
me too much."

"You also told me you'd disappoint me. You were
wrong about that, too."

Just be patient, he almost said. It's only a matter of time.

"It'll be sunrise in a few hours. We'd better get some sleep."

"Not just yet," she whispered. Then she burrowed warmly into the side of his neck, nuzzled a kiss into that sensitive spot below his ear...and all his self-deprecating thoughts and noble intentions sailed away like dandelion fluff on a spring breeze.

Threading his fingers through her hair, Ross brought her lips to his and kissed her deeply. Together they let the moonlight and their quickly heating blood take them where they both wanted to go.

They kept to the high ridges on the way back to the ranch, venturing close to the road only to survey the flood damage and to see that most of the waters had receded into the tall grasses bordering the creek. Maggie's heart sank when she spotted her car a hundred yards from where they'd seen it last, twisted and wedged between two trees. At the same time, she was thankful that her car was the only loss suffered. Without Ross's intervention, it could have been far worse. And, she thought—looking for a bright spot—the damage would be covered by insurance. At least she hoped so.

It was nearly 7:00 a.m. when they rode up to Moe Jackson's back door. Though they'd passed pools of rainwater in the deeper depressions, the Lazy J and Brokenstraw area wasn't as low as Clearcut, and appeared to have come through the storm fairly well. Behind her, Ross slid off the horse, then lifted Maggie down from the saddle as Lila hurried outside, letting the kitchen's screen door bang shut behind her. Words of relief rushed from her lips.

"Maggie! Ross! Thank goodness you're all right. The radio said Clearcut was a mess, and the road was closed. Come inside, you must be hungry."

Sober-faced, her Uncle Moe thumped out onto the back

porch, too, gripping his walker and seeming to stand sentry beside the door.

St. Peter at the gate, determined to keep all evildoers out, Maggie thought. An awkwardness settled between them as she turned to meet Ross's eyes, wondering what to say. By now, her uncle's antagonistic feelings about him were abundantly clear.

"Go ahead," he said softly. "I have to get back. If it's been on the radio that Clearcut was hard-hit, Jess and Casey will be wondering how we made out, too."

"We got a phone inside," a gravelly voice stated from the porch. "No reason you can't call 'em from here, is there?"

Surprise hit her first. Then hope bloomed in Maggie's heart as she turned expecting to see her uncle's crotchety expression—and watched him open the door wide. Maggie's gaze rebounded to Ross. The dark blue eyes beneath the brim of his Stetson were just as stunned as her own. But there was something else in those eyes, too. Moe's unexpected gesture had put a watery shine in them.

"Would you like to use the phone in the kitchen?" she asked.

"Come on, come on," Moe called, "before the house fills up with flies. Hitch your horse to that fence, and come inside, boy. Coffee's hot."

"Thanks," Ross said, swallowing. He looked away for a moment while his emotions leveled out, then he snatched up Buck's reins.

When the horse had been tethered to the rail fence two dozen yards away, and Ross had wiped his boots in the wet grass, they walked up the plank steps to the small back porch. At the threshold, Moe cleared his throat noisily and stretched out a hand to clasp Ross's. "Thanks for bringin' her home safe. Lila didn't sleep all night."

"You're welcome," Ross said sincerely.

A knot tightened in Maggie's throat. To a western man,

a handshake meant respect, acceptance—and being invited to "sit at table" was a notch up from that. Maggie waited until Ross had gone inside, then she hugged Moe gently and kissed his whiskery cheek. "Thank you, Uncle Moe," she whispered. "You're a good man."

"So's he," Moe allowed in a low, rough voice. "Now let's get him to that phone and have us some breakfast."

Breakfast in the Jacksons' blue-and-white country kitchen was a feast. Ross was used to eating hearty in the morning, but Lila's menu had surpassed every breakfast he'd ever enjoyed. She made pancakes and sausage, biscuits and gravy, grits, scrambled eggs and Texas toast with homemade orange marmalade. He felt like royalty with Lila and Maggie fussing over him, and Moe keeping his coffee cup and orange juice glass filled. For the first time in ages, Ross said a small prayer of thanks. Maybe this "town pariah" thing had finally run its course. Maybe this was the first step toward the life he'd wanted since his cavalier life-style had nearly cost him his home and his freedom.

"Full?" Maggie asked, refilling her own coffee mug and returning to the chair beside him. She bumped a playful knee against his under the blue-and-white oilcloth table covering, and he smiled and bumped her back.

"Stuffed." Ross ran his gaze over her, liking what he saw. While Lila had started breakfast, Maggie had washed her face quickly and brushed her hair, then surrendered the bathroom to Ross. But she still wore her wrinkled, soot-marked beige uniform. She could have changed, but she hadn't. Ross thought that maybe she'd remained in those clothes because his weren't in the best shape, either, and she hadn't wanted him to feel uncomfortable. Her sweetness and consideration made him want to wrap her in his arms again.

"So you just holed up in that cave all night?" Moe

asked, taking a noisy slurp of his coffee and pulling Ross's attention from Maggie. "Could have already been occupied, if you know what I mean."

"That's right," Lila said as she put the milk and eggs back into the refrigerator. "Anything from a grizzly to a cougar could have already claimed it."

"Thankfully, nothing did," Ross answered. "We were able to keep the fire going most of the night."

There was a rattly knock at the loose screen door. Then the door swung on its hinges, and Reverend Tom Bristol walked into the kitchen. Dressed in a black polo shirt and jeans, and carrying a suitcase, the trim, slightly graying clergyman smiled from ear to ear. "Happy belated Fourth of July, everybody." His smile turned curious as he took in the unusual smorgasbord filling the breakfast table—as well as the people gathered around it. "What's all this?"

As joyful as Ross had ever seen her, Maggie jumped up and rushed to her father. Ross pushed back his chair and stood respectfully.

"Hi!" Maggie cried, hugging him tightly. "My goodness, I didn't expect to see you until next week. How long can you stay?"

"Only until Tuesday," the reverend said through a chuckle, hugging her back. He winced faintly as he seemed to pick up the odor of smoke on his daughter's wrinkled clothing. "So what's going on here with all the food? Did your freezer break down, Lila?"

Lila laughed, and after pulling the milk and eggs back out of the fridge and setting them down on the countertop, came over to offer her own hug and greeting. "A celebration, that's what's going on," she said. "Are you hungry, Tom?"

"Famished."

Maggie was still glowing. "You remember Ross Dalton, don't you, Dad?"

Reverend Bristol extended his hand across the table to

clasp Ross's, smiling pleasantly. "Yes, I remember Ross. How are you, son?"

"Fine, sir—you?"

"Fine. Sit down and finish your coffee." Turning his smile on Maggie again, he ushered her back to the table. "You sit down, too, sweetheart, and bring your old dad up to speed. What's this celebration all about?"

For the next several minutes, Maggie retold the tale of her car trouble, the blinding rainstorm and Ross's rescue, then moved on to their spending the night together in Ross's "childhood" cave. To Ross's eternal gratitude, she skipped the parts about having to dry every stitch of clothing she'd been wearing—and making love with him. Still, when she ended with "So it looks like I'll be buying a new car," Ross sensed that Maggie's father knew some pertinent information had been omitted from her story. It was apparent in the way his evaluating gaze kept moving between the two of them.

That was why, while Lila scrambled fresh eggs and the reverend and Moe caught up on family news, Ross was eager to help Maggie clear away some of the dishes. He was becoming entirely too uncomfortable sitting across the table from Maggie's obviously adoring and faintly suspicious father.

Lila stopped him when Ross started to wash the dishes. "Oh, no, you don't," she said. "We're already indebted to you for watching over Maggie. Besides, after your call home, you're probably anxious to get back to Brokenstraw. I heard you tell Moe that you'd lost some trees to the wind. I'm sure Jess could use a hand." She heaped Tom's plate and carried it to the table, then checked the leftover sausage she'd warmed in the microwave and retrieved toast from the toaster. "I take it everything else was okay?"

"We lost a few shingles on the old barn, but that's to be expected with winds that high." Ross sent her a crooked grin. "On the other hand, we won't have to check the water troughs today."

Lila grinned back, then went to Ross and gave him a warm hug. "Thanks again."

"You, too, Lila," he answered, surprised by the sentiment tightening his throat. "Breakfast was great." He shifted his gaze to Moe and the reverend. "Reverend, good seeing you again."

Tom Bristol stood and shook Ross's hand. "Thank you for taking such good care of my daughter."

Ross fought the guilty flush rising in his cheeks and simply nodded, then extended a hand to Moe. "Moe...thanks for everything."

"Anytime. And I mean that, boy."

"I'll get your hat," Maggie said, falling into step beside him.

After taking it from one of the pegs by the door, she preceded him outside, then walked with him to the fence. Ross had barely pulled on his Stetson and untied Buck's reins when she snagged his hand and pulled him to the far side of his horse, apparently to shade them from her family's eyes. Chemistry had them in each other's arms instantly, kissing deeply. His body remembered her and began to respond; Maggie fitted herself more closely to him.

Ross sighed as they broke from the kiss, hoping he wasn't facing a brand new addiction. Two seconds in her arms and his blood was on fire. He looked down into her wide brown eyes—eyes that waited for him to say something. But half of him wasn't sure what that was, and the other half was scared to death to say anything that might be misunderstood. He was a loner, and he needed to remember that. "I guess you'll be busy for a while with your dad here."

Maggie nodded, her hair lifting in the light breeze. "We have some catching up to do. It's been over a month since we've had the opportunity to just sit and visit."

Despite his still-conflicted feelings about her, Ross experienced a strange clenching in his chest, and he had the uneasy feeling that something valuable was slipping away. But why should he think that? Her family was less than thirty yards away, and she had just kissed him. "Then you should. Visit, that is."

"He's all I have since Mom died."

"Family's important," Ross said, understanding perfectly. "I'd give anything to have my parents back again...have another chance to say some things I never got around to saying when I was seventeen." He looked back toward the house. "Well...your dad's probably wondering what happened to you."

"Yes, he probably is." With a familiarity that surprised him, Maggie's gaze fell to his mouth, and she stretched up on tiptoe to slide the fingers of her right hand into the hair at his nape. Her collar was open, showing the rapidly beating pulse at the base of her throat. "Bye," she whispered.

"Bye."

Ross lowered his parted lips to hers. But this time, the kiss was soft and gentle, their hands tender and mobile as they stroked backs and touched faces in the way of parting lovers. "Enjoy your time with your dad," he said quietly.

"I will. Thanks."

Then he mounted up, reined his buckskin in a half circle, and headed west, setting his sights on the sprawling pastureland that linked the Lazy J to Brokenstraw.

When he had finally faded from view, Maggie started back to the house, head down, already missing him. Would it always be this way? she wondered, crossing the wet grass. Would she want him every time he looked at her, every time he kissed her? *Please,* she prayed, *let him be feeling some of these things, too. I don't want to be in love all by myself.*

A noise from inside the house—a pan's lid clattering to

the floor perhaps—made her look up. Maggie stilled when she saw her father standing in the screened doorway. His troubled expression said he'd been there for some time.

Tom Bristol walked outside onto the small back porch, closing the door softly behind him. "Looks like the Fourth of July isn't the only thing I missed," he said quietly.

With her lips still moist from Ross's kisses, Maggie ascended the painted gray steps to face her father.

"I just don't understand why you're so upset." Maggie tossed her towel over a wicker porch chair, then combed her fingers through her wet hair to smooth the tangles. At least she'd had a chance to shower and change to shorts and a knit top before her father insisted on speaking to her alone. She settled on the front porch swing beside him and softened her voice. "I'm twenty-eight years old, Dad. In a few months, I'll be twenty-nine. I know what I'm doing."

"You make love with a man in a cave and you tell me you know what you're doing?"

"Yes."

"Maggie, you know how I feel about physical intimacy outside the sanctity of marriage. It's wrong, and it makes me doubt myself as a parent that you can't see the wrongfulness of it. Did I fail you that badly?"

Maggie's spirits sank, not because she'd made love with Ross, but because of the disillusionment she heard in her father's voice. Suddenly she was that little girl again—the one who always surfaced whenever her dad was around. The one who would do almost anything for his approval. "Daddy, I love him. When have you ever preached that expressing love is wrong?"

"Never. But there are more appropriate ways of expressing it until there's a wedding ring on your finger. Your mother, God rest her soul, was the most beautiful, desirable woman I've ever known. But we kept our relationship chaste until we took our vows." He paused, his face lining. "I just can't support this, Maggie."

Swallowing, she picked up the damp blue towel and worked it through her hands. "I'm not asking you to support it. I'm just asking you to understand." Which was probably asking a lot, since she didn't understand it herself. Love had happened so quickly, without any fanfare, without any warning. She was truly in love for the first time in her life...and it was the most amazing thing. She knew now that she'd never really loved Todd, her feelings for him paled dramatically compared to the warmth, and joy, and deep, abiding tenderness she felt for Ross.

"Does he love you, too?"

Maggie kept twisting the towel. "I...I don't know."

The reverend sank back against the swing and, with a shoe to the floor, started it moving. "I see."

"He does care about me, Dad," Maggie persisted. "A man who didn't care wouldn't have come out in the middle of a raging storm to make sure I was all right. Especially since there was no assurance he would even find me. I could have gone back to Clearcut—or I could have caught a ride into town with a passing motorist." Although, she thought, that would've been an extremely remote possibility, considering that few people travelled the Clearcut road.

"He *does* care," she repeated. Then an uncharacteristically mutinous streak reared its head. "And I *am* going to see him again."

For a moment, her father didn't say anything, then he nodded and met Maggie's eyes. His wounded look nearly broke her heart. "Then I don't think I can stay, sweetheart."

For a moment, she couldn't say a word. Then tears welled in her eyes and she murmured, "Blackmail? You're making me choose?"

"No, I would never make you choose. I told you a long

time ago that when temptations arise, you either have to deny them, or decide if you can live with the guilt of embracing them. If this is your decision, there's nothing I can do about it. But you're my only child, Maggie, and I can't pretend that it doesn't hurt and disappoint me.''

Maggie choked out her reply. "But we have sparklers to light, and Aunt Lila and I have been planning a picnic.'' She stopped. Composed herself. Moistened her lips. "Will…will you stay if I promise not to see him while you're here?''

The swing's chains creaked rhythmically as her father lapsed into a long, thoughtful silence, and the insect ring of cicadas punctuated the growing heat of the afternoon. From inside, twangy music from her uncle's old radio joined the ringing and the creaking.

"You'll have no contact at all with him?'' he finally asked.

Maggie swallowed. "None at all, I promise.''

Tom drew a deep breath, let it out slowly, then sent Maggie a sad smile. "All right, honey, I'll stay. Maybe after a few days apart, your head will clear and you'll realize that I'm right about this.''

That night, as Maggie lay in bed thinking about their conversation, she came to realize a lot of things. The first was that this afternoon her dad had been more of a father than a reverend. He'd manipulated her, pushed her buttons, used her love for her mother and her respect for him to get what he wanted. He'd claimed his threat to leave hadn't been blackmail, but in Maggie's mind there was no other word for it.

Suddenly she understood why she'd dropped everything and come back to Comfort. Certainly, she'd wanted to help her uncle and aunt at a time when they needed it. But even more than that, she'd needed to put space between herself and a father who couldn't help being controlling. She loved him dearly, but she had returned to Montana because she'd wanted the opportunity to make her own choices without fear of recrimination. And she had.

Maggie stared at the moonlight-streaked ceiling, wishing with all her heart that she was looking up at granite, not plaster…wishing that her mattress was Buck's saddle blanket, and that Ross was here beside her, turning her limbs to silk with his kisses and his hands.

She thought back to her Uncle Moe's saying that Ross was a good man—and her heart warmed because she believed it, too. Ross had changed in the month she'd known him, for the better. Or maybe…maybe there hadn't been a change. Perhaps he'd been the man he was now for a long time, but had seen no reason to show that side of himself to anyone because no one expected any better from him.

Life would be so much easier right now if she had just lied when her father asked if she and Ross were lovers. But she'd never been able to do that, just as she'd never been able to back out on a promise to him.

Out of respect for her father, she would keep her distance from Ross until Tuesday; she'd given her word. But as soon as her dad was gone, she would find Ross and make him realize a few things, too. Like how much he needed her in his life.

Chapter 11

Ross dumped a scoop of grain into the feed bin in Buck's stall, tossed the scoop aside for the moment, then slipped the leather strap of the currycomb over his hand and started it in a circular motion over the horse's withers and shoulder.

The buckskin nosed into the bin and started eating. In the next stall, Jess's big bay sent Ross an affronted look to protest his sleep being disturbed, then swung his head forward again and closed his eyes.

It was 11:00 p.m., and most of Montana had already retired for the night, probably relieved that the storm, with its high winds and dangerous lightning, had run its course. Ross still had too much energy to sleep. Even after a full day of turning four downed trees into thick, chunky logs, he wasn't tired.

"Probably too much coffee, huh, boy?" he murmured to the horse.

Or maybe sleep wouldn't come because of the emotional high he'd been feeling ever since Moe Jackson shook his hand this morning. After three years of Moe's loathing, a truce had been called. On the heels of Maggie's announcement that she didn't care what anyone else thought about their…what? friendship?…that handshake had been the proverbial icing on the cake. He couldn't recall ever feeling more at peace and more strung out at the same time— the strung-out part being Maggie's fault.

Moving to Buck's right side, Ross repeated the currying process. The smell of horse mingled with the lingering dampness in the air, and the odors of hay and dust in the stall. Through the open window, a slice of moon hovered over the steep ridges above Clearcut, pulling Ross's thoughts back to last night. Maggie's straightforward approach to lovemaking had surprised him. He wasn't sure what he'd expected, but confidence and full, earthy participation hadn't been it.

Frowning suddenly, Ross backed up his thoughts. *Lovemaking?* He had never thought about sex that way before. Certainly never with Brenda or any of the other women with whom he'd slept. But his old cavalier expressions didn't work when he thought about Maggie. She was different, special… And suddenly he felt bad for not telling her so. The physical side of sex had always been good for him. But that deeply contented feeling afterward was something new…and nice.

Maybe that's what he should have said when they were parting at her uncle's fence today. Although…could he admit that and not expect her to place too much importance on it?

Nodding, Ross exchanged the currycomb for a stiff grooming brush. Sure he could. It wasn't like she'd expect him to put a ring on her finger and announce their engagement or anything, right? He'd told her that he couldn't make any promises, and she'd said that she wasn't asking for any.

With renewed vigor, he brushed the dirt and loose hair

out of Buck's coat. He'd give Maggie all day tomorrow with her dad, but she'd probably go back to work on Monday. He'd stop in to see her around noon at the sheriff's office and ask her to lunch at the café. She'd never turn down his aunt Ruby's chicken and biscuits.

"Okay, fella," Ross said to the horse as he reached for the mane comb. "Now that we've got that settled, let's see what we can do about getting the knots out of your tail."

Maggie was on the radio relaying a message when Ross walked into the sheriff's office at 11:45 Monday morning. Something warm curled in his gut when she glanced up, saw him, and smiled all the way up to her brown eyes.

That smile disappeared a second later as her father and Trent Campion walked in behind him.

"Hello, Ross," Reverend Bristol said cordially. "Beautiful day, isn't it?"

"Sure is, Reverend." Ross ignored Trent's smug look. "I hope you're enjoying your visit."

"Very much. I've been making my rounds this morning, and seeing as many of my old congregation as time permits." He clapped a hand on Trent's shoulder and smiled, still speaking to Ross. "In fact, I bumped into your next state representative, here, when I was over at the church talking to Reverend Fremont."

"From your lips to God's ears, sir," Trent chuckled.

Ross tried to hide his revulsion as Campion ambled farther into the room to address him. "I was just over at the parsonage to make a donation. Yesterday at services, Reverend Fremont mentioned that now that the new roof is on, we need to start thinking about replacing the worn concrete steps and patching some inside plaster. You recall him saying that, don't you, Ross?"

Ross stared coldly. Trent knew that he didn't remember; Ross hadn't gone to church yesterday. Considering the small size of the congregation, Reverend Bristol knew it, too.

Maggie signed off and stood, her eyes troubled as she took in the three of them. "Hi, Dad…Ross…Trent."

Tom Bristol walked to his daughter with open arms, and Maggie rounded her desk for his hug, still battling her obvious uneasiness. "Hi, sweetheart, how's your day going?"

"Okay. Yours?"

"Good, good," he said exuberantly, and released her. "You go ahead and take care of Ross, honey. We're not in a hurry." Bristol's affable gaze came back to Ross. "I assume you had a police matter to discuss?"

A police matter? Ross's confused gaze moved from Maggie to her father. Then he saw Maggie's face redden as the reverend sent her a pleasant look which seemed to have something heavier behind it.

"No," Ross said belatedly. "I just came by to see if Maggie would like to have lunch."

"Maggie?" Bristol prodded, that pleasant-but-something smile still in place.

"I…I can't," she said to Ross. "I'm having lunch with Dad."

Ross felt a twinge of disappointment, but he understood; they would only have one more day together, then her dad would be heading back to Colorado. He hesitated for a moment, half hoping they'd invite him to join them—but they didn't. Which was also okay with him. Now that he thought about it, maybe it wouldn't be such a great idea to spend that much time with Maggie's dad. He was smiling, he was friendly…but Ross hadn't missed the silent communication that had passed between him and his daughter. Something was up.

"Well, maybe another ti—"

"Excuse me," Maggie said quickly as she turned to

buzz Farrell's office. "I have to let Cy know I'm leaving so he can answer the phones."

Ross stared at her in complete bewilderment. Why was she so rattled? Then he intercepted another smug look from Trent, who remained standing companionably beside Reverend Bristol—and suddenly Ross knew what was going on. Maggie's head had finally cleared. When there was no one else around, she welcomed him with her eyes and her body. But as soon as her father showed up, Ross was *persona non grata* again. Apparently, Reverend Bristol didn't approve of him, but had a high opinion of Ben Campion's rich, spineless son. They were all going out for lunch together.

"Fine," Ross drawled, forcing a detached tone and adjusting his Stetson as he walked to the door. "Didn't mean to take up your time."

Battling a mixture of anger and indifference—he was *not* hurt—he stalked over to Ruby's and took a seat at the lunch counter. The place was already filling up, already buzzing. "Chicken and biscuits, Sharon," he said to the pretty blonde who hurried over to set a glass of ice water in front of him.

"Anything to drink?"

"Just the water, thanks."

Right on time—and right when he didn't need the aggravation of being reminded again—Ruby and her red high-tops squeaked up behind him. "Didn't see you in church yesterday."

"I know," he answered as patiently as he could. "I was cutting up some trees. We lost a few during the storm. You didn't run into any trouble here, did you?"

"Lost the power fer a few minutes, and the basement took on some water, but that was all. Sump pump took care of it."

"Good. Need me to do anything for you while I'm here?"

Soft laughter rustled behind him, and Ruby scowled as Brenda Larson rose from a nearby table and carried the remains of her salad and soft drink to the counter. She slid onto the stool beside Ross. "Might be a few things you can do for me."

Glaring over her spectacles, Ruby spoke point-blank to the flashy redhead. "I don't need him fer nothin' and neither do you."

The bell above the door jangled as more patrons entered, and a spattering of "Afternoon, Reverend"'s and a few "Nice to see you, Tom"'s interrupted the steady clank and scrape of silverware on china. Maggie's arrival yanked Ross's attention away for only a moment, then he forced his focus back on the two women staring each other down.

"Ruby Cayhill, why are you being so mean to me?" Brenda pouted.

"'Cause sometimes you need it. Yer a nice girl, Brenda, but all you think about is wavin' that caboose of yers around and makin' the men crazy."

"Aunt Ruby?" Ross said through a sigh.

"What?"

"Brenda's my friend, and I'd appreciate it if you'd cut her some slack."

"I just thought she oughtta know you got yerself a girl, and you're through with all that old foolishness."

Was he? Not if he read correctly the actions of the reverend and his prissy off-limits daughter. "Don't sell foolishness short," he answered easily, and took a swig of his water. "Everybody in town knows that's what I'm all about."

Ruby eyed him sharply. "Since when?"

"Since that," he said, jerking a thumb over his shoulder.

She glanced across the room—Brenda's gaze following—and apparently spotted the table he was referring to. Ruby harrumphed Trent's importance aside. "He ain't nothin' to worry about. Fact is, Tom Bristol better count his fingers afterwards if that young scalawag shakes his hand today." She started away, then stopped abruptly to eye Ross again. "And you just concentrate on eatin' your lunch and behavin' yerself."

When she was gone, Ross turned to Brenda. "Things busy over at the insurance office, Bren?"

"Busy enough." With a teasing smile, she picked up her soft drink, her twinkling cat-eyes locking on his as she drank deeply through her straw. "So that's why you stomped in here lookin' so mean and nasty," she said. "You're all worked up over the preacher's daughter."

"Not even a little bit," Ross replied, irritated and wondering what was keeping his lunch.

"No?"

"I said no, didn't I?"

Laughing outright now, Brenda picked up her salad fork and speared a black olive. "Then you've got bigger problems than I thought, cowboy. The only other people at that table are men."

The high-pitched ringing of a chain saw rent the early evening air as Maggie slowed Lila's chestnut mare to a walk and pointed her up the rutted driveway to Ross's log home. Still high in the cloudless blue sky, the hot sun shone down on lush foliage, gleaming natural timbers…and a man's tanned back.

Maggie's pulse stepped up its pace. Thirty-odd yards behind the house, Ross stood in the high grass, taking the noisy saw through a downed tree. His black truck was parked nearby, and he seemed to be alone. At least, she hoped he was. They needed to talk.

Dismounting, she tethered the mare to the base of a sapling, then walked toward Ross.

Why had she never before thought the word beautiful appropriate for describing a man? she wondered. Because from the tip of his Stetson, to his broad shoulders and back, to the scuffed toes on his cowboy boots, that's what he was. Taut skin gleamed beneath a sheen of sweat, and sawdust clung to his lean midsection and body hair, speckled the faded jeans that hugged his seat. To his left, an uneven pile of pine boughs and branches scented the air with a clean, woodsy fragrance.

She watched him raise the saw again, take another cut...

The saw shrieked, bucked and died halfway through the trunk. Ross cursed a blue streak, then swore again when he tried to pull it out and the blade stayed pinched in the wood. Suddenly he whirled, seeming to sense her behind him.

The rugged face beneath his hat could have been carved from granite, his facial muscles were so rigid. Rivulets of perspiration ran from the hair at his temples.

"Hi," Maggie murmured, halting uncertainly several yards away.

Ross stared at her for a long moment. Then he said, "Hi," and snatched up a hammer and long metal wedge from the ground beside him. Shoving the wedge into the cut, he beat it mercilessly, finally spreading the gap wide enough to retrieve the saw.

All right, Maggie thought, he was angry about Monday—and he had a right to be. With her father watching to see if she would encourage his interest after promising to have nothing to do with him, she simply hadn't known how to handle the situation. And she'd ended up handling it badly.

"I've missed you," she said quietly, when he put the saw aside and sat down on the thick trunk.

"All of me, or only specific parts?"

Maggie stood there, stunned. "How dare you speak to me like that."

"How dare you speak to me at all? You didn't dare all the while your dad was in town. Guess he's gone now, huh?"

Sighing, she crossed the needle-strewn ground and sat beside him. He wasn't going to make this easy. "Dad just left for the airport." She tried to lighten the mood. "Thankfully, he had a rental car and didn't have to depend on mine. Pete at the garage said the most humane thing would be to give it a decent burial and try to get on with my life."

To Maggie's disappointment, Ross didn't smile, didn't comment—just let his gaze drift over her loose hair, blue plaid cotton shirt and jeans.

"How have you been?" she asked, once again attempting to put things right.

Pushing to his feet, he walked several yards to his truck to grab the chambray shirt hanging from the side mirror. Then he wiped it over his sweaty chest and shoulders, balled it up and tossed it into the back of the truck. "Fine. Couldn't be better."

"Ross, please don't be like this. If you're angry because I wouldn't have lunch with you—"

"I'm not angry." He carried the saw over and put it in the bed of the truck, too. Then he opened the cab, grabbed soap, a towel and a pair of gray sweatpants from the seat, and headed for the hot spring. "Anger's a waste of energy."

Maggie cast about in frustration, then finally let her own anger out and charged after him. *"How can you be so damn cold!"*

He kept walking. "How can you be such a liar?"

She kept following. "I never lied to you."

"No? How about when you told me you didn't care what anyone else thought of me? Changed your mind pretty quick when your father showed up."

"I *didn't* change my mind."

"Bet he was scared spitless he might have a jailbird for a son-in-law someday. I hope you reassured him on that score."

Furious, Maggie followed him through the long grass to the familiar break in the chokecherries and cottonwoods. They stepped into the dirt-packed clearing where the old fire ring still awaited the next party and the warm, dammed-up creek bed beckoned. "Ross, will you turn around, please?"

"Why?"

"Just turn around! Stop walking and stop talking and *listen* to me! My father never said a word about your past. He was upset because we'd slept together."

He pivoted, his surprised expression lined and questioning. "You told him?"

"No, he guessed. But I admitted it. He was at the screen door and saw us kissing goodbye on Saturday. He...he's almost fanatical about sex outside of marriage."

After another assessing moment, Ross frowned, hung his hat on a tree branch, and dropped to the log beside the fire ring to tug off his boots.

"That's it?" she asked, dumbfounded. "You're not going to say anything?"

"What is there to say?" He glanced up briefly. "You might want to leave."

"I'm not going anywhere until we have a civil conversation."

"Suit yourself." He pulled off his socks, stuffed them into his boots, then stood and unbuckled his belt.

"Ross, I *wanted* to see you while he was here. I really did."

"That's okay. I was too busy for a pity call anyway."

Maggie shot an irritated glance toward heaven. Why did she even care what this overgrown child thought?

He unsnapped his waistband, pulled down his zipper and shucked off his jeans. When he was standing there in nothing but a pair of navy briefs, he sent her a direct look. "Are you leaving?"

"No."

"Fine. Nothing you haven't seen before anyway." Grabbing his soap and towel, he turned away from her, walked to the creek bed, and finished stripping.

Maggie strode after him. "He told me he'd leave if I didn't stay away from you while he was here. Ross, you have to understand—he's a clergyman."

"And a manipulator," he added. Stepping from the bank into mid-thigh-deep water, he immersed himself in the warm eddy. Beyond the dammed-up "hot tub," the shallow, rocky creek babbled its way downstream.

Maggie sank cross-legged to the grassy bank beside the water. Sunlight shone down through the break in the trees as she watched him lather his chest and shoulders. "I don't think he wanted to be manipulative," she said quietly.

"Maybe not. But you're his sweet little girl and I'm the despoiler of virgins. Just ask anybody."

"I'll say it again," she replied evenly. "This isn't about your reputation, it's about mine."

"Which will be ruined if you continue to see me."

"I'm seeing you right now, aren't I?"

Ross laughed and soaped his underarms. "By God, you are. Right out here in front of the squirrels and the blue jays and the occasional wren. Everybody knows what blabbermouths they are."

Maggie felt the swift sting of tears in her eyes. "Okay," she murmured, "that's it for me. I don't need this." She started to get up. His hand was on her wrist in a heartbeat, his expression instantly remorseful.

"Maggie, don't go."

She pulled her hand away. "Why not?"

"Because—" Then all the fight was out of him. "Because I'm the biggest jerk who ever lived, and...I've missed you, too." When she remained frozen in place, he said quietly, "I really am sorry. You were caught in the middle, and I should have realized it." He laid the soap on the bank. "What did you tell him about our being together?"

Relaxing her tense muscles, Maggie sank back down on the scrub grass. She had told her father that she loved Ross Dalton, but she couldn't share those words with Ross until he first said them to her. If he ever said them. "I tried to make him understand that we respect each other, and I told him I felt no guilt for making love with you. But in his heart, he believes it was wrong—so I did what he asked." She met his sober eyes. "I'm sorry I hurt you. It was just easier to hope you would understand than to keep arguing with a man who preaches morality for a living. He...he would have left."

Maggie watched his lips thin grimly, then he spoke. "You did the right thing. As I told you before, family's important. It wouldn't have been right to say goodbye with bad feelings between the two of you." Several long moments passed while their fingers touched and twined and neither said a word. Finally he murmured, "So what now?"

Maggie knew another long moment of uncertainty, then she responded. "You could ask me to wash your back."

Ross's smile came back slowly. "I asked you to do that the last time we were here and you refused."

But the last time, she hadn't been in love with him. Maggie pulled off her boots and socks, then stood, rid herself of her shirt, jeans and underwear, and stepped into the warm water.

Sighing, Ross pulled her into his arms, water sloshing as Maggie's legs came around him and their mouths claimed each other repeatedly—gratitude and anxiety lacing their kisses because the quarrel was over. Finally they stopped to breathe and cling to each other, male to female, hearts beating fast with the quick arousal that three days of abstinence and their very vulnerable location generated. It was still light.

They were almost eye to eye, with Maggie seated on his lap. She lowered her head to kiss his throat and collarbone, and his water-slick skin tasted faintly soapy. "Make love to me," she whispered, moving her mouth up to his ear, nudging his thick, sandy hair aside to find that sensitive spot behind it.

Beneath the warm water, Ross's hands were reacquainting themselves with the span of her hips, sliding up to her waist and rib cage. "Not here," he murmured back.

"Are you expecting someone?" she teased.

"No, but my wallet's back at the house and our protection's in it."

She kissed his jaw, inhaled the citrusy smell of his soap, pressed against his arousal. "We'll be okay. It's a safe time."

"Uh-uh." Easing her away from him, he met her eyes. To her surprise, he smiled, his crooked grin a mixture of humor and longing. "What do you call a man and woman who use the rhythm method of birth control?"

Maggie laughed. "Jokes? Now?"

"Come on, what do you call them?"

"I have no idea," she said through another laugh, loving him so very much. "What?"

"Parents," he sighed.

Ross reached for the soap still lying on the bank. "For now, let's just enjoy the water." His eyes twinkled. "Turn around."

Soap was the most luxurious thing, Maggie thought, lying back against his chest as he lathered her with his wonderful hands and kept every sensation simmering just below flashpoint. He didn't miss a curve or swell; he soaped and rinsed every finger and toe. Eventually, he turned her to face him again and kissed her so deeply that they shuddered, making them both pause to reevaluate the need for protection. Then at Maggie's insistence, Ross gave up the soap and let her hands rove where they would. Minutes later, only the fiercest of determination kept them apart.

"Okay, that's it," he said through a throaty chuckle, as they broke from another kiss. Snatching the soap away from her, he hurled it far into the surrounding woods. "We're going back to the house. The blood's pounding so hard in my temples that if we don't do something pretty soon, I'm going to have a stroke."

Laughing, they splashed out of the water and onto the bank, shared his dry towel, then pulled on sweats, jeans and shirts—foregoing underwear—to half run, half stumble in each other's arms back to the house. They made for the loft.

The setting sun streamed through the window upstairs, turning the natural logs a warm, rosy shade. There was no bed, but Ross's oversize sleeping bag and pillow lay on the floor. Stripping quickly, they dove into it. Maggie welcomed his mouth, his kiss, his tongue as they burrowed deep and twined in each other's arms. They met in the soft folds of the sleeping bag, found a tempo that almost immediately started shudders of pleasure rippling through them. Kissing and tonguing, they climbed that great hill, lungs aching for air, minds floating aloft. Then there was nothing to do but hold tightly to each other while muscles contracted, colors flashed behind their closed eyelids, and they burst, gasping, into radiance.

It was a full minute before either of them spoke. Then Ross made a low sound deep in his throat. "I can't move."

Threading her fingers through his hair, Maggie held him close. "Good," she whispered. "I don't want you to. I think we should stay right here until tomorrow. Maybe the next day."

"That'd be great, except..."

"Except what?"

Rolling onto his back, he slid an arm under her neck,

then gathered her close and kissed her forehead. "Except Lila'd eventually get around to missing her horse and come looking for you." He paused, sighed. "And much as I hate to mention this...it's getting late. I don't want you riding home in the dark."

"You worry too much. I won't cut through the field, I'll take the road."

"I still don't want you traveling in the dark."

"Okay," she finally grumbled. "I'll leave now. Thank heaven for Aunt Lila or I wouldn't have any transportation at all. I have to find some time to buy a new car."

She tried to get up, but he pulled her back down.

Grinning, she tussled in his arms. "Hey—didn't you just remind me that I have to get that horse back home?"

"Yep," he said, returning her grin. Warm breath spilled over her skin as he rolled on top of her again and nuzzled her collarbone. "But it just occurred to me that I could follow you home in my truck. Headlights should brighten up the trip."

Maggie laughed softly, craning her neck to give him more throat to kiss. "My, my, you're just full of good ideas, aren't you, mister?"

"I try."

Goose bumps prickled her skin as Ross's lips inched lower. "I think you do a lot better than 'try,'" she said in a shivery whisper.

Chapter 12

The ride back to the Lazy J was strange for Maggie—not exactly lonely, but a little wistful. At Ross's insistence, he led the way on Lila's mare with Maggie following in his truck. Headlights illuminated his strong back and shoulders, the shadowy outline of his hat. After the warmth they'd shared, it felt wrong to be so close without touching him.

When the horse was stabled, they walked slowly up the dark driveway, passing shadowy outbuildings on their way to the Jacksons' front porch. Overhead, stars twinkled and the moon moved inexorably toward fullness, growing rounder and brighter as the month wore on. A warm breeze rustled the big cottonwoods beside the house, and crickets chirruped in the July darkness.

"I don't know how much time we'll be able to spend together this week," Ross said, keeping his tone low. He laced his fingers loosely through hers. "We're doing the first cutting of hay, and that could take a couple of days.

Then I have to find some time to go out to Roy Lang's and loosen up for Saturday.''

Maggie glanced up at him. "Lang's? Saturday?"

"Roy raises rodeo bulls. He lets me practice on a few of them."

"Oh, that's right. Founder's Day and the rodeo finals are this weekend. When we had lunch at Ruby's yesterday, Trent mentioned—'' Maggie stopped speaking, sorry she'd brought up his name.

"Trent mentioned what?" Ross growled.

"Never mind, it wasn't important."

"Come on, what did he say?"

"He asked if I'd be there for the bull riding. Then I think he read my dad's expression and knew he disapproved of rodeo in general, so he changed the subject."

"Typical politician."

"Actually, I'm sure he was just being considerate. If you had been sitting there and knew the topic bothered my father, you would have changed the subject, too."

"Maybe. But I wasn't sitting there, was I?"

"No," she said, hiding the jealous twinge that she still felt whenever she thought about it. "You were at the lunch counter bumping knees with the redhead from the insurance agency."

Ross was silent for a moment, then he simply said, "Brenda's a friend."

How well she knew. That was another thing Trent had mentioned—twice. Once yesterday, and before that on the day of the church roofing.

Let it alone, that tiny voice in her mind warned. *He's not with her tonight, he's with you. Don't let it spoil the evening you've had.*

They had arrived at the porch steps. Linking his hands at the base of her spine, Ross brought their lower bodies snugly against each other. The familiar contact did much to drive thoughts of Brenda Larson from Maggie's mind.

But it didn't erase the image of Ross being jerked around mercilessly by a bull at the last rodeo she'd attended.

"Can I ask you something?"

"Sure."

"Why bull riding? Why such a dangerous event? You could be badly hurt. Or worse."

"There are safeguards. Everyone wears a vest—like the flak jackets football players wear to protect their ribs. And the clowns make sure the bulls are distracted if a rider's on the ground and in trouble."

"That's not what I asked."

"I know." He paused, moonlight skimming his strong cheekbones, defining his angular jaw. "When I quit gambling, I needed something—" he smiled "—I was going to say 'safer' to get my blood up, but that's probably the wrong word, and I can't think of a better one. There's nothing like trying to stay on a sixteen-hundred-pound bull for eight seconds to remind you that you're alive."

"For the moment," Maggie added soberly.

"Now who's the worrier? Anyway, when it looked like I might be decent at it, I thought about joining the professional bull-riding circuit. You know, ride for the big money. Kansas City, Albuquerque, Las Vegas..."

A sudden fear gripped her heart. Would he leave eventually? Go on the road? "Do you still think about that?"

"Nah. Local events are enough, and I couldn't compete at the pro level anyway." He smiled, his gaze stroking her face. "Besides, I think I might have found something else that gets my blood up."

Maggie felt the strength in his hands as he drew her closer, felt the familiar stirring within her as their warm bodies molded to each other and her arms slid around him. It wasn't the "I love you" she would have liked to hear, but the admission that she had *some* effect on him was reassuring. "You'll ride on Saturday anyway, won't you?" she murmured against his shirt.

"Of course. Trent's expecting me."

Yes, Trent was expecting him. Expecting to beat him handily, in fact. Briefly, Maggie wondered how good Ross would be if he put as much time into it as Trent did. The man in her arms was a natural athlete, blessed with balance, grace and stamina; he seemed to excel at every physical activity he tried.

Ross kissed her hair. "You'd better go in. Moe's probably looking for his shotgun about now."

Maggie laughed softly. "I'm not worried. His feelings about you have changed since we came back from Clearcut."

"I hope so. I don't want to do anything to foul up our friendship again. I've made enough mistakes."

Maggie considered his last statement and realized how much his past still haunted him. "That's why you wouldn't make love to me without protection, isn't it?"

"Neither of us needs the stress of waiting and wondering after our heads clear. I'll leave the baby-making to Jess."

"No babies for you?"

"Nope."

Something squeezed her heart, and Maggie leaned back to meet his eyes. "Not ever? But…you're so wonderful with Lexi."

"Not ever," Ross answered quietly. "I'm not father *or* husband material, Maggie. If you *want* something more, I'm not the guy you should be standing here with."

He was wrong. He *had* to be wrong. When Todd had finally admitted that their relationship couldn't go any further, she'd been disappointed, but she'd accepted it, knowing it was the truth. Family had never been important to Todd.

But Ross—Ross *was* capable of the deep feelings commitment demanded. And not many men had his remarkable rapport with children.

"What are you so afraid of?" Maggie whispered.

His cheeky grin was back in the blink of an eye. "Me? Tamer of sixteen-hundred-pound bulls? Not a thing."

"I don't believe you."

He chuckled. "Okay. I'm afraid of Elvis impersonators and forgetting the words to Alan Jackson's new song—no relation to your Uncle Moe."

"Ross, stop it."

That reckless smile faded by slow degrees while his expression sobered and his eyes held hers. Then his voice dropped to a low, solemn pitch. "All right," he murmured, "I'm afraid of you." He drew a ragged breath, then let it out slowly. "Lady, sometimes you scare me to death."

Chills ran the length of her and Maggie nodded, understanding that kind of fear. "You'll get over it," she whispered. "I did."

But would he? she wondered in the next instant. What if his apprehension over their growing closeness didn't fade?

Needing to show him that he had nothing to fear from her, Maggie touched his jaw and kissed him tenderly, without the crazy tongue thrusts and grinding body contact they'd lavished on each other earlier.

But the kiss became so wholly giving that Ross's anxiety seemed to increase, and Maggie knew she'd made things worse.

Breaking away, he took a few backward steps. "I have to go."

"Will I see you tomorrow?" she asked uncertainly.

Ross stared, not knowing what to say. His heart was a freight train clattering down a fractured track and on its way to derailment. What was he thinking? All he had to do was look in her eyes to know that this woman wanted a long-term relationship. And he could never give her one.

"I don't know. Maybe. Like I said, we're cutting hay, so it'll be later—if I can even get away."

Though he knew that she tried to hide it, Ross saw a flicker of hurt before she grinned, nodded and climbed the stairs. She stopped short of the door to speak again.

"Hey."

"What?"

"I had a wonderful time tonight."

"Me, too," he said. And that was the problem.

Ross watched her go inside, then made for the stables where his truck was parked. He shouldn't have let tonight happen. He should have let her walk away from the hot spring hurt and angry, because now she had... expectations.

He had to end this. That was all there was to it. Something told him that she hadn't been convinced when he'd said marriage and kids weren't for him. And it wasn't fair to let her go on thinking that something permanent could happen between them—when it couldn't.

Ross climbed into his truck, but instead of starting it, he turned the key and coasted it fifty yards down the sloping driveway. Then, when he knew the roar of the motor wouldn't disturb the Jacksons, he popped the clutch, opened it up full throttle, and flew for home. While the mind-bending fragrance of Maggie's perfume tried its damnedest to coax him right back into her arms.

Ross couldn't keep his vow to end things. Less than twenty-four hours later, dog-tired from the sunup to sundown haying—and damning his own weakness—he picked up the phone in the den at the homestead and punched in the number for the Lazy J. She answered on the first ring, sounding anxious, expectant.

"Hi," he said. "It's me."

"Hi." Her voice turned warm and rich, and against

Ross's will, it curled into his ear and slid straight to his heart. "Did you finish the cutting?"

"No, we still have another field to go, then the baling in a day or two when it dries. I just... Well, I had a minute before I climbed in the shower, and thought I'd call to see how your day went."

"Actually, it was a little strange. But we can talk about that another time." She paused. "Can't we?"

"Friday?" he asked, startling himself, then wincing because he'd sounded so eager. Why was it so hard to stay away from her? What kind of hold did this woman have over him? "My water's hooked up at the house now, and some of my furniture's coming tomorrow. If you want, you could meet me there Friday after supper, and see how things are shaping up."

"I'd like that. What time's good for you?"

"Any time after—"

Jess wandered into the den, grinned knowingly, then walked back out again. Scowling, Ross turned away from the doorway, curving himself around the receiver for some privacy. "I need to go over to Lang's for a while, but I plan on being back by eight. Is that okay?"

"Eight's fine," she said, a touch of relief in her voice. "I'll see you at the house."

"Great. See you then."

Ross hung up, raining insults all over himself, and at the same time feeling his exhaustion slip away. Friday. He'd see her Friday. Two more days.

On Friday night, he'd just finished showering away the smell from Roy Lang's butt-bruising bulls when he heard Maggie pull into the driveway. She was a good fifteen minutes early. Ross dove into his jeans, grabbed a clean shirt, and started down the varnished wood stairs, tucking and buttoning on his way. Then he walked barefooted onto the porch where the splashy pinks and purples of sunset streaked the sky and cast a glow on his pine logs...and the exciting woman coming up the steps.

"Hi," he said, catching her fingers loosely in his.

"Hi."

She wasn't dressed any differently from a hundred other women in the county—jeans and a white cotton tank top. But there was something gut-clenchingly sexy in the way Maggie's clothing fit. His eyes took in her firm breasts and narrow rib cage...her tiny waist...the trim curve of her hips. Fragrant hair tumbled black and silky over her shoulders, and long, feathery bangs skimmed her brows and played up her brown eyes. Above toned arms and lightly tanned skin, a hint of sunburn touched her nose. To Ross's conflicting pleasure and chagrin, he was instantly aroused. He read the same eagerness in her eyes.

"Okay," Maggie murmured, "let's see the furniture."

Since the only pieces to evaluate in the great room were his brown leather sofa, two sturdy end tables and a pair of heavy hurricane lamps, they weren't downstairs for more than five minutes.

The furniture showing in the loft, with its massive, hand-crafted, log-and-twig bed lasted until the sun was gone and the steady songs of the peeper frogs shrilled from deep in the cottonwoods.

Eventually, their uneven breathing and gentle sighs ceased, sheets stopped rustling, and low conversation began again. Ross clicked the rustic lamp beside the bed onto its lowest setting. He spoke groggily as they snuggled in each other's arms. "So what was the strange thing that happened on Wednesday at the office? You said you'd tell me about it."

She liked to hear his voice like that: kind of husky, faintly sleepy—a boneless baritone that made her smile. "Ben Campion came in, and he and Cy got into another argument about the re-election rally. Ben backed down to Farrell again."

"What rally? And why would Ben back down to Farrell? Cy's only in the sheriff's office because he has Campion's support."

Maggie frowned, her fingers stroking his chest distractedly as she lay against his shoulder. "I'm not sure why. But about the rally? A couple of weeks ago, I overheard Ben and Cy arguing in Cy's office. Cy was trying to sell Ben on the idea of a political fund-raiser, and wanted Ben to foot the bill. When Ben refused to pay for it, Cy ended up saying that if there was no rally, Trent wouldn't be going to the legislature. What do you make of that?"

"Blackmail."

"I think so, too. When Ben came out of the office, he was still furious, but he said something to Cy like, 'Send me the figures, and I'll take another look at them.' A second later, he looked really startled to see me at my desk. That's when he…" Maggie's voice trailed away as the filmstrip in her mind played back a part of the incident that hadn't really registered before.

"You know," she said thoughtfully, "it didn't occur to me that day, but Ben was crushing a report or something in his hand when he came out of Cy's office. And it couldn't have been the figures for the rally because he asked Cy to send him another copy. The moment he realized I was watching, he folded the papers and shoved them into the pocket of his trousers. Which makes me wonder…"

"Wonder what?"

Maggie scrambled to a sitting position to look down at him. The sheet slid to her waist. "I wonder if those papers could have been the reason he reconsidered Cy's demands? If Cy was blackmailing him—and Ben was resisting—Cy might have shown Ben something to pull him back in line again. Well, not *the* something, but maybe a copy of something—"

"Or," Ross countered, pleasantly distracted as he eased

up on an elbow to nuzzle her softness, "Ben could have had the papers with him when he arrived, and they could've had absolutely nothing to do with the argument."

"True," Maggie allowed, trying hard to concentrate as his warm mouth and talented lips continued their slow exploration of her breasts. "But there was something almost—Ross, stop that, I'm trying to think—almost paranoid about the way he tucked the papers away. As though he didn't want me to know—" his wet mouth fastened on a nipple and he sucked gently, as Maggie drew a soft breath "—what they were."

Closing her eyes, she slid her fingers through his tousled hair and brought him closer, that airy fluttering low in her belly again. My, my…what this man did to her.

"Thought you wanted to think," he teased huskily a few moments later.

Maggie slid down onto the bed again, snuggling close and lacing her legs through his. "I think I'll think later," she smiled, and parted her lips for his kiss.

The fairgrounds were festively decorated with banners and the carnival atmosphere was enhanced by blaring country music, and the wafting aromas of hamburgers, French fries, and cotton candy. There were a few craft displays and leather outfitters selling tack, but most of the craft booths were set up on Frontier Street where the faux kerosene lamps and restored buildings gave more meaning to Founder's Day. Later, covered wagons and buckboards full of "early settlers" and "trappers" would parade down Prairie Street to pioneer tunes by area high school bands. But not here.

This was rodeo.

The barrel racing and calf roping had finished up around noon, and—according to the program Maggie read—after a short intermission, the bronc and bull riding would begin. She climbed the steel risers of the grandstand, feeling the anticipation clear down to her toes. The $1,000 purse would hardly pay off Ross's mortgage, but since he still needed furniture, it would certainly come in handy.

Just as she chose a row and took a seat near the middle, someone called her name over the music and the chatter of converging spectators. She looked around, caught Bessie Holsopple's eye, and waved. But the voice she'd heard had been male. She saw Cy Farrell deep in conversation with Ben Campion...kept her eyes moving...

"Maggie! Down here!"

Maggie glanced down to see Trent wave as he picked his way through the crowd to join her. She waved back. When he was a little closer, she called, "Hi. Nice day."

"Yes, it is." Slickly handsome as ever, he wore a red, white and blue plaid shirt again with his jeans and boots. Maggie decided that she'd been right about his choice of colors at the Fourth of July celebration almost two weeks ago. Trent's—or his father's—political goals were never very far from his mind. Which made her think again of Cy Farrell's threat to keep Trent out of the legislature. Something else flashed briefly through her mind, too—a conversation she'd overheard the last time she'd seen Trent at a rodeo. It was gone before she was able to pin down its significance.

"You're early," he said with a pleased smile as he dropped down beside her. "I don't ride for another hour or so."

Maggie fought a disbelieving smile. No ego there. "I know, but I thought as long as I paid my five dollars to park, I'd take in everything. Did you draw a good bull?"

"Hope so," he chuckled, sliding closer. "It's hard to win on a bad one."

The heavy smell of his aftershave stung Maggie's nostrils, and she eased back a bit.

"Do you know how the judges score the rides?"

"Actually, no," she admitted, trying to pay attention to

Trent and—at the same time—scan the arena for Ross. He was supposed to meet her right before the bronc riding, but so far she hadn't seen him.

"No?" Trent grinned, obviously volunteering for the task. "Then someone should definitely tell you."

A deep, calm voice came from directly behind them. "Someone plans to."

Maggie and Trent both turned as Ross stepped down two rows to sit on a seat above them. Delighted, Maggie's eyes met his, and her heart swelled at the warm glow of connection between them.

His black vest hung open over his green-plaid shirt and faded jeans, and his hat rode low on collar-grazing sandy hair, framing his rugged face to perfection. Two days of haying had deepened his tan, making his eyes seem bluer.

Breaking into the moment, the announcer's voice echoed through the arena, and Maggie suddenly remembered that they weren't alone. She turned back to Trent. "Well, looks like the bronc riding's about to begin. You're welcome to stay and watch with us if you like."

Trent's cold green eyes shifted between Maggie and Ross. "Us? No thanks, I have things to do." His icy gaze fixed on Ross. "I hear you drew Cowboy's Lament."

"And you've got Stampede. He's a good bull."

"No," Trent said coldly. "He's the best."

"We'll see." Ross stood then, and Trent was forced to give up his seat.

With a brusque nod to Maggie, Trent shuffled past the other people in the row and stiffly descended the grandstand. His departure left her faintly unsettled. She'd never intended to hurt Trent or make him angry, but he had to understand that friendship was all she would ever be able to give him. She loved Ross, body and soul.

Then Ross settled in beside her, and Maggie's mind was filled only with him.

* * *

The bronc riding was nervewracking for Maggie, even though no one she knew was participating. The jarring, bucking, back-snapping horses made her glad Ross wasn't riding in that event, too. That faint joy didn't last. Too soon, he was leaving, and she was listening to the folksy drawl of the announcer in the booth introducing the bull-riding competition. Contestants would ride twice, and the five cowboys with the top combined scores would compete in the finals.

The first bull and rider out of the chute didn't make the eight-second horn. The second made it and received a fair score. At least it was a fair score according to Jess, Casey and Ruby, who'd left Lexi with a sitter and arrived late to squeeze in beside Maggie.

Then Ross was up. Maggie's heart pounded until the horn sounded, he landed safely in the dust, and painted rodeo clowns waved the quivering black bull away from him. After the first round, Ross and Trent were the clear-cut leaders, with Ross edging out Trent by two points.

Nothing changed in the second round, except the bulls: they got bigger and meaner. Ross turned in another magnificent ride. Trent matched it, but still remained in second place.

By the time the finals began, Maggie's muscles ached from clenching them, and adrenaline was threatening to burn her up. She looked nervously to the far side of the arena. The ripe smells of sunbaked dust and rank animals rode the still afternoon air.

Pulling on his glove, Ross took his place on the metal rails above the chute as an enormous yellow bull was herded, stamping and blowing, into it. Maggie cringed as it banged off the sides of the chute and attendants tried to settle it down long enough to get Ross aboard. "Dear God," she breathed.

"Relax," Jess said, obviously trying to hide the tension in his own voice. "He's ridden Brimstone before, and he knows his twists and turns—this bull always spins left, never right. He'll be okay.''

''Will he?'' she asked. But she couldn't tear her eyes away as Ross cleared the rails and dropped down onto the bull's broad back.

Suddenly the gate opened, and Brimstone exploded from the chute like fireworks on the Fourth of July. The roar of the crowd and the reaction from the announcers in the booth told Maggie instantly that something was wrong.

Jess shot to his feet, yelling over the din. *''What jackass opened that gate? He didn't have his rope hand set!''*

Maggie watched in horror as the bull heaved his backside high and snapped Ross back against its spine, then wheeled to the left and spun wildly, trying to toss its rider. Ross clung to the rope, hugged the animal with his thighs, and jerked his raised hand for counterbalance and style as he was snapped forward and backward like a pretzel stick riding a paint shaker.

The announcer's voice blared from the speakers. ''What a ride for not bein' ready! And would you look at the size of that animal! That big guy ain't missed many meals. Take him to the horn, Ross!''

A split second later, a scream froze in Maggie's throat as the bull spun viciously to the right. With a powerful lunge and whiplash thrust of its great head, the bull threw Ross into the air and sent him crashing against the metal gate.

Chapter 13

"Ross? Ross!"

Maggie pushed through the knot of men clogging the doorway to the fairground office beneath the grandstand. It had taken her several minutes to reach the sparsely furnished room where they'd taken him, and her heart had been in her throat the whole way. Behind her, Jess kept assuring her that Ross was just shaken up, but his reassurances sounded hollow. She could tell that he was worried, too.

Her concern deepened when she saw Ross seated on a green vinyl sofa. His hair was mussed and hanging over his forehead, his forearms resting on his spread thighs, as George Hellstrom, Comfort's aging general practitioner, checked his eyes with a penlight.

Looking irritated, Trent stepped in front of her and blocked her way. "Maggie, stay back and let Doc Hellstrom check him out."

Maggie jerked away from him. *"Trent, if you don't get out of my way right now—"*

"All I'm asking is that you give him some space."

"Better let her by, Trent," the elderly doctor chuckled as he finished his examination. "Sounds like she means business, and this couch is a bit small for two patients."

Maggie hurried to crouch beside the sofa and slip her hand into Ross's. The look he sent her was a mixture of discomfort, frustration and anger.

"Are you okay?" she asked quietly.

When a scowl was the only reply she got, Maggie glanced nervously at the white-haired man who'd brought her into the world. "Doc?"

"No need to fret, Maggie. Flying seems to suit him— though he might want to work on his landing some before he tries it again."

"But he hit the gate so hard."

Doc nodded. "His pupils are a tad sluggish, but they're equal and responsive, so I suspect he's got himself a slight concussion." Doc's expression sobered as he turned back to Ross. "Sure you won't change your mind about the X ray? A quick trip to the hospital wouldn't hurt."

"I'm fine."

"Ross," Maggie interjected, "if the doctor thinks you should—"

"*I'm fine,*" he repeated.

Doc Hellstrom's shrug indicated it was Ross's choice. "You'll have a headache for a while, I expect." He reached into his bag and took out several sample packets of pain relievers, then tucked them inside Ross's shirt pocket. "You can take a couple of these if you need them."

Hellstrom's diagnosis filtered through the vigilant crowd, and murmurs of relief mingled with the arena sounds carrying into the room. As the crowd broke up, several cowboys called words of encouragement. Maggie was buoyed by their support. Ever since the church roofing, she'd sensed a subtle shift in the way the townspeople viewed Ross. More and more often, a smile was offered instead of a wary look, a handshake instead of a cold shoulder.

Suddenly a timid, unfamiliar tenor voice broke Maggie's thoughts.

"I'm sure glad you're gonna be okay."

Ross's expression hardened, and his blue eyes speared the short, skinny man standing just outside the door. Clutching a beat-up brown cowboy hat, the visitor took a hesitant step inside.

Puzzled by Ross's reaction, Maggie turned to Jess—and was surprised all over again. Jess's expression, too, damned the man—a blonde in his late thirties who reeked of whiskey and obviously hadn't shaved for days. "You the one who opened the gate, Dooley?"

The man nodded miserably. "Lord as my witness, Jess, I heard him say 'go' just like he always does."

Ross bolted to his feet, then sank to the couch again, sucking air. "Dooley, you're a slimy little liar. I didn't say *anything*. I was too busy trying to firm up my rope hand."

"But I was sure I heard—"

Jess grabbed the man by his stained shirt and yanked him up on his boot tips. "You heard something all right— the sound of money crackling."

"No! No, it was an accident, I swear!"

Doc Hellstrom broke in quietly. "This is neither the time nor the place, Jess. I have a concussed patient, here."

Jess froze, then nodded and released the panicky cowboy. "Get the hell out of here," he muttered. "And I don't want to see you anywhere near those chutes again when you've been drinking."

As Dooley made his getaway, Hellstrom sighed, stood and tucked his stethoscope and penlight in his bag. He met Ross's agitated look. "You'd better stick around here a while till your head clears, son. And if you start having a problem with nausea, blurred vision or memory lapses, you get your keister over to the hospital. You got that?''

When Ross didn't answer, Maggie did so for him. ''He'll go. I'll see to it.''

''Good. He's your patient now, Maggie. Keep him quiet for a while.'' Hellstrom paused in the doorway to caution them. ''Don't forget to lock up when you leave. The association will have my hide if this door's left open.''

When the doctor had gone, Jess wandered over to Ross and smiled wryly. ''Nice ride, considering.''

''Didn't make the horn, though, did I?''

Jess shook his head. ''Sorry.'' After a moment, he spoke again. ''Dooley said it was an accident.''

''Right. And the Pope plays tight end for the Dallas Cowboys. We both know Dooley's a coward and a drunk who always has his hand out. I didn't say I was ready, and he didn't open that gate early without some incentive.''

Jess nodded. ''Okay, I'll ask around. Maybe somebody saw something. In the meantime, I'd better let Casey and Aunt Ruby know you're all right.''

''Thanks. And thanks for coming in to check on me.''

When Jess had gone, too, Maggie sat beside Ross on the sofa. Dust from the arena clung to his clothes and streaked his face; on the desktop, his tan Stetson was just as gritty.

''Are you really okay?'' she asked quietly.

''Oh, yeah, I'm just dandy. A thousand bucks just slipped through my fingers and landed in Trent Campion's wallet. I couldn't be happier.''

She didn't know what to say. ''Can I do anything for you? Get you something to drink?''

''No, just leave me alone for a while.''

''I don't think that's a good idea.''

''I do. Go back to the rodeo and watch the heir apparent's golden moment. He's got it sewn up now, and he'll want a big audience for his victory ride.''

Was it sour grapes that she was hearing? Maggie wondered as she studied the cold expression on his face. Or was it something else? "You think Trent had something to do with this, don't you?"

Ross pushed to his feet, winced, then steadied himself briefly with a hand on the desk. "Even if Cy won't let you wear the badge, you're still a trained deputy. Know anyone else with more to gain?"

"That doesn't make any sense. Why would he pay Dooley to sabotage your ride? The Campions have millions. He hardly needs the money."

"It's not the money," Ross snapped angrily. "It's the publicity. I told you before, Ben and Trent have been manufacturing this—this *image*—since Trent went away to college. Winning rodeos, lobbying for environmental issues, showing up at church roofings—those things say 'all-American boy' to the voters, and make them positively giddy to get to the polls."

"But paying someone to give him the edge in a local rodeo is just so extreme. Are you sure you're not—" she backed off "—Never mind."

Ross's eyes darkened like thunderheads. "Imagining things? Ticked off because I lost? Is that what you were going to say? If you were, you're dead wrong. Maggie, I can handle losing fair and square. It just takes me a little longer to mellow out when I know I've been screwed over. Now go find Jess and Casey. I'll see you in the stands later."

She shook her head. "I'm not leaving you alone."

"All right," he said, grabbing his hat and storming out the door, "then I'll leave."

She started after him, and he turned at the door. *"Dammit, Maggie, I'm going to the men's room. If you don't mind, I'd prefer to do it alone."*

"Ross, there's a rest room in here. Use that."

His only response was another glare. Sighing, Maggie

gave up and watched him go, hoping he wouldn't start something with Dooley, or Trent, or anyone else. If he did, concussion or no concussion, Cy would be only too happy to show him the inside of a jail cell again. Heaven knew, he didn't need that. Not when people around here were finally changing their opinion of him.

Maggie turned the lock in the door, shut it tightly, then tried the knob to make sure that it was secure. Then she returned to the stands to find Jess and Casey, cursing herself for not being a more attentive caretaker.

One of Doc Hellstrom's last directives to her had been to keep Ross quiet for a while. She'd certainly done a bang-up job of it.

By the time Ross joined them twenty minutes later on the sidelines, they were all on edge. But no one asked where he'd been or what he'd been doing. Actually, Maggie thought, he probably should have just stayed away altogether. He'd shown up just in time for the awards ceremony.

The announcer's voice reverberated through the hot afternoon, naming the winners of the various events and asking the packed crowd for a show of support. Trent walked humbly to the center of the arena to stand beside the other winning contestants, while attendees applauded and the shutters on a dozen cameras clicked away. Worse, as president of the Fairgrounds Association, Ben Campion made a grand show of presenting his only son with the winner's check.

When it was Trent's turn at the microphone, he thanked everyone for their support and their kind applause—then announced that he was donating the purse, along with a matching sum, to the local 4-H Club.

The voters went wild.

Ross released a disgusted breath as Harry Atkins from the *Prairie Voice* took more photos, and the crowd contin-

ued to applaud. "Sorry, but this is a bit much for me. I'm
outta here."

As his family voiced their understanding, Maggie took
a step closer to Ross. Earlier, Jess and Casey had mentioned getting together at Ruby's after the closing cere-
monies, but Maggie no longer had much of an appetite.
"Want some company?"

His tense look faded finally, and his voice dropped low.
"I'd like that…if I haven't turned you off, blowing up the
way I did."

Turned her off? Not ever. Easing up on tiptoe, Maggie
kissed him softly on the mouth, then smiled at the surprise
in his eyes. How could he think he'd turned her off? She
loved him, and whether or not his suspicions about Trent
were true, *he* fervently believed they were. In Maggie's
mind, that justified his anger.

"Kissing the town hellion?" he asked. "Right out here
in front of God and everybody?"

"Right out here in front of God and everybody," she
repeated. Maggie knew he was thinking of another time
that she'd kissed him, a time when he'd accused her of
waiting until the only breathing creatures around were
birds and squirrels. With a twinge of guilt, she admitted
that he might have been right back then. But no more. Her
love for him grew stronger with each passing day. "Let's
go."

Waving goodbye to Jess, Casey and Ruby, they left the
stands and headed for the cut field where their vehicles
were parked. But just when Maggie thought that they'd be
able to salvage part of the day, they strolled up one of the
grassy parking aisles and came eye to eye with more trouble. A feeling of dread settled over her.

Cy Farrell and Mike Halston were standing beside
Ross's truck.

Maggie sensed Ross starting to boil again beside her,
and she prayed with everything in her that he'd hold his

temper. "Is there a problem, Cy?" she asked when they finally reached the black Dodge.

"Maybe," he answered, removing his mirrored sunglasses. He gestured to the driver's side of the truck. "Mind opening the door for us, Ross?"

"Mind telling me why?"

"Somebody helped themselves to the cash box in the association office."

Ross's expression hardened. "And you're checking everyone's vehicles for it? Or just mine?"

Maggie sent a worried glance toward Mike, and he looked away, clearly uncomfortable with the proceedings.

"Just open it. I'm extending you the courtesy of doin' it yourself, but I can go ahead on my own."

"Without a warrant?"

"Probable cause," Farrell said. "There was no sign of a break-in, and accordin' to Doc Hellstrom, you and my brand-new deputy here were the last people in the office. I trust Maggie. I don't trust you. Now open the door."

Glaring, Ross shoved past Farrell. "This is ridiculous. I wasn't anywhere near the office after Maggie and I left." He yanked the unlocked door wide open. Then Maggie's heart dropped, and Ross went pale beneath his tan. The corner of a gray metal box stuck out from beneath the front seat.

Farrell looked almost as stunned as Ross did. Then he recovered and caught Halston's eye. "Get it out of there."

Halston took a handkerchief from his back pocket and used it to remove the box. He examined it. "Still locked," he said to Farrell.

"Good." Farrell still looked deeply puzzled as he turned back to Ross and began to recite his Miranda rights.

But in the past two months, Maggie had grown to know Cy well, and she saw that Farrell was hesitant to make the arrest. In fact, unless Maggie missed her guess, until Cy spied that cash box, he'd only been playing his usual game of harassing whichever Dalton was handy.

"...have the right to an attorney. If you can't afford an attorney..."

Blood pounded in Maggie's ears. Had anyone seen Ross during the time they'd been apart this afternoon? Could anyone corroborate his whereabouts? Her mind snagged something positive, and she told herself he'd be okay; they wouldn't find his prints on the cash box. Then that small hope died as she recalled that he'd worn a glove during the bull-riding event. The absence of fingerprints on the cash box could easily be explained away.

As Farrell finished advising Ross of his rights, Maggie's thoughts were reeling. Cy had called her his brand-new deputy. That meant he'd made his decision to hire her over Harvey Becker's newly graduated son. What convenient timing.

What very convenient timing.

Taking a deep breath, Maggie backed away from the truck—and in doing so, backed away from Ross. Farrell had made his decision, now she had to make hers. No matter how difficult it would be.

Maggie's eyes met Ross's, and she saw the trapped look that he was trying to hide beneath his anger. "I thought I knew you," she said coldly. "How could you do this?"

The hurt and betrayal in Ross's eyes nearly destroyed her.

Three hours later, Maggie thanked Mike Halston, squared her shoulders and crossed the reception area in the sheriff's office to the cell alcove. Farrell was out having a late supper, and she'd convinced Mike that she just wanted to end things with Ross once and for all.

A feeling of déjà vu struck when she saw him stretched out on the cot, long and lean, still dusty from his fall, much the way she'd encountered him on the first day he'd come grinning back into her life. His booted feet were crossed at the ankles again, and his tan Stetson rode low over his eyes. She knew without a doubt that he knew she was there, but he didn't acknowledge her or look up. He made her speak.

"Ross?"

"Get out."

Maggie moved to the bars, keeping her voice low. "Not before I have a chance to tell you why I said what I did. There was a good reason for it."

"Catchy little tune, but I've heard it before, and I didn't like it all that well the first time."

Yes, he had heard it before, she thought—the day her father had pressured her not to see him anymore. "Ross, please, if you hear me out, I can explain."

"Explain it to someone else. I'm through with you."

Tears welled in Maggie's eyes, and suddenly she was so hurt and so angry...*that she knew exactly how he felt*. If there had been any other way to handle things this afternoon... But there hadn't been.

"Well, I'm not through with you yet," she answered, trying to control the trembling in her voice. "If I hadn't made it look like I was backing away from you, I wouldn't have Cy's trust, and I wouldn't have a job here anymore— a job I need if I'm going to help you."

He exhaled derisively.

"I have a few ideas, but I need access to this office to check them out. I think...I think that if you're right about Trent paying Dooley to open the gate early, Trent could be behind the robbery as well. I'm not sure why. Maybe he's angry about my relationship with you, or maybe he's still holding a grudge over the horse-beating incident. Maybe both. But I think it wasn't enough of a payback to see that you lost the rodeo. He wanted you shamed."

Maggie waited for him to comment—hoped that he'd leap to his feet and agree with her. But when another long moment passed in silence, she sighed in frustration. "Aren't you going to say anything?"

Ross lifted the brim of his hat long enough to pierce her with cold blue eyes. "Yeah. Goodbye."

The tears stung a little more. "Okay," she murmured, "if you're determined not to understand, fine. But you do have to listen. Ross, I...you're important to me. And whether I get your cooperation on this or not, I won't let you pay for a crime you didn't commit."

Mike was at her desk when she came back into the room, his face showing a mixture of sympathy and—curiosity? Rising and walking around the desk, he handed her several tissues; for the first time, Maggie realized that she needed them. She wiped her eyes and forced a grin. "Sorry."

"You okay?"

"No, but I will be." She wanted to tell Mike to see that Ross was permitted to take a shower—to make sure that he got some medication for pain if he needed it. But she couldn't do that without appearing to care for him. "When's the arraignment?"

"Earliest we can get him before a judge is Monday at three."

"Who's representing him?"

"Mark Walker. He was in here ten minutes after Ross phoned Jess."

Thank God for Jess. But Ross would have to remain in custody until Monday. After his innocent plea at the arraignment, he would almost certainly be released on bail, but sitting in a cell tonight and all day Sunday would be incredibly frustrating for him. The knot in Maggie's chest tightened. "I'd better get going. See you."

"You, too. And if you need a shoulder..."

Maggie stared in surprise, and a momentary flush stained Mike's cheeks. "No, not me—although I can't say I haven't thought about it." His expression sobered again, and something inscrutable moved across his eyes. "I was talking about Trent. He and Ben were here earlier. When they left Cy's office, Trent asked how you were holding up. He's interested."

The prospect of touching any part of Trent Campion's anatomy—even a shoulder—made Maggie ill. Because for the past three hours, she'd been trying to tie up all she knew about Ben, Trent and Cy. The strange things she'd seen and heard in the past month and a half were connected; she was sure of it. And she was convinced that clearing up the mystery of Ben's bewildering association with Cy was the key to Ross's freedom.

Any law enforcement official with a brain could see the frame. No criminal—not even a novice—would steal something, put it in his own vehicle with the doors unlocked, then go back inside the rodeo arena to wait for someone to realize that it was missing. So why wasn't Cy looking for another suspect?

"Maggie? Something else bothering you?"

Maggie pulled her thoughts back to the here and now, and shook her head. "No, just tired. It's been a crummy day. See you tomorrow."

Between worrying about Ross, feeling sick about his attitude toward her, and trying to come up with a plan to free him, Maggie slept fitfully that night. There was also the added guilt of staying away from him all day on Sunday. She wasn't scheduled to work, and any interest on her part might be perceived as support. She couldn't take a chance on Farrell or Mike realizing that she still cared for Ross. Although, it was possible that Mike had his suspicions; that might explain those skeptical looks of his.

By the time Monday morning rolled around, Maggie had an elaborate list of queries in her purse that might just persuade Ross that she was on his side. If she could convince him of that, he might be able to help her by filling in some of the blanks in her reasoning. She'd lived elsewhere for the past eleven years, but Ross had never left Comfort. He had memories that could be useful.

When Cy and Mike were both called out of the office just after lunch, Maggie moved quickly to the lockup. Ross didn't react when she entered, and Maggie didn't speak to him. She simply slipped her notes through the bars and left again.

She'd posed several questions, and had included her own views and answers. The first one was, why would Trent want to frame Ross?

Her answer had expanded on the reason she'd mentioned two days earlier: jealousy. For whatever reason, Trent seemed to want her. Maybe a relationship with a minister's daughter was another ingredient in his calculated march to the legislature.

Another question: Why was Ben so eager to hush up the horse-beating incident? Pride? Or his grand plan for Trent?

Eventually, that question had led her to the possibility that Trent had been involved in other wrongdoings, and that Ben had concealed those as well. As for Cy—if the sheriff had covered up crimes in return for payment or favors from Ben, that could be what Cy held over Ben's head. Exposure could mean the death of Trent's political ambitions.

Except that exposing Trent would ruin Cy as well. Falsifying evidence was a serious offense.

The question she'd written at the bottom of her notes was one that had made her heart pound: Had Trent ever left the association office? She'd lost track of him in her concern for Ross. What if he had stayed behind when everyone else left?

Maggie gave Ross several minutes, then walked nervously to the lockup and peeked through the small mesh-and-glass window. To her relief, he was reading. She waited until he'd finished, then stepped inside, leaving the door to the office ajar so that she could monitor the front door. If Cy or Mike returned unexpectedly, she could always say that Ross had called her in to request a visit from his lawyer.

"So, do you have any thoughts?" she asked quietly.

Ross glanced up from his seat on his cot, but his look wasn't friendly. Maggie understood. She'd hurt him twice, and it would take some time to regain his trust.

"You think Trent ducked inside the rest room in the office while everyone was distracted, then took the cash box after you locked up."

Maggie nodded. Ross had thought of the rest room, too. There'd been no other place to hide in such a small room. "There was no sign of forced entry, other than the drawer where the cash box was kept. Whoever took the money either had a key, or was inside when I left."

After a thoughtful pause, Ross spoke grimly with reference to another question on her list. "There was a rumor circulating about Trent a while back, but it died out quickly. If it was true, and Cy covered up the incident, that might make Ben grateful enough to hand over some money, do a few favors."

Maggie's heartbeat picked up speed. "Tell me."

Ross rose from his cot to brace his hips against the small porcelain sink in his cell. He'd showered, shaved and been given clean clothes for his upcoming arraignment; the black jeans and gray, black and white plaid Western shirt looked good on him.

"When Trent was in college, he was a partier—used to get all rummed-up on weekends. No one ever admitted there'd been an accident, but he used to have this flashy red sports car that really tore up the roads. Then one day...he didn't. I remember some bruises on his face and arms that he claimed came from bedding a coed with a boyfriend. But rumor had it that he'd hit another car—and hurt someone pretty badly.''

A drunk driving offense? An injured party? Trying to temper her excitement, Maggie walked to the cell. "Do you remember the month and the year?"

Ross handed Maggie's notes through the bars. "It was in the spring. June, maybe, but I don't know the year."

"Could it have been five years ago? I overheard Ben browbeating Trent at the rodeo preliminaries. He said something about pulling Trent's fanny out of the fire five years ago."

"It's been at least that long. Aunt Ruby'd know if anyone would. But if you're thinking about checking the files, you're wasting your time. Farrell would've either made the accident go away altogether, or turned it into an innocent fender bender."

"But if he did turn it into a fender bender, the victim's name would be in the file. I could contact him. Or her."

He sent her a cynical look. "And this will help me how?"

"If we can prove that Farrell falsified evidence, we can use that as leverage to get you out of here."

"Blackmailing the blackmailers, Maggie?"

After a night without sleep, his caustic remark irritated her. "Do you have a better idea?"

"Hell, yes! I want the bastard who set me up to—"

Maggie spun around as the door suddenly opened and Mike Halston's lanky frame filled the doorway. "Mike, I—I didn't realize you were back. I was just seeing if the prisoner needed—"

"No, you weren't," he said gravely. "I know exactly what you were doing." He paused. "Give me the papers, Maggie."

Chapter 14

Maggie was afraid to breathe. "The papers?"

"Yes. Let me see them."

"Why?"

The deputy sighed. "Because if I'm going to help the two of you, I have to know where you're headed with this."

Maggie exchanged a wary look with Ross. "What do you mean—if you're going to help us?"

Mike walked into the narrow aisle beside the cells, his eyes on Ross. "I know you didn't have anything to do with that theft, and so does Cy. It doesn't make any sense."

Exhaling in relief, Maggie offered up a silent prayer of thanks. "We think Trent was involved. Which I'm sure you'll think makes even less sense."

"Trent?"

"Yes."

It took a moment for the deputy to digest that. Then he

inclined his head toward the office. "We'd better talk out there."

"Wait!" Ross snapped. "I need to hear this. This is my *life* you're talking about."

"I realize that, and I'm sorry," Halston returned. "But Cy's due back in a few minutes, and we can't risk his finding us in the middle of a discussion. Not if what I overheard the two of you saying is true."

Maggie cringed as Ross slapped a palm against the bars, then turned away in frustration and disgust.

"Just so you know," Mike advised Maggie, "if we try to nail Farrell and it backfires, you're the one with the most to lose. I'm leaving anyway. But Cy has friends—not to mention the connections the Campions have. If this goes bad, you'll never work in law enforcement again."

The reminder didn't deter her in the least. "Then I guess we'll have to make sure it doesn't go bad."

When Mike stepped back into the office, Maggie turned to Ross again. She stilled when she met his troubled gaze. "What?"

"Don't do it. Let Farrell alone. Someone must have seen me when I was walking around the fairgrounds cooling off. He won't be able to make the charges stick."

"He's still an immoral man who thinks he can do whatever he wants because he wears a badge. Knowing that, how can I let it go?"

"Maggie, I know how much you want this deputyship."

"Could you let it go, if you were in my place?"

"Yes."

"You're lying," she said quietly. Then she pressed her fingertips to the bars because he was too far away to touch, and left.

By the time Mike and Farrell returned from Ross's arraignment, Maggie's shoulders ached with the tension that she was trying to control. Red-faced, Cy strode past her desk and headed straight into his office, slamming the door behind him. Apparently, something hadn't gone well. Maggie wondered if it had anything to do with Ross.

When Mike approached the desk, she kept her anxious voice low. "How's Ross?"

"Out on bail, and royally ticked off," he murmured with a half glance toward Cy's office. "The last I saw him, he was heading into the café."

Probably to question Ruby about Trent's accident, Maggie guessed, though he probably wouldn't get the answers he needed. She'd already phoned the café, and Ruby's memory of the gossip surrounding the accident was sketchy. "Does Ross have anything to do with Cy's mood?"

"Ross could be part of it, but I think something else is going on, too. I get the feeling that whatever it is, it's coming to a head."

Farrell's angry seclusion worked to their advantage. It gave them time for several quick searches through the old files in the storage room at the rear of the office. There was nothing incriminating under Trent Campion's name, but Maggie hadn't expected there to be. Cy would more likely have misfiled the accident report under a heading that he alone knew, or have hidden it under the victim's name. They took turns checking through the folders and manning the phones—and watching for Farrell to emerge from his office.

Just before four o'clock—shortly after a nameless caller put in an urgent personal call to Cy—Maggie found what they'd been looking for. Heart pounding, she scanned the document, memorized the phone number, and jammed the folder back into the file cabinet.

Trent Campion's victim was Mildred Tenney, and she lived two miles off the Clearcut Road!

Maggie was reaching for the phone when Cy burst out

of his office, headed straight for the hat pegs on the wall, and grabbed his Stetson.

"I have to leave for a while," he said gruffly. "Radio me if anything major happens." He spared Mike a brief glance, but never broke stride on his way to the door. "Can you cover for me if I'm late getting back? If not, call Joe in for a few hours."

"I can stay."

"Good. I should be back by seven—seven-thirty at the latest, but you never know." Then he was out the door and shutting it tightly behind him.

Maggie waited until Cy moved past the window, got into his Jeep and backed out onto the street. Then she grabbed the phone and dialed, bringing Mike up to speed on the accident report while she waited through a half-dozen rings.

"Mrs. Tenney?" she said breathlessly when an elderly voice answered.

"Yes?"

"My name is Maggie Bristol, and I'm with the sheriff's office in Comfort. Would it be all right if I came by this afternoon to speak with you?"

"The sheriff's office?" Tenney repeated, something fearful creeping into her voice. "Have…have I done something wrong?"

"Not at all. I just have a few questions for you regarding an accident you were involved in several years ago. I'd be happy to explain when I get there."

When the woman reluctantly agreed, Maggie said goodbye and hung up. "Mike?"

He understood her unspoken question. "Go ahead. Find out what you can. Just remember, according to the file the accident was nothing: minor damages, no one hurt, no booze. If Mrs. Tenney doesn't tell you anything different, we'll have to let it go."

Maggie grabbed her purse. "I'll let you know what I find out."

Mildred Tenney's home was an aging white clapboard that sat back from the road, with a dozen cats roaming the banisters and lounging on the sagging porch. But it wasn't the number of cats that startled Maggie as she spiked her brake at the foot of the long driveway. It was the cherry-red truck roaring toward her, and the determined-looking cowboy behind the wheel.

Ross skidded to a stop in the loose gravel, then pulled Ruby's truck up beside Maggie to speak through the open window. There was a palpable tension in him, an agitation that matched her own. "Guess we both had the same idea."

"How did you find out it was Mrs. Tenney?"

"Aunt Ruby. She finally remembered hearing that Mrs. Tenney had been hurt a while back, and that right afterward she came into some serious money."

Maggie glanced at the house. "Serious money?"

Ross nodded. "You can't tell from the exterior, but everything beyond the front door is expensive and new. Apparently, she wasn't flaunting the fact that her financial situation had improved, but the gossip got out anyway."

Maggie's heart hammered. "I have to speak to her."

"You can if you want, but she's already told me everything—implicated Trent, Ben, *and* Farrell."

"Oh, Ross, that's wonderful. But she has to come in and make a statement."

Ross handed a sheet of paper through the window. "Good enough for now? She's not up to traveling."

"The accident?"

"I'm afraid so."

Quickly, Maggie scanned the page. It read like a diary. If the woman was nervous, her strong, fluid handwriting gave no indication of it.

"I have no complaints," it began. *"I was treated fairly."*

Maggie's pulse quickened as she read about "a dreadful night, filled with fog and rain," and the car crash that had left Mildred Tenney wheelchair-bound. There were several references to Mrs. Tenney's appreciation for the kindness shown her by the Campions—*and one brief admission that Trent had been driving drunk.*

Maggie glanced up from the page. "What about Farrell?"

Ross's jaw tensed. "It's in there. In a nutshell, Trent called home from his cell phone, Ben relayed the message to Cy, and our illustrious sheriff took it from there. Cy convinced Mrs. Tenney she'd get better treatment in a city, and before she knew it she was in a private hospital up north."

"Cy wasn't concerned for her well-being," Maggie said coldly. "Ben wanted her out of the way so Trent's political ambitions wouldn't be derailed."

"You bet." Ross inched the red truck forward. "Now Farrell and I are going to have a little talk."

Maggie glanced toward the house, then back at Ross, vacillating between interviewing Mrs. Tenney herself and going with him. The storm in his eyes made the decision for her. If he let his temper get the best of him, things could go badly. "I'll follow you."

Mildred Tenney's statement was only a stepping-stone, but it was a big one. Maggie prayed that once they confronted Cy, everything else would fall into place. And Ross would be cleared.

When Cy walked into the sheriff's office at 9:30 that night, Maggie glanced at Ross and knew that it was a struggle for him to control his rage.

Farrell's cool glance touched everyone seated around

the dispatcher's desk: hers, Ross's, Mike Halston's and attorney Mark Walker's.

"Are we havin' a party?" he drawled through a scowl.

Ross tossed the altered accident report that he'd been reading on the desk. "Yes, and it's in your honor."

Returning Ross's stare, Farrell ambled over to pick up the report. He paled for an instant, then recovered and let the document slip through his thick fingers to the desk.

"A little mishap five years ago? That's what this pow-wow is all about?"

"No," Walker said, "it's about falsifying a police report—possibly concealing the truth about Saturday's theft at the fairgrounds."

Cy started a blustery reply, but Walker spoke over him.

"Ross just came from Mildred Tenney's home." He held up Mrs. Tenney's statement. "She said Trent Campion was drinking the night he swerved into her on Clearcut Road. She also said that her accident required a hospital stay and months of physical therapy. There's no mention of any of that in your report, Cy. Why is that?"

Ross stood to prowl the room. "The word cover-up comes to my mind. What springs to yours, Cy?"

Tension was evident in the gray eyes behind Farrell's glasses as he stood there, seeming to evaluate his position. Then, apparently realizing that denial was useless, he sagged into the chair they'd set out for him. Cy wiped a hand over his thick cheeks and chin stubble. "The charges against you are going to be dropped. I've already phoned Brokenstraw and told Jess."

"Not that I mind," Ross said, unimpressed, "but why?"

"Because you didn't take the money."

"That didn't stop you from arresting me."

Farrell bristled defensively. "I *had* to arrest you. The evidence was in your truck! If you'd locked the damn thing, none of this would have—"

Mark Walker broke in. "Look, I don't want to be here all night pulling details out of you, Cy. Why are you dropping the charges?"

Farrell, obviously trying to regain his poise, squared his shoulders. "Ben called me out to his place today. He needed me to do some damage control. Seems Dooley Spence was drinking himself stupid near Ross's truck when Trent shoved the cash box under the front seat. Apparently, Dooley found some courage this afternoon and tried to shake Ben down."

Ross's face turned to stone as he walked to the desk, towering over Cy. "Then why isn't Trent behind bars?"

Looking up at Ross, Farrell moistened his lips and shifted uneasily for a moment. Then he looked away. "He, uh, took off. I don't know where. I expect his daddy does, but Ben's not saying."

Maggie saw Ross's expression, and knew that he, too, was wondering about Farrell's guilty break in eye contact. Was Trent really gone? Or was Farrell still protecting him?

"Look..." Farrell said. "This is a mess, for sure. But I think we can settle things without too much fuss if we just look at the facts."

"What facts are those?" Mark Walker prompted.

The sheriff's voice grew more confident. "Since the fairgrounds association never lost a cent, and Trent *did* donate his part of the prize money to charity—even pledged to match the funds—Ben and I thought it would be best for everyone concerned if we—"

"*Just covered this up, too?*" Ross lunged forward and banged both fists on the desktop. "*No way.* You're resigning, you son of a bitch, and Trent's going to be front page news if I have to buy my own newspaper and print only one issue. I've done some stupid things in my life, but stealing was never one of them. I don't want people thinking I cut a deal or that charges were dropped because of insufficient evidence."

Maggie rose and eased Ross back from the desk. "That's not going to happen."

"No, it's not," Mike Halston agreed. His firm look shifted to Farrell. "Sorry Cy, but I need your badge and gun."

Cy's first reaction was shock. Then his angry eyes bored into Mike's. *"Who gave you the authority to—"*

"You did. You're under arrest. Conspiracy, withholding evidence and impeding a criminal investigation. After I talk to Ben, I expect we'll be adding extortion to the list."

As Cy was advised of his rights and led to a cell— loudly and furiously demanding to make a phone call— Walker spoke to Ross. "Mike and I can take it from here if you and Maggie want to go." He shook Ross's hand. "I'm really sorry you were put through this. I'll be in touch about the particulars, but as far as I'm concerned, the matter's settled. And don't worry—we *will* find Trent."

"Damn right, we'll find Trent," Ross muttered a few minutes later as his long strides took him out of the office and into the warm night air. "Can I get my truck out of impound?" They'd dropped off Ruby's vehicle at the café, and once again Ross was without transportation.

Maggie hurried to keep up. "Not until everything's been resolved. No exceptions, I'm afraid."

"Then I need to borrow Lila's rig."

"Why? What are you going to do?"

"I'm going out to the Campion ranch. You saw Farrell's reaction when I asked where Trent was. I think he lied about Trent leaving. Maybe that's why he's so hot to make a phone call. Ben could be waiting to see if Cy can smooth things over before he ships Trent off somewhere."

Maggie disagreed. "How could Cy smooth things over? There was a witness to Trent's crime."

"Dooley Spence?" Ross released a short, flat laugh as

they reached Lila's truck. "How hard would it be to discredit the town drunk's claims as hallucinations? If we'd all agreed to go along with the sweet little scenario Ben and Cy cooked up, Trent would've gotten off scot-free. *Again.*"

Maggie tossed him the keys as Ross strode to the driver's side, and he caught them neatly. They both climbed in. "Okay, say, for the moment, you're right and Trent's still at the ranch waiting to hear if he's in the clear. When Cy doesn't phone within a certain amount of time, Ben could get nervous. The Campions have a small plane and airstrip near the boundary of their property, and Trent's a pilot. He could already be in the air."

Ross hit the key, and Lila's '68 Chevy roared to life. "I can't worry about that right now. Hang on."

The imposing grounds around the Campions' sprawling Spanish-style residence were softly lit, as was the long, paved driveway that marked the last quarter of a mile to the house. Earlier, as they'd driven the curving, wooded access road, they'd passed white plank fencing, handsome outbuildings and the shadowy outlines of horses in the pastures. Everything about the place shouted "wealth."

Ross extinguished the headlights and shut off the truck just short of the first light pole and the heavy iron gate that hung open. A row of pines followed the driveway nearly to the house.

"Okay," he said quietly, "we won't get anywhere knocking at the door to the castle. If Trent's still here, no one's going to admit it." He got out of the truck, and Maggie followed. "We'll make our way up to the house through the trees in case someone decides to look out a window."

Suddenly Maggie was chilled to the bone, though the daytime temperatures were still holding. Shivering, she followed Ross into the pines and spoke in a whisper. "Ross, this is trespassing. And if they have an airstrip, they almost certainly have security cameras on the grounds."

"If they spot us, they spot us. You're a deputy sheriff searching for an alleged felon."

"I'm not officially a deputy yet."

"You will be soon enough. And if this pans out, no one will worry about trespassing. Besides, it's not posted and the gate's open. Looks like an invitation to me."

They proceeded stealthily through the pines, using the elaborate landscaping and shrubs for cover. Finally, they were quietly circling the house and, to Maggie's discomfort, peering through the lighted windows.

They saw no one until they reached the kitchen and viewed the housekeeper wiping countertops. Then, off the veranda at the rear of the house, they noticed Ben sitting stonily at the desk in his study. He was alone, his expression despondent, as classical music pulsed against the glass doors. Maggie could almost feel his misery.

But there was still no sign of Trent, and they'd run out of lighted windows. Somewhere down by the stables, a dog had begun to bark, stirring up the horses. Maggie's nerve endings thrummed. As desperately as she wanted Trent to pay for framing Ross, she wanted to leave.

Ross didn't.

"Now what?" she rasped a few minutes later, when they'd checked out the dark, silent garage.

Ross swore in frustration. "I don't know. Maybe Cy was telling the truth. Maybe Trent's already gone. It's too dark to see anything inside the damn garage, so I can't tell if his fancy Lincoln's in there or not." He swore again.

Maggie pressed her forehead to his warm shoulder and yearned for the closeness she'd been missing. Ever since that horrible scene with Cy at the fairgrounds, their relationship had deteriorated into something that wasn't quite platonic, but that was heartbreakingly far from intimate.

"I'm sorry," she murmured. "I know how badly you wanted to bring him in."

Ross tugged her close for a moment, then released her. "It's okay. This was a long shot anyway." Taking her hand, he dipped to a crouch again. "Come on. Let's just go back."

They had just emerged from the trees above Lila's truck when an engine roared to life and a vehicle shot down the driveway toward them.

Maggie turned swiftly, instantly blinded by headlights. The driver swerved toward them. With a hoarse cry, Ross tackled her, and they tumbled into the safety of the trees. The black Lincoln Navigator roared on.

"You okay?"

"Yes!" Maggie answered. *"What on earth—?"*

"It was Trent," Ross shouted, scrambling to his feet. "Stay here!"

"No! I'm coming with you!"

But he was already yards ahead of her, climbing into Lila's truck.

"Ross! Dammit, don't you do anything stupid!"

"I'll come back for you! I don't want you in the truck when I try to stop him!"

Adrenaline pumping, Ross hit the key and backed onto the access road. Then in a flurry of gears, spinning tires and spraying gravel, he was fishtailing up the narrow road after Trent.

He gripped the steering wheel in a stranglehold and pushed the old truck as hard as he could. The Navigator was streamlined and built for power. But the road was a corkscrew, and Ross prayed that would slow Trent down. *It had to.* The preppy bastard had to pay for what he'd done. These last few weeks, Ross had regained some trust and respect in this town, and it had felt damn good. Trent's vindictive act had almost turned Ross into the town pariah again.

Distant brake lights flared briefly in a thick cloud of road dust, and in the high beams Ross saw a blur pass in front of Trent that might have been a deer. He thanked nature for the delay. What was it that Lila had said about her truck? That it was a gutsy old girl that could take anything Ross drove?

"Come on," he muttered to the truck. "Come on. Make Lila proud."

Ross took the next turn on two wheels; coming out of the turn the old truck hit the road hard, but he was gaining on the Lincoln. Trent was hell on bulls, but he obviously couldn't make a vehicle do what he wanted. Ross punched down on the accelerator and Lila's old Chevy did things that it should never have been able to do. The distance closed between them.

Suddenly, in a haze of road grit and taillights, Trent was right in front of him.

Ross jerked the wheel hard to the left and came abreast of the Lincoln, both of them still speeding. Trent lunged ahead as they came into another sharp turn. Ross was back on his tail in seconds.

Up ahead, the gullies along the road were deeper and the trees were thicker. Ross braced himself and floored the gas pedal. Trent glanced out his window and shouted as Ross came even with the Navigator again. Then Ross cut the wheel hard to the right, struck the Lincoln's front fender, and the Lincoln went bouncing up and over the ditch and into the trees.

Ross was out of Lila's rig in a moment, running to stop the man climbing out of the Lincoln. Trent tried to run, but he was no match for Ross's adrenaline-fueled anger.

One roundhouse punch settled it once and for all.

Breathing hard, but exhilarated, Ross shook his stinging hand, then dug behind Lila's seat and found some rope. It gave him tremendous pleasure to hog-tie Trent and to drag, hoist, then shove him into Lila's rusty truck bed. Then he slammed the old tailgate and slipped in the pins.

"Finally," he whispered in the darkness, his breath coming in shallow gasps. "Finally a little justice."

Ross climbed back in the truck, then turned it around on the narrow road and headed back for Maggie. She'd be spitting mad that he'd left without her. But if she had come along and then been hurt during the chase, he never would have forgiven himself. An emotional knot rose in Ross's throat. She was everything to him.

But he couldn't have her.

When Ross and Maggie left the sheriff's office for the second time that night, Ross's relief at being cleared was tempered. Trent was locked up and screaming profanities at the ex-sheriff in the cell next to him. But there was still another matter to be settled tonight, and he wasn't looking forward to it.

Maggie slipped her hand into his and squeezed, and emotion tugged hard at his chest. After she'd finished chewing him out for leaving her, fuming about Lila's dented fender, and ranting that he could have been killed, she'd flown into his arms. And fool that he was, he hadn't been able to stop himself from hugging her back.

Now, with his truck still impounded, she was taking him home.

"All set?" she asked through a bright smile.

Ross nodded, feeling a stab of guilt because he would have to take that smile away.

The ride back to the house was interminable. It didn't take many long silences from him before Maggie's high mood faded and she seemed to realize that something was wrong. Several times, he nearly plunged right in and told her. Then the coward in him—the one who didn't want her hurt—vetoed the idea.

But he couldn't delay their discussion any longer when she got out of the truck and started up the steps to his log home.

"Maggie...I don't think that's a good idea."

"What isn't?"

"Your going inside. I don't think we should see each other anymore."

He watched her expression change from confusion, to disbelief, then finally to hurt. Slowly, she lowered herself to the top step of the porch. Jess had apparently turned on the porch light, and moths fluttered near the door, some clinging to the gleaming logs. In the post-midnight darkness, crickets chirruped nonstop.

"You were quiet all the way back from town," she murmured. "Are you still angry because of what I said to Cy at the fairgrounds?"

Shaking his head, Ross walked slowly over to the steps. "No. And most of my anger was frustration because you were out there fighting my battles for me. I hated feeling helpless. It reminded me of all the times—" His gaze fell to the log handrail and he ran his thumb over a raised nub. "It reminded me of all the times I screwed up, and Jess had to make things right."

"That's ancient history," Maggie replied solemnly. "Why shouldn't we see each other anymore?"

Regret tightened his chest as Ross met her eyes again. She was so beautiful, so sweet, so strong. And it would be so easy to reach out, pull her into his arms, and keep her there forever. But that would be the selfish thing to do—and he was through being selfish.

"I've had a lot of time to think lately," he said. "And most of the time, I thought about you. Maggie, you're the best person I've ever known. You deserve a lot better than me."

She was on her feet in an instant, dark eyes flashing as she, too, gripped the handrail. "Don't you *dare* say that about yourself. If you really want me out of your life, don't make excuses. You tell me the truth.''

"It *is* the truth. I'm telling you this for your own good.''

"Really? Well, I'm sick to death of people doing things for my own good. First my father decides what's best for me, now you're jumping on that bandwagon. I make my own decisions, and I've decided I want you.''

Frustration made him grab her by the shoulders. "Maggie, for God's sake *look* at me. I'm not the kind of man who can commit to a lifetime of wedded bliss. I was the biggest tomcat this town ever saw—a partier and a gambler who didn't give a fat fig about anyone but himself.'' He released her. "Is that the kind of man you want?''

"No!'' she shouted, already missing his touch. "I want the man he's become. The decent, hardworking, caring man he's become.'' Once, her uncle had called him an accidental hero, but that simply wasn't true. Not then, and not now. Maggie drew a deep breath, and swallowed. "I don't need a wedding ring and an organist. I just need to know that you'll give us an honest chance.''

Reaching up, she touched his face tenderly, feeling the faint scrape of his beard beneath her fingertips as poignantly as she felt the ache in her heart. "Ross,'' she repeated in a whisper, "why can't you give us a chance?''

The phone rang.

And rang.

And rang.

To Maggie's dismay, instead of replying, Ross went inside to take the call.

When he came back out, he was still subdued, but he managed to dredge up a weak smile. "That was Lila. There was an emergency meeting of the town council a few minutes ago. Congratulations. You're the interim sheriff's new full-time deputy. Mike wants you to call him.''

What should have been happy news made little impact on her, although she wondered vaguely who she would eventually be working for. Mike was leaving in a month, so the council would be looking for another lawman to take his place. It wouldn't be Joe Talbot; Joe was satisfied being a part-time deputy. And it wouldn't be her. No one went from dispatcher to sheriff in two months.

"Where's Mike now?" she asked.

"Still at the office. You can use the phone inside."

After all they'd been to each other, he was now giving her permission to use his telephone? How very sad, when only a few days ago…

"That's okay," she answered quietly. "I'll just drive back into town. I'm sure there are things Mike and I need to discuss in person." Ross followed her to Lila's truck, then closed the door behind her.

Maggie started the engine and met his eyes through the open window. "I'll come by for you in the morning and take you to pick up your truck."

"Jess can do that."

A deep hole opened in her heart, and Maggie swallowed again. "Ross, this isn't over."

"I'm sorry, Maggie," he said gently. "But yes, it is."

She was sure that he would come to her in the morning and tell her that he'd changed his mind. That was the only thing that got her through the night.

But he didn't, and for the next three days Maggie threw herself into her work. One of the first things she and Mike did was question Ben Campion.

When Campion learned that Cy wouldn't protect his son anymore, Ben became very cooperative—and Maggie learned the significance of that mysterious false drawer. The day Cy pressured Ben to fund the election rally, Cy had unlocked the drawer and pulled out a copy of the original—and factual—accident report. It was that copy that Ben had tucked into his pocket—just a gentle reminder from Cy that in their game of mutual blackmail Ben had more to lose.

The work was rewarding. But it didn't fill that empty space in her soul that ached for Ross.

Late Friday afternoon, Maggie was so frustrated and unhappy that she went to the telephone and called Brokenstraw for help. "Casey, how do I get through to him?" she asked, utterly beside herself.

"I wish I knew," Casey answered, "because you're good for him. Jess was just as stubborn about making a commitment to me. In fact, if I hadn't completely lost my mind the first night I met him, we probably wouldn't be—" there was a long pause before she continued thoughtfully "—together today." A smile seemed to enter her voice. "Well, now. Maybe there is something you can do."

"What?"

"It's really drastic."

"Being patient certainly isn't getting me anywhere. Tell me."

By the time Casey finished her tale, they were both laughing, but Maggie's laughter was tinged with apprehension. What if Casey's plan backfired, and Ross wasn't as agreeable as his brother had been? What then?

"Maggie?" Casey added. "You *do* know why he's so afraid of a permanent relationship, don't you?"

"I think so. It's because of the gambling, isn't it? He's afraid he'll revert to his old habits, and any woman he marries—any children he has—will suffer because of it. He doesn't trust himself."

"That's what Jess and I think. He heard a lot of horror stories at those Gamblers Anonymous meetings."

"But he must have heard some success stories, too. He's strong now, Casey, I know it. And I love him more than

I can say."

"I'm glad. I hope you can convince him of that."

Tense and exhausted, Ross swung off his horse and led the buckskin into the corral, then loosened the saddle cinch. He'd been working for three solid days like a man possessed—mending fences, rousting strays and splitting cordwood for the winter. And he still couldn't get Maggie out of his mind. What was it about her that wouldn't give him any peace? Any air? Especially since he knew this breakup was the best thing for her? He wasn't cut out for the kind of life she deserved. She needed a man whose past indiscretions couldn't be recounted in detail by everyone in town. She needed a man who wasn't scared blind of screwing up again.

With a soft grunt, he pulled the saddle off of the buckskin and slung it over the fence, then piled Buck's saddle blanket and bridle on top. When the horse loped off to join the chestnut mare at the end of the corral, Ross sighed at the symbolism. Sometimes it seemed as if the whole damn world moved two by two.

He shut the gate and lugged his tack into the barn, with its faintly comforting smells of dust, leather and hay. Maybe he'd walk up to the house and see if Casey had any leftovers from supper. See if Jess wanted help painting the back porch.

Ross flopped his saddle over a low partition and hung his bridle on a hook. He just needed to keep busy now, that was all. If he buried himself in work, his preoccupation with Maggie would have to go away. He'd fill his mind with so much other stuff that there'd be no room for her.

But as he turned to leave, he stopped dead and stared at the blanket he'd dropped on the tack-room floor. A thick, woven-hair, horse blanket that triggered a vivid memory of another blanket...and warm, Sunday-afternoon grass.

The longing in his heart became a deep, hard ache. Suddenly he was back in the churchyard with Maggie, eating her fried chicken, teasing her to distraction, loving her smile. What a vision she'd been that day in her white dress, with her long black hair falling over her shoulders. Almost like... Ross exhaled raggedly.

A bride.

A second passed. Then another. And another.

Finally, he smiled and gave his head a self-deprecating shake as a feeling of contentment washed through him, more powerful than doubts, more satisfying than yearning. More profound than empty promises from a heart too weak to resist her. Who was he trying to kid? He'd never be able to stay away from Maggie Bristol. Not today, not tomorrow, not ever.

He *could* make her happy. All he had to do was transfer the energy he'd been using to forget her—to loving her. Because he *had* changed—before she'd come into his life, and even more afterward because he'd wanted her respect. How incredibly stupid he'd been to push her away.

Hurrying to his truck, Ross climbed in and drove hard for home and a shower, praying that it wasn't too late to get her back. She had to give him another chance. She just had to. There was only one cure for what ailed him. Maggie.

The moon had just begun its climb in the sky when Maggie and her jittery nerves arrived at the house. Thankful that Ross wasn't around to object, she carried her suitcases upstairs to the faintly lit loft. The sound of rushing water came from the master bathroom where the door was slightly ajar, the shower nozzle spraying full force.

Heart pounding fiercely, she hurried across the room and threw her bags on the bed, right on top of the clothes he'd laid out—just as Casey had done the night she'd gone head-to-head with Jess and staked her claim to her half of Brokenstraw.

Then, in a way Casey had *not* behaved—nor suggested—Maggie drew a nervous breath, shed her clothing, and walked into the steamy bathroom.

Ross's lean form shimmered behind the foggy glass doors, and the clean citrus smell of his soap wafted on the air.

He whirled as the rear shower door opened, then stared in shock as Maggie stepped inside behind him. He seemed oblivious to the spray pounding the nape of his neck and shoulders. "Maggie? What—?"

Lifting her chin and stepping into the diffused spray, she took the soap from his hand. "My clothes are in the bedroom. I'm moving in." A pulse-beat later her courage deserted her, and Maggie's voice became small. "So don't try to send me away, okay?"

Ross's blue eyes warmed with his smile. Exhaling in relief, he pulled her close. "Now, why would I send you away? I was on my way to you."

The soap bounced and echoed off the floor of the tub as Maggie filled her hungry arms with him. Then, mindless of the spray running over their hair and faces, careless of it streaming down their bodies, they clung tightly in the steamy shower stall. Water wet their lips as they repeatedly drank from each other, kissing deeply, sighing and murmuring soft words. Sighing again.

A more perfect man didn't exist for her in all the world, Maggie thought several minutes later as they moved in that gentle prelude to lovemaking. It wasn't just his physical beauty that she was drawn to, but the decency and integrity that lived in his heart. Yes, this was love. And he felt it, too. She knew he did. Even if he couldn't say the words she wanted to hear.

But now, with his hands working their magic on her water-slick skin, it didn't matter. They would take care of one need now…and the other later. Breaking from the kiss, Ross reached back to shut off the shower spray. And they kissed all the way to the bed.

The window was open—a big, broad rectangle that framed the fresh moon and a few bright stars. There were no drapes to rustle in the warm night breeze, no fabric to block the moonlight streaming into the loft.

"We're going to soak your bed," she whispered as he knocked her suitcases to the floor and lowered her to the spread.

"It'll dry."

Eager lips found each other again. Then Ross inched lower, trailing tiny kisses over her collarbone and breasts. Maggie drew a soft breath, threaded her fingers through his wet hair to hold him close.

Legs intertwined, and hips strained for closer contact.

Hearts beat faster, and grateful hands relearned each other's curves and textures.

Then Maggie welcomed him inside, closing her eyes as he filled her, then opening them again as he hovered over her. In the dim light, his shadowy face was all hard angles and planes, but she could see his smile.

"You make me so happy," he whispered, brushing a strand of hair from her cheek. "Why is that?"

"Because you know I'm going to love you forever," she whispered back. "No matter what."

"I'm a gambler, Maggie."

"No, you *were* a gambler," she murmured. "Now, you're just mine."

With a trembling sigh, Ross buried his face in her neck. And finally, the words he'd been so hesitant to say rustled near her ear.

Maggie's heart swelled to near bursting. *He loved her.* More than the heat building inside her, she clung to that thought. More than the airy pleasure flowing through her, she floated on that knowledge. Moments later, when the lovely shudders turned their minds to satin and their limbs to silk, Maggie knew perfect contentment. For the first time in her life, she felt whole.

Later, they lay facing each other in the moon's dim light.

"You love me," she whispered.

"Of course, I love you. How could I not? You jeopardized your job for me. You defended me to your father." He paused for a long moment. When he spoke again, his low voice was troubled. "I want to marry you, Maggie."

Faintly unnerved by his tone, Maggie touched his face in the semidarkness. "I want to marry you, too. Why don't you sound happy about it?"

"I am happy about it. But it could be a very long time until we're together. I won't marry you without your dad's approval."

New love filled her heart. "Oh, Ross, he never *dis*approved of you. He only disapproved of our sleeping together without being married. When I tell him we're living together, he'll move heaven and earth to see that you make an honest woman of me."

"No, he won't. Because you're not moving in."

Maggie scrambled to a sitting position. Hadn't he just said that they would be married? "What are you saying?"

Ross took her hand and held it fast. "I won't dishonor your father that way. I won't *let* you move in here with me. Not until he walks you down the aisle and personally puts *this* hand in mine."

That was all? Snuggling down with him again, Maggie sighed happily and pillowed her head on Ross's shoulder. "He's going to love you. When he sees how happy you make me, he's going to love you as much as I do." Then, craning her neck, she nuzzled the warm cleft below his earlobe and murmured, "Now, how do you feel about August weddings?"

Epilogue

Ross stood in the shade of the huge cottonwood beside the homestead, looking down on the people gathered some fifty yards away. Most of them were laughing and talking in groups, but to their right, several women carried food to the buffet table. Beyond, rows of chairs with a grassy aisle between them were decorated with puffy white bows. Baskets of pink and white flowers sat on long linen-covered tables.

Jess ambled across the grass toward him, and Ross chuckled softly. "Don't you look pretty."

"Almost as pretty as you do."

They stood for a time, both of them dressed in Western-cut tuxedos, watching the activity below. In front of the chairs, Casey and Aunt Ruby were putting the final touches on the white lattice arch. Cars and trucks continued to fill the grassy field beside the corral. Guests began to take their seats.

"Scared?" Jess asked.

"Nope. Ready." In fact, he'd never felt more ready for

anything in his life. Maybe he wasn't nuts about all the flowers and chairs with ribbons. But he wanted Maggie badly enough to put up with all the fancy things women seemed to need.

Briefly, he wondered again how Maggie's dad really felt about giving her away today, then put it out of his mind. He'd done the best he could to convince Tom that he loved his daughter and wanted to make her happy. If Tom had reservations, time would have to take care of them.

"Moe's walking pretty well these days," Jess observed, nodding toward the seats. "And I don't think I've seen Lila in a dress since my own wedding."

"Me, neither."

Jess's brow furrowed. "Who's the guy with Mike Halston and his girlfriend?"

"Where?"

"Down by the corral—getting out of the white Blazer."

Ross shifted his gaze to the tall, black-hatted cowboy slamming the driver's door. He scowled. "That's our new sheriff. Maggie invited him."

Jess sent him an amused look. "So what's the scowl about?"

"I don't know, I just don't like him."

"Would you rather have Farrell back?"

Ross grinned. "Okay, maybe he's not so bad."

Bessie Holsopple left a group of women near the tables and walked to the organ. Jess clapped a hand on Ross's shoulder. "Okay, little brother, it's time. Does the groom have any last requests before he takes his final walk as a free man?"

"Yeah," Ross said through another grin as they left to take their places. "Stay away from the hot spring tonight."

Bessie played something soft and pretty as Ross and Jess approached the rose-and-ivy-covered arch. Then Reverend Fremont, smiling and all decked out in his "marrying whites," walked over to Ross and shook his hand.

"Ready, son?"

"Yes, sir."

"Good." With a wink, Fremont took his place, opened his missal, and the wedding march resounded in the mid-August afternoon.

Friends and neighbors stood as the tiny, dark-haired flower girl walked down the aisle holding the matron of honor's hand. Wearing a pink-and-white gown that matched her mommy's, Lexi smiled shyly at everyone she passed.

Then Ross's heart began to pound…the music swelled, murmurs rustled through the crowd…and Maggie walked toward him on her father's arm.

Her black hair was pinned up in a delicate bun, with loose curls framing her face and trailing down the nape of her neck. Above soft bangs, she wore a band of tiny white and pink flowers. Plain white satin shimmered in the sun.

With every step she took, Ross's heart grew fuller. She was so beautiful…so giving. And she was his.

"Hi," Maggie said softly when she reached him.

"Hi," he murmured back.

Ross's throat knotted with emotion as Tom Bristol drew his daughter close and kissed her cheek. Then, blinking back tears and smiling tightly, he shook Ross's hand, and finally placed Maggie's hand in Ross's.

"Be good to each other," he whispered.

"We will," they both answered.

Then, to Ross and Maggie's confusion, Tom stepped up on the low platform where he and Reverend Fremont exchanged chuckles and handshakes. And Tom Bristol took the white-robed clergyman's place before the congregation.

A radiant smile lit Maggie's face, and Ross felt the lump in his throat get bigger.

"Dear friends and neighbors," Reverend Bristol began, his eyes glistening as he smiled down at the couple before him. "It is my heartfelt pleasure today to join in marriage my daughter, Maggie, and Ross Dalton…a man I've come to know and respect."

Ross didn't hear another word of his own wedding ceremony—didn't remember repeating his vows or saying "I do." He was too busy thanking God for second chances, and gripping Maggie's hand for dear life. Besides, words didn't bind two people together; the feelings they held in their hearts did.

So with watery eyes, Ross just kept smiling down at Maggie.

And Maggie kept smiling up at him.

* * * * *

Well, two down, one to go....
But while Katie and Dana have already
broken their vows—
and gotten themselves engaged to doctors—
Lee is going to be different.
She'll never succumb to a doctor's charms.
Or will she?
You can find out in

CHRISTINE RIMMER's

DR. DEVASTATING

the wonderful conclusion to

PRESCRIPTION: MARRIAGE

available from
Silhouette Special Edition
in December

Meanwhile, turn the page
for a sneak preview....

"**W**hy are we playing this stupid game, Lee?"

"Uh, game?"

"Yes. Game. You looking at me the way you do, and me pretending I don't see. What's the point, when you're attracted to me and—well, I suppose I might as well just say it. I'm attracted to you, too."

"Huh?" Lee almost dropped her water glass. The thing slid through her fingers and clinked on the edge of her plate. Awkwardly, at the last second, she caught it by the rim and somehow managed to ease it to the table without spilling any.

Derek watched her struggle with the glass. And then he nodded, still rueful, a little abashed. "It's true." His expression said it all. He couldn't understand what in the world he saw in her. He considered her totally beneath him, since she was neither gorgeous nor blond. For goodness' sake, her eyes weren't even blue. "I don't know how it happened, but I'm attracted to you."

Amazing, Lee thought. The man really did have an ego every bit as hefty as the two-hundred pound barbell he bench-pressed each time he worked out. But then, he was a doctor, after all. Lee recalled an old joke she'd heard back in nursing school: Imagine an arrogant doctor. But I repeat myself....

Derek went on, a little bewildered, but still utterly sure of himself and his power over disease, injury—and the feminine gender. "I guess what I'm saying is, I think this is something we might as well just go ahead and deal with straight out. I think we can see each other in private and still maintain a viable working relationship. Because I really do believe this is something we're just going to have to get out of our systems."

"Like a viral infection, you mean? Something that has to run its course?"

Lee had meant to inject a note of irony, but Doctor Taylor failed to pick up on it. "Yeah. You could say that. We could agree that whatever happens between us, we won't allow it to affect our work at the clinic."

"Whatever...happens?"

"Yes." He narrowed his eyes at her, in one of those reproving looks he reserved for patients who balked at the course of treatment he'd prescribed. "And what's the problem? Am I not making myself clear?"

"Well, no. I think I'm getting the picture just fine."

"You do?" He looked doubtful.

"Yes. You want to...date." The word sounded so incongruous to her that she had to choke back a burst of hysterical laughter as soon as she said it.

He blew out a breath and gave her a reproachful frown. "Lee. You're behaving very strangely about this."

Strangely. He thought she was behaving strangely. Well, all right. Maybe she was. Derek Taylor was her fantasy. Her mind candy. She'd had a very good thing going with him. A safe, secret, harmless, one-sided, totally mental love affair. It had been great.

But he just couldn't leave it that way. Oh, no. He had to go and make it dangerous. Make it *real*.

And beyond that, there was the little matter of his attitude about the whole thing. His arrogance and his ego simply knew no bounds. It was written all over his too-handsome face; he thought he was doing her a big favor to give in and go out with her.

Well, she didn't need any favors from him.

What she needed was out of here, stat.

"Lee. Say something. Please."

Carefully, she pushed her glass and her plate toward his, in the center of the table. Easy, she thought. Tread cautiously. Remember, you do have to work with the man.

"Lee?"

"I, um...."

"Yeah?"

"Well, Dr. Taylor—"

"Derek."

No. She was not going to call him that. *"Dr. Taylor,"* she repeated, a real edge in her tone.

They stared at each other. At last, he said too quietly, "Go on."

She reached for her shoulder bag a few inches away on the Naugahyde bench of the booth. She pulled it into her lap, all ready to go. And then, choosing each word with agonizing care, she told him, "Dr. Taylor, I'm sorry if you imagined I had some...romantic interest in you. But I promise you, I never intended for you to think I wanted anything more than a strictly professional relationship with you. I love my work. And going out with you is way too likely to cause problems—for me, for you, and most important, for the work we do."

His fabulous face had taken on a totally blank, disbelieving expression. She thought of how a Ken doll might look if Barbie went and told him she was leaving him for GI Joe. "You're telling me you won't go out with me." Clearly, getting turned down was a new experience for him.

"Yes. I think it's for the best. I think that we—"

"Just a minute." The words were pure ice. She did her best not to flinch at the sound of them. And the blank look was gone. Suddenly, he bore no resemblance to a Ken doll at all.

"Yes?"

"Are you saying you're not attracted to me in the least? That I *imagined* those looks you're always giving me?"

Lee knew what she should answer: That's exactly what I'm saying. But she just didn't have it in herself to tell a lie that big. So she hedged. "Whether I'm attracted to you or not isn't the issue here."

"I think it is."

"Well, I'm sorry, but I can't agree with you."

"You *are* attracted to me. Admit it. I just want the damn truth, that's all!"

FOLLOW THAT BABY...

the fabulous cross-line series featuring the infamously wealthy Wentworth family...continues with:

THE SHERIFF AND
THE IMPOSTOR BRIDE
by Elizabeth Bevarly
(Desire, 12/98)

When a Native American sheriff spies the runaway beauty in his small town, he soon realizes that his enchanting discovery is actually Sabrina Jensen's headstrong *identical* twin sister....

Available at your favorite retail outlet, only from

Take 2 bestselling love stories FREE

Plus get a FREE surprise gift!

Special Limited-Time Offer

Mail to Silhouette Reader Service™

3010 Walden Avenue
P.O. Box 1867
Buffalo, N.Y. 14240-1867

YES! Please send me 2 free Silhouette Intimate Moments® novels and my free surprise gift. Then send me 6 brand-new novels every month, which I will receive months before they appear in bookstores. Bill me at the low price of $3.57 each plus 25¢ delivery and applicable sales tax, if any.* That's the complete price, and a saving of over 10% off the cover prices—quite a bargain! I understand that accepting the books and gift places me under no obligation ever to buy any books. I can always return a shipment and cancel at any time. Even if I never buy another book from Silhouette, the 2 free books and the surprise gift are mine to keep forever.

245 SEN CH7Y

Name	(PLEASE PRINT)	
Address	Apt. No.	
City	State	Zip

This offer is limited to one order per household and not valid to present Silhouette Intimate Moments® subscribers. *Terms and prices are subject to change without notice. Sales tax applicable in N.Y.

UIM-98

©1990 Harlequin Enterprises Limited

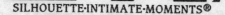

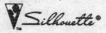

For a limited time, Harlequin and Silhouette have an offer you just can't refuse.

In November and December 1998:

BUY **ANY** TWO HARLEQUIN
OR SILHOUETTE BOOKS and
SAVE $10.00
off future purchases

OR BUY ANY THREE HARLEQUIN OR SILHOUETTE BOOKS
AND **SAVE $20.00** OFF FUTURE PURCHASES!

(each coupon is good for $1.00 off the purchase of two
Harlequin or Silhouette books)

···

JUST BUY 2 HARLEQUIN OR SILHOUETTE BOOKS, SEND US YOUR
NAME, ADDRESS AND 2 PROOFS OF PURCHASE (CASH REGISTER
RECEIPTS) AND HARLEQUIN WILL SEND YOU A COUPON BOOKLET
WORTH $10.00 OFF FUTURE PURCHASES OF HARLEQUIN OR
SILHOUETTE BOOKS IN 1999. SEND US 3 PROOFS OF PURCHASE AND
WE WILL SEND YOU 2 COUPON BOOKLETS WITH A TOTAL SAVING OF
$20.00. (ALLOW 4-6 WEEKS DELIVERY) OFFER EXPIRES
DECEMBER 31, 1998.

···

I accept your offer! Please send me a coupon booklet(s), to:

NAME: _____

ADDRESS: _____

CITY: _____ STATE/PROV.: _____ POSTAL/ZIP CODE: _____

Send your name and address, along with your cash register
receipts for proofs of purchase, to:

In the U.S.	In Canada
Harlequin Books	Harlequin Books
P.O. Box 9057	P.O. Box 622
Buffalo, NY	Fort Erie, Ontario
14269	L2A 5X3

PHQ4982

COMING NEXT MONTH